MASS

A NOVEL

MASS

A NOVEL

Kristin Durfee

ORANGE BLOSSOM
PUBLISHING

Cover: Red Raven Book Design
Formatting: Battle Goddess Productions
Editing: Arielle Haughee

Published 2021 by Orange Blossom Publishing
Maitland, Florida
www.orangeblossombooks.com

eBook ISBN: 978-1-949935-20-2
Paperback ISBN: 978-1-949935-21-9

Library of Congress Control Number: 2021902942

Thorn Coyle

Dedication

To all those searching for what they believe

CHAPTER ONE

S o, I'd consider myself a religious person. I go to church. I
actually *love* going to church. The singing, getting to be
surrounded by beautiful stained glass, seeing my friends. The
free snacks.

I help out in youth group when I can and always, *always*, pray
before a big test. I guess I took my faith for granted, it was just a
thing that was there, that both felt a part of me and separate from
me. I'd participate, but then leave, focusing more on school or
what else I needed to do that day. I believed in God, but I wouldn't
go so far as to say He was in my every thought and action. So, it's
an understatement to say that nothing prepared me for meeting
Mary for the first time. Like, *the* Mary, mother of Jesus.

She came to me in what I first thought was a dream, light pul-
sating around her, muffling her features. When she smiles though,
I feel the jolt of recognition in my heart.

I've seen paintings of her my whole life, but that isn't how I
know it is *her*. She fills me with a light of knowledge. In an instant,
everything becomes clear—my life, my purpose, the history and
future of humanity. I can't put words to the knowing, but it feels
like a physical thing resting in me. The place we are in is warm and
comforting. The heat radiates through my body, coursing as it if is
a part of me. Maybe it is. Flowing through me alongside my blood.

I look around, but I can't make out anything that surrounds
us. Just soft forms. Objects without clear borders, existing on the
edges of my vision.

She is the same softness, features barely discernible beneath
her purple robes. The fabric looks lush and heavy, and I want to

reach my fingers out to touch it, but find I don't have the energy to lift my hand. Instead, I just sit and look at her, and enjoy being in her presence.

I'm not sure how long we stay there, her standing and me staring, but when I feel wakefulness pull at me, I fight it. I don't want to leave this place. I want to live here forever. When my lids open, I frantically search for her. My eyes dart to each corner of my darkened room, but she is gone, the knowledge she brought dissipating into the nothingness around me.

·······•••••••(●∕◉)•••••••·······

My body feels like it's trying to separate from my mind at school the next day. I walk from class to class, going through the motions of my day, but my focus is completely shot. There's a combination of lack of sleep last night plus a mix of fear and hope that Mary will come to me while I'm sitting in class, which makes me useless for learning.

Part of me desperately wants her to visit, to validate what happened last night was real. But a larger part of me is scared that it'll cause some visible fit and everyone will think I'm nuts. As much as I long to see her, I decide to put all my attention toward willing her away.

By fifth period, my best friend Stacey pulls me aside. Not so gently, causing me to almost trip over my feet and fall to the ground.

"Stevie, what is going on with you?" she whispers as she drags me to our next class. She's concerned about me, but not so worried as to risk getting detention by being late.

"Huh? Oh, nothing." I try to sound nonchalant, oblivious to her reason for questioning.

"Liar."

I sigh. "No, really, just didn't sleep well last night. That's all, I swear."

"Nothing to do with Jorge?"

As if her words could magically materialize into a person, my boyfriend Jorge rounds the corner. Deep in conversation with two other guys dressed in the same basketball team jacket, he looks up at the last minute and beams when he sees me.

"No," I say out of the corner of my mouth to Stacey. "We're all good."

To put an exclamation point on what I told her, when we pass he stops and kisses me before moving back down the hall with a quick wave to Stacey.

See, my smile to her says.

She narrows her eyes at me, unconvinced that I'm not keeping something from her, but resigned that if I am, I'm not going to tell her. At least not yet.

Halfway through chemistry and I change my previous prayers. I beg Mary to come and take me. Take me anywhere. Anywhere that isn't this classroom hearing Mr. Brown drone on about the periodic table and how important it is to memorize the common elements with their atomic numbers. As if we all are dreaming of becoming lab rats without the use of the internet or may be future contestants on Jeopardy.

Since I have aspirations of neither, I tune him out.

Somehow, I make it through the day. Jorge has an away game tonight, so he's not able to give me a ride home, and I'm stuck taking the bus. Luckily, since most seniors drive themselves, my fellow juniors and I get first dibs on the good seats at the back. I choose my when-Jorge-can't-give-me-ride seat and slide all the way in, resting my head against the cold glass.

I've had a headache building all day. At first, I thought maybe it was because I forgot to eat breakfast this morning and didn't drink enough water earlier, but I remedied both of those without any dissipation of the pain.

I'm not getting them super frequently, but they are certainly becoming more intense than the previous ones I've had on occasion. I have to take more than the recommended dose of pain meds usually to take the edge off now. I read some stuff online saying that it was common for girls my age to get migraines and might be diet related. Or, of course, it could be a tumor.

I rolled my eyes when that diagnosis came up. I swear, I could WebMD a stubbed toe and they'd probably say that undiagnosed foot cancer was the root of the pain, not the bloodied nail from jabbing it into my bed frame while walking in the dark.

As far as the migraines go, the diagnosis I'm most apt to believe is that doctors aren't really sure why they happen, but that people typically grew out of them.

As I close my eyes and lean harder into the cool windowpane, I hope it will happen for me sooner than later.

CHAPTER TWO

······••••••(e/•)••••••······

I sit in church between my mom and stepdad running my fingers mindlessly over the gold embossed cover of the missal. My back is sore from sitting upright against the hard, wooden pew for the better part of an hour. I long for a prayer that will allow us to lower the padded velvet knee rests just to change position. Not quite time yet.

The priest talks about the mission trips some of the college students are leaving on the following week. They're going to South America. Or was it South Africa? My mind wanders, making it hard to pay attention. Either way, they are going to build houses and hand out Bibles. Or was it to build a church and pass out shoes? I shake my head from side to side and try to snap out of my stupor. But I can't stop thinking about *her*.

My eyes glance up for the umpteenth time to the statue on my right. Mary, in her blue robes, eyes half-closed in prayer. Her features are well-defined, sharp edges carved into the wood. Her expression is calm and peaceful, and while she is beautiful in her own way, I can't help but think how she doesn't look quite like *my* Mary. Close, but without the same warmth and lightness.

In the three months since my first vision, Mary has visited me on seven occasions. All at night. As if she's daring me to think they may be dreams and not real. But I know the truth. Even if I haven't told a soul.

I'm not sure what it is about our relationship, but I don't want to share it with anyone. Not yet at least, not until I can figure out what it means.

Because while in the moment, I feel this overwhelming sense of knowing and clarity, but as soon as I wake up, the feeling starts to float away. By the time I'm able to rush to a piece of paper or open the note app on my phone, it's gone. A ghost of the memory of purpose she gave me without any of the foundation to know what it was.

It's becoming increasingly frustrating. I almost yelled at her the last time, but found as soon as the anger entered my thoughts, she floated it away like those weird Febreze commercials. Which typically would make me even madder, but I find it impossible to feel anything but love toward her while I'm in her direct presence. Sigh.

This last week I've coached myself each night on what I'll do if I see her. How I'll remain strong and logical and *make* her tell me what the point of coming to me is. Unfortunately, since I've been working on this plan, she's been silent. As if she knows and is avoiding me.

I look back up to the statue and for a moment I swear she's moved, tilting her head in my direction ever so slightly. My heart leaps, and the hairs on the back of my neck stand. Is this going to happen now? Finally, will she appear when I wish her to? Or is this proof that I'm crazy and falling down some insane rabbit hole?

I lean forward and stare harder, but it's just the fake candle by her playing tricks with shadows. Relief and disappointment mingle, and the feelings confuse me.

An elbow in my side jostles me back to the present. I lean forward and join my mom on the kneeler, arching my back to stretch it. *Relief.* After a few more songs, the service is over and we make our way down the long aisle to the open room just outside the sanctuary. My mom and stepdad fill Styrofoam cups with coffee and go talk to a group of parishioners while I load up on lemonade and cookies. I make no attempt to hide that this is my favorite part of the service.

It's not that I don't enjoy going to Mass, some of the songs are okay and I typically get a little boost in feeling connected to

God, but I do also skip breakfast on Sundays just so I don't ruin my appetite. Priorities and all.

I've just placed three vanilla sandwich cookies on a napkin and shoved a fourth into my mouth when I feel a tap on my right shoulder. Anticipating the trick, I turn to the left and see the smiling face of Jorge. Behind him Stacey holds an assortment of cookies herself.

"Hey!" I say, trying not to spray crumbs as I talk with a full mouth.

"What are you up to today?" Stacey asks.

"I don't think anything." I look over at my mom. "Guessing she's probably planning something."

"Universal?" Jorge asks.

"Yes," I say without hesitation. Of course, I'll need to ask if I can go to a theme park unplanned, but it'll be more of a formality.

"We just need to pick up Malik on the way," Stacey says.

It's the first weekend of summer for us, but a lot of schools aren't out yet in the rest of the country, so the crowds shouldn't be bad. I've had a season pass for as long as I can remember, but until this year when Jorge got a car, I didn't get to go all that much.

Naturally, it's almost too hot to be outside in Florida in the summer, but it's a small price to pay to be able to ride roller coasters all day and basically get to live in Hogwarts whenever you want.

Now that school is out, I have a feeling we'll be spending the better part of the summer there. At least the first half. I'll be spending most of the month of July and half of August at my dad's place in Nashville. It's pretty much how I spend most of my summers since my parents split up seven years ago.

I'm lucky though, my parents divorce was as amicable as it could probably get. I spend alternating holidays and half of my summer with my dad and his new wife. We also talk pretty regularly between our visits.

My mom's new husband Reg is nice. He certainly cares for my mom and me, but I don't feel like I have a whole lot in common with him. But he usually doesn't try to tell me what to do and is laid back, so he's pretty okay in my book.

I leave Stacey and Jorge, stuffing one more cookie in my mouth, to ask my mom. She's in mid-conversation with someone, so I wait until my stepdad catches my eye before I jump into their conversation.

"Hey, do you guys mind if I go to Universal with Stacey, Jorge, and Malik?"

"Did you get all your homework done?" my stepdad asks. I sigh as the group of parents around him laugh.

"Will you be home for dinner?" my mom asks.

"Ugh, you guys know it's summer, and yes, doubt we'll make it past four."

She nods, and I hug and kiss both of them before walking out with Stacey and Jorge, extra cookies tucked in my pocket.

CHAPTER THREE

············(●✦●)············

Sweat trickles down the back of my neck and we haven't even gotten inside the park yet. Luckily our church is pretty casual, so I was able to wear shorts and a t-shirt to Mass, but I'm wishing I had a tank top and hat on now.

The walk from the parking lot to the entrance is winding, especially with the way Jorge likes to weave and dive through the crowds of meandering people. I catch a whiff of popcorn, and even though I'm not hungry at all, my stomach grumbles and yearns for the buttery goodness. I tuck the sleeves of my shirt into my bra strap to get a bit of relief as I leap off the people mover to keep up with Jorge. I must have the shortest legs in our group, because when I look over to Stacey and Malik, they appear to be keeping up without effort.

We've just dodged a family in matching denim shorts and shirts, the parents clad in neon fanny packs, when we get stuck behind a group in matching red shirts announcing a local summer camp. I laugh and make a faux exacerbated face to Jorge, but am secretly glad for their roadblock so I can catch my breath.

Jorge groans. "It's like this all the time. How are you con-stantly surprised and annoyed?" I say.

He throws up his hands, gesturing to no one in particular. "Seriously, all the time. Don't these people actually want to get *in* the park? It's like they have no agenda."

I pull him forward to follow Malik and Stacey, who have deftly broken through a space between a few of the kids. Having season passes allows us to skip the first ticket line, but we are herded toward one equally long for security. So much for crowds being low today. I motion to the far end, but Stacey shakes her head.

"You always pick the wrong one," she says, rolling her eyes.

I start to protest, but Jorge lightly touches my arm.

"You do." His words are without malice. I know he's right, but I fake defiance anyway and start to move. He holds my arm tighter and I turn and kiss him, laughter making our teeth click together. A sharp ping resonates from the middle of my forehead to the back of my right ear, and I fight a yelp escaping from my lips.

I must have made a movement to clutch my forehead because he turns to me and lowers his voice in concern.

"Headache?"

I nod, but infinitesimally, so as not to shake my brain any further. The migraines having been coming in clusters lately. The few times I've laid in bed aimlessly clicking through the internet, it's said migraines can happen that way. A few different prescription medications were suggested, but so far I've kept their presence between myself and Jorge.

I know if I mentioned something to my parents it would just freak them out. I'm pretty sure they'd suggest that maybe I shouldn't ride roller coasters, and naturally that's not an option. So I complain to Jorge about it sometimes, but basically just suck it up and move on with my day.

"You wanna go home?" Jorge whispers. His forehead is inches from mine, making sure his voice is low so only I can hear it. In front of us Malik and Stacey place their fingers on the infrared scanners that ensure we aren't illegally using someone else's tickets, so we have a moment to ourselves to talk.

"No, thanks, it's not that bad, just might take it easy today." Which in my language meant maybe I'd only go on each ride maybe two or three times. My headache is already starting to fade, they tend to come in intense waves then recede. Plus, I know they sell medicine at some of the kiosks.

I decide to press my luck and do all the rides with them.

After going on a ride that just shoots you straight up and down, there's a bit more of an intense throbbing in my head. As if sensing it, Jorge leans over and kisses my forehead. The weight from his lips gives a small reprieve to the pressure building. If it wouldn't cause everyone to look at us weird, my friends included, I'd wish he could stay like that all day.

It's funny, we've gone to the same school and church for years, but I'd only met Jorge a year ago through Malik. They play basketball together, and he kept talking about his friend and that I needed to meet him. Finally, to shut him up, I agreed to a double date.

We went to Universal of all places and immediately bonded over our love of thrill rides. He's in the grade above us, which means while Stacey, Malik and I will be seniors next year, he just graduated. While we're only a year and a half apart in age, him going to college in the fall makes it feel like much more of a gap. He doesn't seem to mind, and my mom and stepdad love him.

He's over at our house most weeknights for dinner as his parents tend to work late. He fit into my family so quickly, it's almost like he'd been there all along.

When his lips leave me, I replace them with my hand, giving gentle pressure to the spot. Worried that it'll be noticed, I parlay the move into retying my ponytail. I give it one sharp tug, tightening the hair until I feel my scalp move slightly back, as if the elastic is now holding some of it in closer. It helps a bit.

Hand still hovering, Jorge pulls it down and plays with the small ring on my pinky finger. It's a simple gold band that my mom and dad, back when they were still together, gave me for my First Holy Communion. I remember thinking it would never fit, and how it slid off when I had it on my thumb. Now it barely fits on my pink finger. I'd probably have to stop wearing it soon, but I'd gotten so used to having it, mindlessly twirling it anytime my mind wanders or I got nervous. It's a habit my mom's been after me to break. I mess with it so much, Jorge also took to playing with it.

With the burst of pain luckily subsided, we decide to hit one of the water rides before the line gets too long. Half the time we don't even get to go on them because the wait is so crazy, but we luck out and only have to stand around for fifteen minutes before we get on.

We sit in a circular boat along with a family of four. The parents frantically stuff their belonging in the waterproof basket that sits in the center while the two kids talk excitedly about who is going to get the most drenched.

The answer, it turns out, is me.

I get stuck under three waterfalls, my shoes so wet by the end of the ride, I leave small puddles in my wake. Jorge tries to be sympathetic, but he literally can't stop laughing at every squeaking step I take.

"Shut up," I grumble. Which naturally just makes him laugh harder.

"Sorry, babe." He leans down to kiss me, but I move my head, feigning annoyance.

"Hey, at least you don't need to take a shower today!" Stacey says brightly.

I glare at her.

"Log flume?" Malik asks, running a few steps ahead. I'm annoyed to see he only has one small wet patch over his right shoulder and wonder how the hell he managed that.

"I literally don't think I can handle one more drop of water." I ring out my shirt for the third time for emphasis.

"You guys go," Stacey says and links her arm in mine. "We're gonna get a snack."

"What if I want a snack?" Malik asks.

Stacey rolls her eyes and points to the clock under the sign for the ride. "Get one when you're off. Wait is only twenty minutes. You'll live."

"You care if I go?" Jorge asks me.

"Nope. Hope you get drenched."

"Love you too," he says as he runs to catch up with Malik.

I feel my cheeks flush with heat.

"*Love you?*" Stacey asks, her lips inches from my ear.

The shrillness of her voice brings a ping of pain in my head, but it passes through quickly.

"Come on, I need some Dippin' Dots in my life." I turn to walk away, but she grabs my wrist and pulls me to her.

"Nope. Spill, now. When did you first say you love each other? Do you love him? Oh my God, I'm dying."

"Oh, come on, you and Malik have been saying it for years."

"Yeah, but we've been together since we were like six."

"Okay, we said it last week, right after graduation."

Her eyes widen. "Did you sleep with him after?"

I slap her arm. "*No.* We were out on a nice simple date. He said it, I said it, and we kissed."

"Just kissed?" she asks.

"Get your mind out of the gutter. Let's get some ice cream."

CHAPTER FOUR

•••••••••◆(◉╱◉)◆•••••••••

J orge and Malik, now almost as wet as I am, join us and get
their own cups of futuristic ice cream before we work our way
to the back of the park. We hit a few more rides we know will get
busy later in the day. I go through two Cokes which helps take the
edge off my budding headache.

I hesitate before we go on one of the more intense roller
coasters, but decide against my better judgement and do it. It's
the last one we're going to ride before figuring out what to do for
lunch. It was a lesson we learned the last time we were here, filling
our bellies then tossing them upside down in tight loops moments
later. It was a miracle that none of us threw up.

As we lower ourselves into the row of seats and pull the head-
rests down, the pain starts to swell again, against my temple this
time. My arm is trapped at an awkward angle, so I'm not able to
rub it into submission. I wonder, in a moment of panic, if a person's brain can explode if you couple a headache with g-forces.
Luckily, the thrill of the ride seems to momentarily suspend whatever is happening inside my head. Other than feeling a little dizzy,
I determine I've come out unscathed, brain intact and all.

Standing on the cement under the blazing sun, the last damp
patch on my shirt dries out. My jean shorts are hopeless though. I
think my butt is going to be wet until I can get them off and hung
up at home. Stacey and Jorge are arguing about where we should
get food from. I'm just about to put in my two cents when I see her.

Mary stands at the far end of what I know should be the faux
street, but it has melted away to nothingness. Panic washes over
me. *Not here. Not now*, I think. I'm not prepared for her in this

moment. The stores that should be to my right are covered in gray, fog-like discolorations. No one clutters the road and the silence puts me on high alert, my ears straining to hear if she's saying anything. Then I notice she isn't alone.

Her hand clutches that of a small boy. I squint, feeling like I should know who he is, but not quite being able to make out his face. I go to walk toward the pair, but my feet are rooted in place. When I look down to figure out what the problem is, I see the ground has started growing over them, swallowing my shoes up to the laces.

My panic builds—how am I ever going to get them freed again?—but then the calm that happens each time she visits washes over me. She is far away, but I can see she is nodding at me. I return the gesture, glad that it doesn't cause pain to shoot through my head. She's taken the pain away, pulling it inch by inch out of my brain and replacing it within the gray fog. She's taking care of all of it. I know this as a deep truth. Even my feet, my feet will be fixed by her. I needn't worry about how I am going to move. She will take care of it.

The overwhelming feeling of importance and purpose fills me. I need to know why. The faint reminder of my rehearsed confrontation whispers in the back of my ear, but the previous frustration isn't the catalyst for it anymore. I *need* to know why this is happening.

"You will show them," Mary says without prompt. Her voice is muffled and I wish I could walk closer.

"Show them what? Who?" I try to shout over the noise, but I can't even hear myself talk, so I doubt my words reach her.

She smiles. "You will show them."

I open my mouth to call out to her again, but a lightness meets me, preventing my mouth from forming words. Sounds pour into my ears. I hear footsteps running, shouts, far-off screams of children. Is it the little boy? A mechanical whirl. What is happening?

I shift, and notice that my feet are no longer covered, but they also aren't standing on the ground anymore. No, they are on the ground, but they aren't supporting my weight. I realize instead of looking down the street, my eyes stare straight into the blinding light of the sun and sky. I am lying down.

These truths come to me slowly, along with the knowledge that I am no longer in whatever vision one would call the place my Mary lives in. This, this here is real. There is no more gray fog. The stores have returned as people yell. I close my eyes and pray that my fit, or whatever it should be called, went unnoticed. As the voices come into better clarity, I realize no such luck, they are yelling about me. The footsteps, they are running toward me. The whirring sounds, I hope that has nothing to do with me.

I blink my eyes and they lock with Jorge's, dark brown and filled with fear, as he leans over me. I try to smile at him, but I either don't do it successfully, or it does little to make him feel better. Stacey and Malik are standing behind him, her pressed against Malik's side with his arms around her.

They make a good couple, but I wonder if they will last past senior year. It's a thought I hadn't had previously about Jorge, but now it's all I can think about. Am I going to be with him through college? Beyond? Life? Heavy thoughts for a sixteen-year-old, but the ground will do that to you sometimes I suppose.

A man in a deep blue uniform leans over me and shines a light into my eyes, temporarily blinding me.

"Miss, can you tell me your name?" his voice is higher pitched than I would have thought. I shift and try to prop myself up on my elbows, but he shakes his head. "Why don't you just stay where you are for now?"

"I feel okay," I say. My throat is strangely sore, like I haven't spoken for months and my vocal cords have atrophied. I wonder how long I was out for, if that is in fact what happened.

"I'm glad to hear that," the guy says. "Let's start with something simple, though, your name?"

"Stevie," Jorge answers for me. I can tell in the guy's face he isn't pleased.

"Stevie," I echo.

"Good. Hi, Stevie. My name is Lewis. I work with the EMT department here in Orange County. Do you know where you are?"

"Orange County? Like in California?" I can tell my joke is a dud as soon as I say it. "I'm kidding." I ignore his protests and sit up. "My name is Stevie Albie. I am sixteen years old. I came to Universal Studios in Orlando today with Stacey, Malik, and my boyfriend Jorge. I had a bit of a headache when I got on the ride, but didn't think much of it, then felt a bit dizzy getting off. I am guessing maybe I fainted or something?"

I try to feign a casual tone to my voice, but inside I'm freaking out a bit. I passed out? I'm pretty sure all the times Mary's come to me before I've been close to sleep or already sleeping. I always wake up after, but I've never wondered what happened to me *while* the visions were happening.

But passing out?

No, it must just have been that I glazed over from what happened to me and people freaked out a bit. Maybe I just laid down for a second, but I didn't lose consciousness. Unless the ride had something to do with it? If this means that my roller coaster days are behind me...

I can't entertain such thoughts. We haven't eaten lunch yet. I've probably taken too many aspirins and thrown off my electrolyte balance with soda. After the ride I'm guessing it was just a bit too much. Like the puke lesson of last time, this was a learning experience that I'll make sure not to repeat. Done and done.

"Are your parents here with you, Stevie?" Lewis seems unmoved by my dramatic recovery.

"No." Luckily, I was smart enough not to shake my head. It feels a bit better, but I can sense the pain waiting on the cusp of my brain like a tiger in tall grass. There is no way I'm poking it.

"I recommend you come with us. I think we should check you out at the hospital." Lewis looks up and addresses my three friends, now all standing close to one another. "Can one of you call her parents and ask them to meet us at the Orlando Health hospital? Just let them know it is precautionary."

"Her dad doesn't live here," Stacey says, a quiver to her voice that breaks some of my defiant resolve. I'm not sure what my episode was just yet, but the fear on the faces of my friends tells me all I need to know. I won't argue with the EMT. I will go.

Jorge offers to ride with me, under the claim that he can relay info to my mom when she arrives. I know the hospital staff will do that—I've seen enough TV shows and movies. I can tell Lewis thinks it over for a moment before relenting. Probably taking pity on us and allowing it.

The gurney shakes as the legs folder under it when they load me in. The jostle scares me and sends a bolt through my brain that dissipates like lightening. Tears pour down Stacey's face as I give her a thumbs up. The moment I do it I feel like an ass—what am I, some fallen sports figure exiting an arena?—but the doors close before I am able to do anything else. We speed away as I watch her collapse into Malik's arms.

CHAPTER FIVE

········•••••••••(৫✦๑)•••••••••········

For all the times I'd wished I could ride in an ambulance—the rush of careening through traffic, the hustle and bustle going on inside—it was actually quite boring, which I guess is exactly how you'd like your ambulance ride to be if you could choose.

Lewis hooked me up to a few monitors as he talked to the woman driving us. They spoke in a shorthand that was likely to keep me in the dark about whatever terrible thing I may be dying from. Jorge's skin turns a tint of green and his eyes go in and out of focus. I worry he's going to throw up, and he's not one I've ever known to get motion sickness.

"So," I pause, mustering up the courage to ask my question. "What do you think happened?"

"Well," Lewis talks to me as he fiddles with machines and items around me.

It's strange that after being so focused on me moments ago, it now seems like he's gotten bored with my situation and is looking at things to pass the bumpy ride. Apparently dodging traffic on a highway isn't as smooth as I envisioned it to be. Each bump, hit of the break, and curve of turns, jostles me around the gurney. I wonder how people who are in actual pain handle this.

Lewis turns, maybe sensing that I want his focus. "From the way your friends and bystanders described it, it appears you had a seizure. They are going to confirm that at the hospital and run some tests to see what exactly is going on." Shock must have been evident on my face because he rushes to continue. "Sometimes this happens and it isn't a big deal, just a one-time thing. Maybe the rides caused a spike in temperature. There can be explanations that don't mean long-term treatment or changes to your lifestyle."

I nod, but get the feeling he doesn't believe the words he's saying. *A seizure.* Nothing I read on my web searches mentioned seizures from headaches. I was always too afraid though to Google anything about the visions, worried whatever entity watches the internet would flag me as crazy and cart me away. Or just show me a bunch of targeted ads for psychics.

Maybe the visions have nothing to do with it and the seizure was just a fluke?

Jorge leans forward and holds my hand. I look over at Lewis, making sure this doesn't break some ambulance rule I don't know about, but he says it's okay as long as Jorge stays in his seat. I'm dying to whisper something about the visions to Jorge, feeling ridiculous for not sharing them with him before. Maybe he'd have some insight into what they are about. He's like the perfect supportive boyfriend. I know he'd have the exact right thing to say, but something has kept me from telling him before. Now, with Lewis here and us banging around the inside of a wailing vehicle doesn't seem like the right time. When I get out, I'll tell him everything.

We arrive at the hospital what seems like an eternity later. A team of people in dark green and blue scrubs come and get me then wheel me into the back, leaving Jorge and Lewis behind.

As the doors shut behind us, I wonder what happens to Lewis now. Does he wait to get his gurney back? Surely, they would give him another? He and the driver will probably head back out and save another life. How strange to be such a huge part of someone's life, possibly even the reason why they get to keep living, and yet it be such a small moment for the person doing the helping.

I wonder if he's already forgotten about me.

They put me back in a room and run what I expect are the typical gamut of ER tests. Blood pressure, temperature, take about six million vials of blood from me, yet leave the PICC line in just in case they need more. I wonder why more stories don't have vampires as doctors in them. Where else can you say, "I need four more vials of blood" and no one questions it? Clearly an untapped market for the undead.

My mom arrives just as they are wheeling me up to get a CT scan. Her face has no color as she rushes up to me.

"Oh baby, what happened? How are you feeling?" she doesn't wait for me to answer and pulls out her phone, checking the screen quickly before putting it back in her purse. "Reg is on his way. After church he went with Mr. Albright to run some errands. They're heading back to his house now so Reg can pick up his car."

"Mom, it's okay. Really, my head doesn't even hurt anymore."

"I can probably see if he can be dropped off though..." her voice trails as she takes out her phone again and types a rushed text message. "Why didn't I think of that before? Why would we want two cars here?" She laughs, even though she hasn't made a joke, and throws her arms in the air. She's acting really strange.

"Mrs. Albie," the nurse pushing my bed says, interrupting my mom's panicked flailing.

"Laurel," my mom and I say in unison. The nurse looks at us quizzically.

"I remarried," my mom says. The nurse nods, no further explanation needed. "Where are you taking her? How long will it be? Can I go?"

The nurse is unphased by the harried questions thrown at her. She probably does this ten times a day. Tries to do something, get a patient somewhere, and gets interrupted by that person's family member.

"I'm taking her up to get a scan of her head, very routine in cases where we have unexplained events. It will take about thirty minutes. You'll have to stay here, but I'll be bringing her right back to her room, four-two-three, as soon as we are done. You can either wait for us there or in the waiting room. I can have someone get you as soon as we get back."

My mom nods, fresh tears in her eyes.

"Mom..."

"Oh, Stevie." She leans over me and kisses my cheek. "I love you, baby girl. I'll be right here waiting for you. It's all going to be okay. Everything is going to be fine."

It's odd for her to make such a statement. Because really, who is she to know?

CHAPTER SIX

························

W e're in my curtained room for what feels like hours. My mom and stepdad take turns sitting at the foot of my bed, checking if I need more ice—which I don't—and leaving for phone calls. I wonder if they are about me, but honestly, I don't know what kinds of lives they have. So maybe half of themselves are moving on with their day while the other half freaks out about if I am parched or not. Which I am not. Because they have forced me to eat about twelve cups of ice.

Jorge looks like a stray dog in the corner, behaving for the simple fact of not wanting to be kicked to the streets. Any time my mom suggests something, a snack? A magazine? Jorge's out fetching it. I wish he would just sit still, or sit on the end of my bed blocking it from anyone else. It's as if I'm radioactive for as far away as he's staying from me. I would laugh if it didn't kind of piss me off.

I'm just about to say something to him when a woman in a lab coats walks in. She holds an iPad-sized device in her hands, stethoscope slung over her neck like a stole.

"I'm Doctor Miller. Mr. and Mrs..." her voice trails as she looks at her screen. "Laurel." She pauses, seeing Jorge in the corner, and asks him to leave. I nod when he looks over at me. He rushes forward and kisses my forehead.

"Stevie—"

"It's okay, I think you should get going," I cut in. "I know you have work tomorrow. I'm sure it will all be fi ne. I'll give you a call tonight, okay?" I keep my voice low so he has to lean in to hear me. He nods. "Will you text Stacey and Malik that I'm all right?"

"Of course. I'll talk to you later. Bye, Mr. and Mrs. Laurel." He waves and slips out, Dr. Miller pulling the curtain closed behind him as if the illusion of privacy is as good as the real thing.

I want to call for him, beg the doctor to let him stay. For some reason his absence makes me want to cover my ears with my hands and refuse to listen to whatever it is this doctor is about to say.

Mary, full of grace, please, please, please let everything be okay.

I repeat the prayer over and over in my head until the words jumble together.

My phone pings, breaking the spell of my mantra. I can see it sitting on the rolling table next to my bed. Stacey's name flashes along with about a million lines of text.

I fight the urge to snatch it up and respond. If I pick up, maybe I can delay whatever they are going to tell me. I can pretend that everything is fine for a little while longer. I start to stretch over, but my mom either thinks I'm going after her hand, or knows what I'm about to do and stops me. She smiles and shakes her head as she squeezes my hand. The vibration stops and my phone goes black.

In the background, the doctor speaks as she pulls up the images from my CT scan on a large TV screen.

She takes a breath, and I shut my eyes, not quite ready to hear what it is she has to say.

CHAPTER SEVEN

•••••••••◦(℃✐◎)◦••••••••••

My head swirls. My head that is filled with cancer.

Okay, maybe filled is a bit dramatic. And I suppose cancer isn't a guarantee yet until every single test comes back, but from the images the doctor showed us and her current prognosis, she's pretty sure that's what it is. More tests will need to be run. Of course they have been wrong before, not typically, but it has happened. Of course, of course, of course.

But I see it. Dark and dense in the front of my brain. I say "it," but it has a name, albeit a barely pronounceable one. *Oligodendrogliomas*. The doctor sounded it out bit by bit. Olah. Go. Dendrow. Gli. Oh. Mah.

I dub him "Ollie." Sounds friendlier that way.

Ollie resides in my right frontal lobe and is responsible for the lightning headaches I have been getting. That's actually what they call them, and I am satisfied that my description was correct. They are very rare, only about four percent of brain tumors are in this category, and even less seen in people my age, making up only about six percent of all diagnoses. They are slow growing, so that's positive, and are good surgical and chemotherapy candidates. The five-year survival rate, which I gather is the going figure for how screwed you are, is ninety percent, a figure that doctors say in such a way that we are supposed to sigh in relief.

But I'm not relieved.

If you would have asked me a few hours ago, I would have told you that my five-year survival rate was one-hundred percent. As I see it, this Ollie jerk just cut my rate by ten.

Tension fills the cloth-walled room as my mom starts to cry. The doctors assure her there is a wonderful team in Atlanta they've already spoken with that is willing and eager to take on my case.

"Atlanta?" my stepdad asks.

"They are more well-versed in this type of cancer and treatment, especially for someone her age. She'll be in very good hands there." The female doctor gives my mom a piece of paper with scribble all over it.

My pulse and breath quicken. How can they talk about this so cavalier? There is a mass of cells named Ollie living in my brain, pushing on the space between the precious tissue that holds everything that makes me, me, and the thick skull my dad would argue also makes me, me. For once, the internet doom-and-gloom was right.

Does this mean the world is also going to end soon in a zombie apocalypse?

My breathing increases so much that I am soon gasping for air. As if suddenly remembering that I'm still there, the doctor rushes over and places a mask over my face, coaching me on how to take long, measured breaths.

I want to take the mask off and yell, but the oxygen is intoxicating, thick like humid air. It calms my insides and flushes out my bad thoughts. It makes my skin tingle and a warmth radiate through me. As each breath pushes in and out, my vision clears to white-sharpness.

"Is that better?" Her words don't so much infiltrate my ears, but my being.

"Yes." I am relieved my voice is clear. I was worried that she wouldn't be able to hear me through the mask. Though, now that I reach my hand up, I realize the mask is gone, my fingertips rubbing against my rough lips.

As I turn toward the sound, it's not Dr. Miller I see, but Mary.

"Good, you gave us a bit of a scare." Her voice is light and magical, what I'd expect butterflies to have if given speech.

Us.

The word rattles around inside me for a moment before it registers, and I notice the other figure near her. The boy, or who was the boy, now much older, maybe my age.

Jesus, a voice whispers in my head.

I know it's right, but I'm too afraid to even think it.

"Why," is all I can muster, all previous scripted brevity escaping me now. *This isn't the time for confrontation*, a voice murmurs. *Just take it all in.*

"Oh, my darling child, don't you know how special you are? How perfectly needed?"

I don't. I've never been special. Mediocre is pretty much my middle name. I can't name a single thing I've excelled at. Every sport I've ever played, I've come off the bench. I've never gotten honor roll in school or was named student of the month. Don't get me wrong, there is something to be said for just doing enough. I enjoy myself just fine without having to expend the kind of energy I see others doing around me. Being good at something looks exhausting. Okay is fine with me.

I don't think I've even gotten the "you can do anything you set your mind to" talk from my mom or dad. Sure, they are proud of me in a way that only parents can be, but if you ever asked them, they'd probably shrug to come up with something that I had enough talent in to warrant being highlighted.

I shake my head.

"Oh, my sweet, sweet child," Mary says. There is pain in her voice, like I've hurt her by my own ineptitude. I feel her glowing love start to leave, like tendrils loosening on my body.

"No," I gasp. "No, I'm sorry. I'll try harder."

"Harder? Honey, what are you talking about?" My mom's face hovers over mine.

I look around. Mary and Jesus are gone.

The room is back in soft tones and quiet beeping. The tingling has ebbed away and I wonder if it had anything to do with the oxygen, or if the sensation was brought on by the vision.

I pull the mask off, suddenly feeling suffocated. My eyes turn to Dr. Miller, her brows nearly touching each other in concentration.

"What happened there, Stevie? Can you describe it?"

"Was," I pause, "was that another episode?"

She nods. "They can happen just that quickly. That's why it's important for you to get yourself checked out soon. It's possible these seizures may happen with more frequency and increasing violence to your body." She turns to my mom. "We're going to send you home with some medicine that should help control it. Her doctors in Atlanta may change her to something else, but for now, this is the best thing to give her."

"She just looked sort of out of it, but I didn't see movement," my stepdad says, taking a half-step closer to me.

She nods. "That can happen as well. It's not always like the movies, Mr. Laurel. Seizures don't necessarily have a lot of jerky motion. They can be almost still. That's why sometimes they can be hard to diagnose, as it may not be obvious the person is having an episode. Though patients can report lost time, often accompanied with other indications—winding up on the floor, urinating oneself, things like that."

Oh God, did I pee myself? I casually drop my eyes, but no, the bed sheets appear dry. I think to when I was first put on the gurney, my jeans still damp from the water ride. Oh lord, does Lewis think I peed myself? So now I not only have to worry about dying from a brain tumor, it might also make me sporadically piss myself? Double ugh.

"You spoke just now," the doctor says, interrupting my spiraling thoughts. She moves closer to my bedside and stares me straight in the eyes. "Who were you speaking to?"

"No one," I lie. I'm not ready yet for them to know everything that's happening to me. I feel possessive of Mary and Jesus. Like if I share them with anyone else, it'll lessen how important they are, or worse, make them go away.

"Sometimes people report visions, which can seem sort of like daydreams, and even euphoric episodes during these types of seizures." She must have seen a flicker of acknowledgement in my eyes because she presses on, words rushing in her excitement. "Are you having both, visions and euphoric feelings?"

I nod, making the decision to let them in a little bit, but not all the way.

"What does that mean?" my stepfather asks. "Is that a good sign?"

"No, not necessarily. It can just happen sometimes. I haven't had a patient yet report that. Most people with seizures complain about lost time. They are doing one thing, everything goes to black in a manner of speaking, and they come to later. But there is a small population that report complete lucidity during episodes and even have memories, almost dream-like but more real. It is fascinating, the brain."

I nod again, because what else do you do?

"And how long have you been having these visions or episodes?" she asks.

My mom takes my silence as confusion and decides to speak for me.

"She had her collapse yesterday," my mom says. "I'm sure it says on her chart."

The doctor nods. "Yes, but have you had visions before that? Sometimes people have them and don't realize they may be related to a seizure or event."

They all turn to stare at me.

I go through my options as quickly as I can. Tell the truth? Tell some of the truth? Flat out lie? I decide on a combo.

"A few weeks."

"What are you talking about, Stevie?" my mom practically shrieks.

"I, I..." the words stammer and then I remember what the doctor said at first. "I thought maybe they were dreams. I don't know, maybe they were, but now that she says they may be something more, they did feel a bit different. More real."

"That definitely happens sometimes."

"Why didn't you tell us?" my mom asks.

"I thought they were just vivid dreams. I didn't pass out or anything. It never happened at school or when I was out anywhere," I say, the latter part at least true.

"Like I said," the doctor continues, trying to defuse the situation, "that's not uncommon for patients to experience. Sometimes it takes a larger event, like the one Stevie had yesterday, for them to realize what they're seeing is something more."

I can tell my mom isn't totally on board with what the doctor is saying, but she relents. I'll have to be more careful about how I talk about the visions in the future so I don't contradict myself.

"I think our best course of action right now," the doctor says, "is to keep her overnight, that way we can observe and adjust her medication as necessary. We will plan on releasing her to your custody in the morning. Dr. Oppenheimer in Atlanta is able to fit her in on Friday. I know that will probably take some coordinating."

"It won't be a problem," my mom says curtly. I know she's lying. She has work, and I'm sure my dad will want to fly from Nashville. I wonder if she's called him. Maybe he's who some of the calls have been from?

"Can we stay with her tonight?" my stepdad asks. His question takes me by surprise. It's not that I've ever had a problem with him, but I wouldn't say we're particularly close.

"Yes, yes of course," a nurse answers, who until this moment I didn't realize had even joined our sad little party. Dr. Miller says she will check in with me later and slips away, fingers already typing notes into the pad. "We'll be moving her to a private room shortly. I'll make sure there is a cot set up for you as well."

We thank her and she leaves us alone with the knowledge that our lives have changed forever.

CHAPTER EIGHT

•••••••••◦(ℰ✧❀)◦••••••••••

The windows outside the hospital are pitch black when I'm finally wheeled into my new room. My insides have a strange numb feeling, like the overload of information has zapped my synapses. A nurse removes one of my wristbands and exchanges it for a bright orange one that says "Fall Risk" in large block letters. I wonder if I'll have to get a permanent one, like a medical bracelet, and if my mother will ever let me out of her sights again.

As soon as the nurse leaves, my mom pushes past her, leans over, and kisses me, an answer to my question.

"Okay baby, Reg and I are going to make a trip home to pick up a few things. Can I get you anything? Some socks, maybe Al?"

I'm mortified she knows I still sleep with my stuffed rabbit. I thought I'd kept it a secret, but also never having spent more than the stray sleepover without him, I nod wordlessly.

As soon as they are out of the room, I slide to the edge of the bed to get up to use the bathroom. A note on my whiteboard implores me to call for a nurse anytime I need to get up, but I ignore it. You would have thought I was stealing the Mona Lisa. The second I stand, before I'm even able to take a step, loud alarms go off. I've barely taken three steps when four nurses rush in.

They explain that there are weight sensors in my bed that alert the nurses' station if a patient gets up. Especially a flagged patient like I am. One of the nurses makes a big show of turning the alarm off. Like it's way more complicated than just putting in the four-digit code. Another stays to "help" me, which really entails hovering while I awkwardly try to pee without dislodging any of the sensors taped to just about every part of my upper body. When

I'm done and back in bed, I get a lecture about how important it is to follow the rules, they are in place for my own safety. Blah, blah, blah.

Before she leaves, I ask if she can pass me my clear plastic hospital bag containing all the items I came in with. I fish my cell phone out and thank her. She leaves, but not before warning me once more about getting up. Yeah, yeah, yeah.

I stare at my phone, hesitant to unlock it and make the phone call.

What I am supposed to say? How can I possibly explain what is going on when I have no idea myself? About twelve hours ago, I was riding roller coasters, and now I'm sitting in a hospital room wondering how long I have to live.

And the visions. I haven't even begun to unravel that aspect of it. Could it be this foreign thing in my head is giving me some sort of power, a window into another world? A world I have been surrounded by my whole life, but now I get to be a part of it, an actual part? I can live in it, speak with Mary, maybe even Jesus. If another vision happens, I will talk with Jesus instead. Mary, for whatever reason, thwarts my attempt at questioning. Maybe He'll tell me what the heck is going on and why.

I toggle the phone on and off three times before going through with the call. Jorge picks up before the phone even rings on my end.

"Tell me everything. How are you feeling. Are you back home? What did they say?" I smile despite myself and wonder how the words I'm about to say are going to change our relationship.

"They are referring me to another doctor, in Atlanta actually, so we won't know a hundred percent until then." I can't do it. I practiced it over and over in my head, but I just can't do it yet.

"Okay, so no red flags yet. That's good, right? Maybe it'll be nothing."

His words are so hopeful. I take a deep breath. I can't keep this from him.

"Well, not really. I think it's more confirmation than they think it's something else."

"And what are they confirming?"

I sigh. "Cancer. It's got some funny name. I can't even pronounce it."

Silence.

I pull the phone away from my face, the screen lights up, and the call time ticks away second by second. He's still there, but says nothing.

How silly. Just hours ago I was wondering if we'd stay together through college, get married maybe. I'm not sure if we'll even last to the end of this phone call.

"Okay," he says in a long exhale. "Okay. So now what, Atlanta?"

"Atlanta," I repeat.

"And then?"

"They are really hopeful. Surgery, maybe chemo, but the success rates are really high."

"And you don't know what the cancer is called?" he asks. I can hear movement in the background and picture him sitting in front of the computer, cursor poised over a search bar.

"Um, it's Oligo-something. I've been calling him Ollie."

"Ollie?"

"Yeah," I say.

"Screw Ollie."

I laugh despite myself. "Yeah, screw Ollie."

We hang up the phone a few moments later, and I realize that I broke my promise to myself, still not telling him about the visions.

CHAPTER NINE

·······●●●●《◎ ◎》●●●●·······

T he night in the hospital is strange. For some reason, nurses keep coming in to check on me through the night, like I'll suddenly worsen and die under their watch. I keep trying to explain that I feel fine and don't need to be woken up every thirty minutes.

"Sorry, honey," the 2 a.m.-guy says. "We just have to double check, make sure your seizures are under control, and that there isn't anything odd cropping up. Plus," he lowers his voice and leans in, "my ass would be on the chopping block if I didn't follow protocol."

I know they all try to be quiet, but they wake my mom and stepdad each time, too. I think we're all about to sneak out or figure out how to barricade the doors.

After twenty hours, the millionth check of my vitals, and a two second once-over by a doctor I hadn't seen before, I am finally released.

For as terrible as I feel, my back stiff from sleeping uncomfortably, my mom and stepdad look a million times worse. The circles under my mom's eyes, already a makeup struggle for her, are deep purple and sunken. My stepdad's hair, for the first time since I've known him, is unkempt, his face darkened with stubble.

We drive in silence, Al clutched in my lap while I rub his ears.

It's only been a day, but the house feels different when we walk through the front door. The air, slightly stale. My mom turns down the AC, the movement of the fans breathing some life back into the place.

They hover in the kitchen and I sense they want to talk. I can't. I ask to go to my room and sleep a bit, and while I can tell they'd rather us all be uncomfortably seated on the couch so they can keep tabs on me, my mom nods.

"I'll bring you up some lunch a bit later. That sound good?" my stepdad asks.

"Yeah, great." I'm actually starving, but I feel nauseated at the same time. Maybe after relaxing a bit I'll be up for eating something.

In my room, I bypass my bed and go straight for my computer. It takes several pages, but I finally find what I'm looking for.

The blog is old—the last entry from two years prior—but the content is all still there. The woman, I judge to be in her mid-forties by her picture, speaks frankly about her diagnosis and treatment of grade II oligodendrogliomas. But that's not what interests me, or not the only thing that interests me. One particular entry seems ripped from my own internal thoughts.

Wednesday, November 16ᵗʰ: The doctors have scheduled my surgery for next week. So, I'll have to spend Thanksgiving in the hospital. Joy. As if sensing the end is near, my episodes have been clustering together into a steady stream of events. Gosh, how am I going to give this up? I feel so good, what I imagine those on drugs experience. I think my husband worries I will turn to something like that when all this is over. Chasing the high. It doesn't seem right that I have to trade this though. Totally unfair that what makes me feel alive is actually killing me.

In her couple of post-surgery entries, she writes longingly for those feelings, that part of her is empty and lost without them. She wonders if she will find joy again, find anything that will make her feel that good again.

Her last post simply states: *In saving my life, did I also doom it?*

Going down the rabbit hole and clicking around a few other sites, I even find an article that calls them "Magic Tumors" because of the incredible ways they can affect their hosts. There are even several mentions of God.

I know, *know* that Mary is here for a reason. She wouldn't show herself to me if she didn't want me to do something, use the knowledge of her presence for some kind of good. I just need to figure out what it is.

But part of me can't help but question what I've been seeing. Which came first, the visions, or the tumor? And if Ollie is really causing all of this, what will removing him also take away?

CHAPTER TEN

········•••••◦(●∕◉)◦•••········

I must have fallen asleep at some point, because the next thing I know, it's morning. A glass of water sits on my side table, the only indication I've been checked on during the night.

My neck and back crack when I stretch. It's amazing to sleep in my own bed, but I'm still feeling the crappy night's sleep from the day before. I down the glass of water in one deep gulp, some of the liquid spilling and running down my neck.

I know I should go downstairs and face the day, but I delay it a little longer, standing under a hot shower until it turns cold. Normally, my mom would have come up and yelled at me for taking so long, but today she's silent.

Point one for cancer.

In the kitchen, my mom and stepdad stand as I enter the room as if I'm some kind of royalty. I awkwardly motion for them to sit back down. There's only so much weirdness I can handle.

"How are you feeling?" my mom asks.

I grab a waffle from the freezer and move to put it in the toaster. "Fine, I guess."

"Here, honey," Reg says as he takes the waffle from me. "Let me make you something."

"Okay, cut it out."

They both look at me like I just made them watch a bunch of kittens drown. I sigh.

"I feel good, better since getting to sleep in my bed," I say.

My stepdad laughs. "Yeah, those hospital beds are the worst." He drops the waffle in the toaster then moves to get me a plate. Apparently, he can't help himself.

I eat my food in silence, but sense them watching me. When my mom offers some grapes, I grudgingly agree. At least I can bet on not going hungry any time soon.

"Hey mom," I say into my plate. For some reason I'm finding it difficult to look at her. "Do you think you can drive me to St. Francis?"

I look up only because of the complete and utter silence in response. Tears pour down my Mom's face and my stepdad rubs her arm.

"Mom?" I am confused. We go to church at least once a week. If there are youth group events or fundraisers, sometimes we'll be there two or three times. It's really not that big of a deal.

My mom wipes her face, but does a poor job keeping up with the fresh tears. "Honey, you are going to be fine."

Oh, I get it. I have to stifle a laugh. "No, oh God, no. I don't think I'm dying or anything. I mean, I guess I'm kinda dying?" The response on their faces says this was the exact wrong thing to say. "I'm kidding. Okay, look, I just want to talk to Father Hugh about something. I know I'm fine. I know this is all going to be all right, okay? I just," I pause, wracking my brain for an excuse, "I said I would help with some youth group stuff, but I want to let him know in person that I might not be able to. That's all, promise."

The lie tastes bitter on my tongue, but it gets the desired effect.

She steps toward me and wraps me in another hug. Apparently, she just can't help herself either. "Sure, baby, of course I'll take you."

My mom drops me off, pretending she has errands to run, though I know she will just park at the far end of the lot and wait for me to call. I don't say this to be narcissistic, she's done it before, and I know in my current state, she won't want to be far from me. Just in case. Just in case.

I walk through the empty halls to the sanctuary. The doors echo as I push through. The room is eerie in its still darkness. The scent of polished wood and burned incense fills my nostrils. The only light that pours in is through the stained glass from outside and a single spotlight, poised to illuminate Christ on the cross.

His eyes lowered in pain or contemplation, yet a peaceful slack is on His face. I walk forward until I'm standing directly below it.

"Hi," I whisper. His face looks both young and old, and while the image is like hundreds I've seen before, He's nothing like *my* Jesus. He's too skinny, ribs and bones showing all around the cloth tied around His waist. And He lacks the hopefulness of the Jesus I know. This one almost looks like it's resigned itself. Given up.

I open my mouth to ask Him a question, when I hear my name called behind me.

Father Hugh walks in dressed in jeans and a black shirt with the small white tab in the center. It's odd to see him in street clothes, like he doesn't quite fit in in his own body unless it's draped in black robes.

"Stevie! To what do I owe the pleasure?"

I smile at him and pick a thread off my shirt. Why am I here? It seemed like such a good idea in the morning, that he would be the exact person to answer my question, but now standing under the wooden sculpture, I'm not sure if I want to share my secret with anyone.

"Stevie?" He leans forward and places a hand briefly on my shoulder to snap me out of my stupor. His expression is a mixture of worry and confusion. "How about we go in my office? It's right through here."

We make our way down three stairs to the right of the altar and through a door. For all the years I've been coming to this church, I've never been in this part of it. His office is small and contains a wooden desk covered in papers, a chair on each side.

I'm not even sure if he's asked me why I'm here before I let the words pour out of me. I start speaking quicker and quicker as I go through the events of the last few days. The seizure. My diagnosis. And the visions. The hour is a blur.

He nods, face becoming more and more drawn as I continue. Unexpected tears well when I tell him about the cancer, but I don't pause for us to talk about it. Sure, that is part of why I'm here, but what I really want to speak with him about is what I've seen.

"So, what do you think?" I ask, afraid of what he may say.

"Stevie, I am so sorry. I'm sorry that you are having to do this, but know that me, the entire congregation, and more importantly, God, are on your side."

I nod, though I pretty much could have guessed that. This isn't news. But what I need is information. "What do you think about the visions?"

He sighs and takes a moment, I assume to collect his thoughts and have some much-needed piece of wisdom for me.

"I think when people go through stressful matters their brains try to do anything to help," he says.

I'm sorely disappointed.

"So, you don't believe they're real?" I ask.

I'm crushed. I figured he must have heard a million stories about visions and miracles and such when he was in seminary school.

"Of course I believe you saw these things," he says in a measured tone. He shifts in his seat and I wonder why this, of all things, is making him feel uncomfortable.

"But?"

"No but. I've heard stories of visions and such, but I don't have any experience with these things, I'm sorry to say."

Maybe it was jealousy then that made him so aloof. Is he upset that I've seen Mary and Jesus and he hasn't, despite years of loyal service?

"I don't really know what to do about them. Or the tumor, for that matter," I say.

This causes him to sit up. "What do you mean, *do* about the tumor?"

I wasn't expecting such a change in reaction. "Umm, I just mean, some of my research with people with similar conditions said that their visions went away when the tumor was removed."

"Stevie, you can't possibly be considering *not* removing it." His voice is even-toned and his eyebrows pinch together like I'm a crazy person wielding a gun.

"No, of course not," I lie without hesitation.

I should have learned my lesson. I should keep what's happening to me to myself, but I had no idea. There was no way to know in this moment that these visions would change my life yet again.

The conversation comes to a stalemate. Father Hugh clearly has no idea what to do about my predicament, much to my dismay, and I find myself twirling my ring.

To break the tension, I ask about the upcoming activities in youth group. I promise to make all I can. He shuffles a few papers, keeping eye contact with me, but clearly implies our conversation is coming to an end. I thank him and say I can show myself out.

Turning the corner from his office to go back up the steps, I run straight into Miss Rosa, the choir director. A few papers with music notes on them flutter to the ground along with her phone and I scramble to pick them up, apologizing.

Miss Rosa is a woman who's always on a mission, and looks like she just smelled something unpleasant, but this time her face is softer, nervous almost. There's a bit of pink in her cheeks like she'd just run from somewhere.

Her eyes shift from me to the illuminated screen on her phone. I would normally receive a stern lecture about careening around blind corners. *Odd*, I think.

It's not until I'm waiting outside for my mom that it hits me. Maybe she overheard our conversation. I groan. The only thing Miss Rosa loves more than God and choir is gossip. If she knows, there's no telling who else had heard my secret, probably the whole congregation by now.

Maybe it's just a coincidence. Maybe my secret is still safe.

CHAPTER ELEVEN

················(€/ ⊙)®············

Light floods my room, illuminating my basketball trophies and snow globes I collected when I was little. I can tell by the slants on the posters on my walls that I've slept in much later than normal. For some reason, even when it's summer, my mom gets it in her head that I should still wake up at a reasonable hour and "get started on my day!" Whatever that means.

I know I shouldn't complain, especially since sleeping in is something I begged for every day each previous summer, but it feels strange being allowed to sleep so late, especially in the middle of the week.

It's like Sunday was a lifetime ago. Strange to think that this time last week my biggest stressor was trying to figure out how to avoid getting a summer job. I was going to work a few of the church summer camp sessions, but that only ate up three weeks total. I'd made the argument that I wasn't even going to be around that much this summer, but my mom and stepdad said I could work something part time for now and then continue working there once I got back from my dad's. I reminded them I'd be going to school, but they seemed to think that was inconsequential, and I could just keep a few hours during the week and work weekends once the year started back up.

"Wait. You want me to get a job, explain that I can only work for a few weeks with modified hours, leave for a while, and they will hold the job so I can work during the school year?" I was incredulous. Who had they been talking to that this seemed like a good idea? I didn't know a single person getting a job this summer. A couple of people were working camps, I guess, but that didn't really count. Usually it was unpaid, and you got to participate in the program for free. But then to also work during the school year? Insane.

"You know," my stepdad had said. "I started working when I was thirteen delivering newspapers."

"That was like a million years ago. Do people even read the paper anymore?"

My mom sighed. "It will be good for you. I had a summer job, too."

I groaned. "Mom, I think I'm going to be busy enough. Plus, once the school year starts, don't you want me to focus on classes and studying? And getting into a good college?" It was insane that I had to explain this to them. I had friends that wanted jobs and their parents refused, citing the same reason I'd just given.

"You can't spend all your time studying," my stepdad said. "That won't make you a well-rounded individual."

"And working at the grocery store will?"

"There are life skills you get from a working environment, yes. Skills that are good to learn now and not when you're in your twenties. You'll be expected to have these skills. Where do you think you learn them?"

They had let the matter go, but I would find applications sitting on my desk as the school year came to a close. As this was the first week of summer, I expected the onslaught of pressure to kick into high gear, but they've understandably let the matter drop. But this? Letting me sleep in til almost eleven? This is too much. They've lost their minds the other direction.

I shuffle my way downstairs and find them both in the living room.

My mom is about to say something when there's a knock on the door. I'm the closest, so I move to open it. The image in front of me is so bizarre, it takes me a moment to realize what's happening.

A woman with perfectly quaffed hair despite the climbing humidity holds a microphone out to me. Another woman stands behind her holding a camera up with a bright light illuminating the top portion of it. She must have repeated the same phrase several times before everything catches up with me and I can figure out what she's saying.

"Are you Stevie? Stevie Albie?"

I nod. "Who are you?"

She smiles broadly and takes a step forward, as if my question is a green light for whatever is about to happen. "I'm Patricia McIlvey with Channel 3 News. I wanted to ask you a few questions."

My mom appears over my shoulder, putting a hand on my arm, my stepdad right behind her.

"Can we help you?" he asks.

"We'd like a moment of your time, a quick interview if we can?"

"Interview?" I ask. None of this is making any sense.

She smiles again, her white teeth in perfect rows. "Yes, Stevie, we want to talk to you about these visions of God you've been having."

A cold sweat breaks out over my entire body. I think back to Miss Rosa and the illuminated phone. Her nervous face. She must have texted or called someone.

"I..." My voice trails, unsure of how to respond.

"We're going to have to ask you to leave," my stepdad says. He moves forward and gently takes control of the door from me and closes it in the woman's face. This does little to deter her as she continues to yell questions through the door.

"Is it true that you're communicating with God? Our viewers want to know! Does God speak back to you?"

The thin film of sweat freezes, making me shiver.

"Kitchen," my mom says, and we wordlessly follow her, Patricia McIlvey's voice fading to the point where I can't tell if she's given up and left. I hope she has.

My mom takes a deep breath. "Sit." I obey. "Now, tell us what she's talking about." Her voice is measured, but I can tell she is working hard to keep it under control. Never my mom's strong point.

"Umm." Where do I begin?

"Stevie, what's going on? What's that lady talking about?" my stepdad asks.

"Okay, so I wasn't totally going to talk to Father Hugh just about youth group stuff. I mentioned at the doctors that I've been having these visions, right?"

"Yes, but you also said you thought they were just dreams, and you didn't think much of them. Stop lying to us. This is too important. You can't hide what you're going through. There's no way we can help if you don't tell us everything that's going on. You know they're more than dreams." She says it as a statement.

"Yes," I say.

"Tell us," she implores.

My resolve drains, the energy to hide leaving me. "They're religious." I say in a rush.

There.

"Religious?" my stepdad asks. "Like God? Is that what that reporter lady is talking about?"

"Sort of? Mary and Jesus, so far."

"So far?" my mom's voice is shrill. "So, what the hell is this reporter doing on our doorstep? Did you call them?"

"No Mom, of course not. I'm guessing that Miss Rosa did. I ran into her when I was leaving Father Hugh's office. I bet she overheard my conversation. She must have been outside his office and ran when she heard me. I should have known." I think back to the exchange between us. The flushed look on her face. "I hoped she hadn't, but well..." I gesture to the front door.

"I'm going to need you to help us a bit more here," my stepdad says. "You're having visions of Mother Mary and Jesus, decided to talk to Pastor Hugh instead of your parents or doctors, and what exactly did he help you with?"

I didn't think they'd be thrilled by my revelation, but I certainly didn't expect them to be angry. My mom paces the kitchen, taking random items out of the sink and putting them—not so gently—into the dishwasher.

"Mom..."

My words hang in the air. What was I going to say to them? Maybe I'd hoped they'd never find out and this could be my secret. So much for that.

"It's not like they've been happening for a while. I thought they were dreams. It wasn't until the doctor mentioned visions that I put two and two together and thought maybe that's what it was. So, I went to Pastor Hugh to get his thoughts on it. That's all." I piece half-truths in with the lies. I hate having to do this to them and Mary. I hope she knows I don't believe what I'm saying to them and I don't think for one second I'm doubting her.

To seal the deal, and put myself in the running for an acting award, I sigh. "Look, I know you guys are worried about me, and I didn't want you to be *more* worried." There is some truth to this.

My stepdad comes forward and envelops me in a hug. I can probably count the number of times on one hand that he's done that. He's not really the touchy-feely kind of guy. Honestly, I guess none of us are, but my mom comes and joins him, still clutching a dirty glass. I stay motionless, hoping whatever strange display of affection they are bestowing upon me will end soon.

"Sweetie, this is a tough time for all of us," my mom says, finally breaking up the little hug-fest. "But keeping secrets doesn't do anyone any favors, okay? We appreciate you trying to protect us, but that's kinda our job." She smiles and kisses me on the cheek. "Next time, instead of Father Hugh, come to us."

I must be wrapped up in the moment, because I say the next thing without even thinking.

"I just wanted to talk to him because I've been struggling with going through with the removal surgery."

I regret the words the second they pass my lips.

CHAPTER TWELVE

························

The sound of the glass breaking as my mom drops it reverberates around the kitchen, but not a single one of us jumps.

It's so quiet, I think maybe the glass dropping was a separate incident. For a split second, I think maybe they didn't hear me, and I can pretend I just coughed weird, but then they explode.

"What the hell are you talking about?" my mom shrieks.

"Young lady, that isn't even an option!" my stepdad hollers at the same time.

Shit.

"I don't know. It's major surgery. The tumor is low-risk right now." I'm rambling, but can't stop. "I'm not sure if I want them cutting into my brain."

My mom throws her hands up and walks out of the room. It may be worse than if she started yelling more.

"In the morning, you are going to Atlanta," my stepdad says. "And you *are* getting that surgery."

Anger flares in me and I stomp upstairs to my room, purposefully crashing each bare foot on the step so it echoes through the house. I know they hate this. Drives my mom crazy.

"You're a teenager, not an elephant!" she would holler at me.

I channel my inner pachyderm the whole way up to my room. Taking small pleasure in the added annoyance they must have now.

I look around my room for something to throw. The snow globe I got the Christmas we spent in New York? The trophy from a million years ago with the soccer ball on top? Maybe a few picture frames or some of the glasses I hoard in my room?

My eyes land on about a dozen objects before I run out of steam. The gravity of the last two days leeches the energy from me. I sit on my bed instead and reach back for Al, knowing instinctively where he sits without looking.

I clutch him to my chest and allow his fur to tickle the bottom of my chin.

I have cancer.

The words repeat over and over like my prayer to Mary did. I am only sixteen, three months shy of my seventeenth birthday. I'm about to enter my senior year of high school. College brochures are stacked ten high on my desk.

Brain surgery should be the furthest thing from my mind.

I grab my phone and call Stacey, but she doesn't pick up. The loneliness I feel is all-consuming and I wish Mary would show up. I shut my eyes and try to make the tingle feeling happen. Or bring on a headache. Or whatever calls her to come to me. But when I open my eyes, the only thing staring back at me is my clock, ticking away.

The vibration from my phone makes me jump like it's shocked me. I reach for it and see Stacey's name and picture flash across my screen.

"Hey," I say. There's a few beats of silence on the other end.

"You scared the shit out of us," she says.

"I know."

"I don't think you do. I've never been so scared in my life. I thought Malik was going to have to carry me back to the car. Holy shit."

"I know."

She sighs. "Jorge filled me in. Cancer. Shit."

"Yeah." A desperate desire to escape floods me. The need to be alone replacing the previous one of wanting company. I don't feel like talking about this anymore. I want to burrow myself in the covers and forget what's happening.

"Well..." her voice trails, probably feeling my reluctance for conversation.

Stacey and I know each other so well, it's strange to feel this awkwardness building in our silence that was always so comfortable before. This is a big deal, obviously, but we've gone through some tough stuff together. Stacey's parents divorced a few years after my own did, and if you had to describe their spilt in one word, it would be—ugly. I'd only seen the kind of venomous nastiness in movies, so it was shocking when two people I thought I knew seemed to lose their minds when the split happened.

Any time we spent at her mom's was filled with her mother talking about how terrible her father was. How he never paid for child support yet expected her to give him money any time Stacey was with him. Embarrassed tears would flow down Stacey's face as she apologized for her mom's behavior. Then if we were with her dad, all he did was talk about how Stacey's mom couldn't wait to run around with other men now that he was out of the way.

When I say we sat in uncomfortable silences before without issue, this is what I mean. Because really, there wasn't anything I could say to her to make it better or ease her pain. All I could do was be there. And I was. Eventually her dad got remarried and her mom seemed happy to casually date. Things got better after that, but every now and then a hint of their past hatred would creep up.

We never really talked about it, but I'd squeeze Stacey's hand in the back seat as we drove to the movies or sat at the table just to let her know without words that I was here and not going anywhere.

But now, the silence builds around us. A moment ago, all I wanted was to be surrounded and share everything and have her make me feel better. Now I wish the whole world would go away and leave me alone so Mary could come to me and the two of us could figure this out together. I need her. Desperately. I need her to explain why this is happening and why I feel this deep-seeded need to keep the tumor. What is the meaning of all this?

"Look," I cut in, saving her having to end the conversation. "I'm sorry, I haven't been sleeping well and stuff's been crazy over here."

"Yeah, of course. Let me know if you need anything. If there's anything I can do."

I thank her and hang up.

Realizing that no, there isn't anything she can do. Nothing that anyone can do. I'm on my own.

CHAPTER THIRTEEN

W e're almost at the end of the seven-hour car ride to Atlanta, and I think my mom and I have spoken only a half-dozen words to each other, and those involved food and bathroom breaks. Not exactly riveting conversation.

I figured she was still upset with me, but didn't realize how upset.

At one point I ask her if I can change the radio station as it's gone from warbled music to just straight fuzz.

"Since you obviously know what's best for everyone and can make your own decisions, I don't see why not," she says without hesitation.

My hand freezes in the air for a moment before I drop it back down. Static surrounds us for the rest of the way.

At this point I'd give almost anything to have another person with us just to break the tension. My stepdad had to stay home — he was part of a big project at work and had already missed quite a few days — but my dad is going to meet us. I'm looking forward to the distraction of another person. Though I am a bit nervous. I haven't seen him since spring break, and well, with the cancer and all I know he's anxious to see me.

We've texted a bit, but I haven't told him about The Disagreement, as I'm referring to it. Not that I try to pit my parents against each other, but when push comes to shove, I have a feeling my dad will side with me.

When they got divorced, it all seemed to go strangely smooth. They sat me down and calmly told me they were splitting up. They gave me the whole "this isn't your fault, we still love you" spiel as if it were some after-school special and not our actual lives. I can't remember if there were any tears, but I feel like there weren't. My dad moved out to an apartment on the other side of town. I spent every few days there, but after his lease was up, he moved to Tennessee.

Now that I think about it, I wonder if the move to Nashville was always on the agenda, if the apartment was just a way they could both keep an eye on me and my "adjustment," as they called it. There were times when it seemed like this split was decided by them years before, like a prenup for the end of their relationship.

We'll do this in phases, and after that, once we're sure Stevie isn't going to off herself, or maybe either of us, we'll move on with our lives as stated in article seven, subsection twelve—the inevitable and planned dissolvement of our relationship. Too perfect.

My dad got a place with Karen, a name that was new to me but presented as if I should know who this woman was, and Reg moved in. It may not have gone precisely this way, but in my memory, these events happened at the same time. One day our old lives existed, and the next, completely new ones emerged from the ashes.

But it really did seem like the best for everyone. I can't remember my parents ever being happy together. They were more into hissed voices and long stretches of silent treatments than screaming at each other. But the intent was the same. They punished each other every chance they got. And it never seemed one-sided to me, not in a way I could figure out who was at fault for one argument over another.

And then one day, it was over. I'm not sure what the catalyst was. Karen? Maybe they were both just too tired to keep up the charade of being married. Had Mom met Reg yet? I think it was a while before he came into our lives, but was it?

I know I have it way better than a lot of kids with divorced parents. Stacey wasn't the only one whose parents let their drama play out for all to see. I remember a kid in our third grade class being dragged out by his mother as she loudly talked about how his father wasn't going to get his hands on them ever again. He never came back.

When my parents broke up, our lives settled into a sort of quiet I couldn't remember being there when I was little. I split time between them, which really wasn't that bad. When it first happened, I prayed every night that they would somehow get back together. I never wanted to have two birthdays or Christmases. I wouldn't have to worry about shuttling opposite weekends or summers. I envied my friends whose parents were still together, as if this single fact made their lives so much easier, when really, I had no idea what was going on in their houses. Maybe the togetherness made their holidays miserable.

Even on the rare occasions we were all together, instead of arguing, my parents acted like a long-rooted friendship connected them. Or maybe it was just a show for me. I wondered if I died, if they'd still see each other, or if I was the only thread keeping them together.

Morbid thoughts, I know, but I can't help my mind wandering.

We get to the hotel and I realize when we head up to our room using one of the two glass tubular elevators, that I recognize this place from a few recent movies. The room is massive, by far the nicest I've ever stayed in. It's a two-bedroom suite with a living room in the middle and a small kitchen. My dad's already settled in, taking the room with the one king, leaving the two queens for my mom and me. The kitchen is fully stocked and the drinks in the fridge are even cold. I open a Coke and down half of it in a few deep gulps. I've been dying of thirst, but didn't dare break the silence after the radio fiasco. The last thing I wanted was an excuse to give my mom to talk my ear off about how irresponsible I was being when there was no escape route.

I may be young, but I'm not completely stupid.

My dad crushes me to him after I put the cap back on the drink. I hug him back just as hard. This is a thing we always do, but feeling his tight grip makes me realize how much I needed to see him. The past week has been insane. Somehow, he brings a bit of calm to the situation just by being here. I take a deep breath, filling my lungs with his cologne, bringing myself back to when

I was little and he'd sit with me during a thunderstorm because I was scared.

"So, how was the drive?" he asks. Of course he knows it's been terrible. I bet my mom texted him during our two stops, but he smiles anyway.

"Fine," my mom says, which is universal code for *the most terrible thing, but I can't admit it.*

He looks at his watch, the silver one I'd gotten him for Christmas last year, and nods. "Well, I made dinner reservations for us at six. You guys ready to leave in a few minutes? If you want, we can walk. It's not too far, and then we won't have to worry about parking."

"That sounds great," I say. "I'm starving."

"Thank you, Edward."

My mom and I change, hit the bathroom, and the three of us walk out the door a few minutes later. I let my parents chat as I trail behind them. If I squint, I can pretend we are a complete family, doing normal family things, and that none of us are currently being invaded by a brain tumor.

CHAPTER FOURTEEN

••••••••••《②/⑨》••••••••••

I bury my stress in dinner rolls and pasta. Which, in the great wide-world of options, really isn't the worst one. My parents go through updates like they were old high school friends catching up—I guess in some ways they were? I'm only half listening as my dad talks about Karen and what random new fitness craze she's become obsessed with. My mom speaks about Reg and how he's getting on at work. I sit in blissful silence, eating probably my twelfth buttered slice of bread. I don't even think that's an exaggeration.

It takes my dad repeating the same question twice for me to realize he's been speaking to me.

"Huh? Sorry, what?" I ask, hurrying to swallow.

He laughs.

"Other than, you know." He gestures with his hand as if there were a universal signal for *you know, the brain cancer in your head.* "How's stuff going?"

"Umm…" I trail. Really, what is there to say?

"Stevie is looking to get a summer job," my mom chimes in.

Apparently, that topic hasn't been forgotten. Great.

"I guess. I was going to look for something, but, well, I don't know."

"What about one of those sign twirlers?" my dad offers, mock seriousness in his voice. "I know how much you love twirling things."

I roll my eyes. This is the joke that will never die. My declaration when I was like four or five that I wanted to do baton. My parents signed me up for classes and at the very first one I wasn't listening to the teacher, threw my baton in the air with the notion that I'd catch it perfectly and wow the masses.

It hit me right in the face and gave me a terrible black eye. I never went back.

"Well, you're going to help out at church with summer camps," my mom says. I sit frozen, unsure of what direction she's going. This topic is paper-thin ice. "Maybe you can ask Father Hugh if there are any office jobs you can help out with as well. You should have asked him when you spoke the other day."

It was as if she lobbed an easy underhand ball toward my dad who was at the ready.

His eyebrows inch toward each other. "You went to see a priest the other day? What for?"

Look, I know my parents don't keep secrets from one another when it comes to me. It's a given that my involved co-parents will keep the other one informed in matters of me, but just once, just one time, I'm hoping my mom will neglect to tell him this thing. I'm surprised she didn't call him right after our conversation yesterday, but maybe she wanted it to come from me and watch me writhe in misery once more.

"Oh, you know, just to talk," I say. I look at my mom, begging her not to.

It may be my imagination, but it looks as though she shakes her head the smallest amount.

"Stevie has been seeing visions of God and is now questioning whether or not she wants to have surgery to remove the brain tumor that will surely kill her if she doesn't." My mom speaks so fast, it's as if it all comes out as a single word. She's seriously going to do this here? In a crowded restaurant? The food in my stomach expands and makes it feel like I've swallowed a bowling ball.

My dad doesn't respond to her. I foolishly hope he hasn't heard her. Maybe she can get it off her chest without us having to talk about it? But I know that's too much to ask.

He wordlessly signals the waitress for the check and hands over his credit card without looking at the bill. My mom makes no movement to fight him over who's going to pay. I sit in silence, wishing I hadn't eaten so much.

The walk back to the hotel feels like an eternity. I trail behind my parents as they have a strained, yet quiet, argument in front of me. My dad's hands flourish in the air like they do when he's super angry and my mom randomly throws hers up above her head. It's like they are in some sick puppet show, unable to control their appendages due to the course of emotion running through them.

When we get back to our room, I've barely taken a step toward the bedroom before my dad stops me.

"Stevie, sit." His words are firm, but not unkind. I obey and pick at a hangnail on my right pointer finger, tearing the skin until it bleeds. "While that may not have been the best time to bring such a matter up," he pauses and throws a glance at my mom. "I need you to tell me what your mother is talking about. In your own words."

He sits in one of the chairs across from me, picks up a pen from the table next to him, and mindless caps and uncaps it. My mom goes to sit on the couch, but hesitates and chooses instead to perch on its arm like she needs to be poised for a getaway.

"I've been seeing these visions and, well, I'm not really sure what they are yet, but I'm sure they're important."

"And your health isn't?" my mom asks. My dad reaches over to touch her hand to silence her.

"Please, go on."

"They've been happening for a little while. At first I thought they were dreams, but now I'm not so sure."

"And what happens to you when these visions occur? Are you sleeping?" he asks. He returns the pen to the table, but picks it back up a moment later.

"I thought so because I'm not really present with what's around me anymore. Like, if I'm standing in a room, it kinda fades away, but from what the doctor in Orlando said, it may be while I am having a seizure." He nods and I continue, not making eye contact with my mom. "But the tumor may be triggering them."

He nods again. "That makes sense, based on where it is. I did quite a bit of research after your mom told me about your diagnosis, and I read that visions can be a side effect."

"Right." I'm excited. Maybe he will side with me. I lean toward the edge of the chair. "And I'm sure you also saw that these types of tumors grow incredibly slow. There are loads of brilliant people who've had them and have used these visions to tap into something within."

"And you think that's what you're going to do? Become some brilliant visionary?" The bubble pops. He's only humoring me.

"I don't know..." I trail, sitting back. How do I explain that, yes, part of me hopes that this is some special window into the other side? A connection to God that I alone have, so how can I turn my back on that? "I'm not ready to give up on what this may be." I feel panic pushing the food up the back of my throat and have to swallow hard.

"Sweetie," his voice is infuriatingly low. It makes me want to scream. "This, this *thing*, it's cancer. The only solution, the only thing we need to focus on, is removing it."

"It's not your brain they're cutting into!" my voice comes out louder than I anticipated. I didn't realize how angry and hurt I am.

My dad takes a deep breath. "I think that's enough for tonight. Why don't you get ready for bed? We have a big day tomorrow. We'll speak with the doctor and hopefully he'll alleviate your fears."

I nod, because what else is there to say?

Chapter Fifteen

························(C∕O)···············

I slip under the covers and pull out my phone. I'd texted Jorge a few times during the drive, but I'm not really in the mood to talk now.

Heading to bed talk tmrw?

A few minutes later a ding comes in.

K, nite

I know I should feel guilty, but I've been feeling so isolated lately, it's hard to want to be around other people, and for some reason, especially Jorge.

Should I just break up with him? Save him the trouble of having to stand by my side for whatever my future will hold? If I get the surgery, what if they mess something up and I become a vegetable? I don't want him to feel obligated to stay with me, or beat himself up for choosing not to. And on the flip side, if I decide not to get the surgery right now, what will that mean? Will he have to sit by as I struggle through increasing seizures and go deeper and deeper down the rabbit hole of whatever this is?

I hear my parents talking quietly in the other room. It's muffled at first, but they must either assume I'm asleep, or have forgotten that I'm in the next room, because soon their voices rise to an audible level.

"You know, there was a better way you could have told me. Like, a phone call?" my dad says.

I hear a sigh. "I just don't know what to do. Obviously, she is getting the surgery, but I'd rather not have to strap her down to the table to get it. How do we convince her this craziness isn't worth her life?"

"And does she really think she's seeing God? Or does she realize this is just a delusion caused by the cancer? From what I was reading it can mess with reality."

Delusion? Where does he get off? How the hell does he know what I am experiencing and its validity?

More sighing. "Well hopefully the doctor will knock some sense into her. I wonder if I can talk to him beforehand, tell him to really emphasize how important this surgery is to her overall health and survival. Make it seem like it is her idea?"

"I guess," my dad says. "I'm all for her agreeing to it, but I'm with you. She's getting the surgery either way. She's a child. She's just thinking like a child."

"A scared child," my mom says softly.

"Still…" his voice trails.

Some glasses clink and a bottle cork pops. They must have gotten a drink and settled back down, but lowered their voices again to where I can't hear them.

I clench and unclench my fist in rhythm. How dare they. Yes, of course I'm not an adult-adult, but a child? Really?

My phone vibrates and I groan. I am even less in a mood to talk to Jorge than I was a few minutes ago.

I look at the screen and don't recognize the number. Usually, I never pick up—way too many solicitors have my number for some reason—but some curious pull makes me slide the green icon to the right. Like I knew this call was different.

"Hello?" I whisper so my parents don't hear me.

"Hello," a woman's voice says on the other end. "Is this Stevie? The girl who sees God?"

CHAPTER SIXTEEN

••••••••••◦◖◐◗◦••••••••••

M y heart races, which is strange, because it's just a phone
call and I can always hang up. No real pressure, but my
chest tightens anyway.

"Who is this?"

I check my watch. It's late, but from the noises outside I'm
guessing it will be a bit before my mom comes to bed. I bury
myself under the covers just in case.

"My name is Dot, and I am with a group in Florida called the
Church of the Eye." Her voice is much too bright for this time at
night. I picture her slightly overweight and wearing a sweatshirt
with some sort of appliqué on it. Cats maybe? Or a horse? I'm
probably being unfair, but I can't seem to get the image out of my
head as she continues. "We are a group of True Believers, but the
really exciting part, the part that I'm calling you about, is that our
leader has spoken of a prophet who sees the Lord. This prophet
will lead us into the future, teach us, and prepare us for The After."

My head is swirling. "Is this a joke?" I ask, because what else
is there to say?

"I have a sense of humor, Stevie, but the Lord is something I
never joke about."

Puppies, I decide. Her shirt definitely has puppies on it.

"Right, of course, sorry. But I still don't understand what you
want with me."

"I said, a prophet that sees the Lord."

"And you think that's me?" I half snort a laugh.

"We know it's you." Her voice is even and serious. She is
serious. "I would like to meet with you and show you what our

leader has shown us. Let you know how you fit in and see if you would be interested in helping us."

I am speechless. I hear movement and muffled voices from the living room. My mom must be back.

"I need to go." The words rush out and I hang up the phone.

I hold my breath, listening to see if either of my parents caught me talking. Their muffled conversation along with glasses being picked up and replaced on the coffee table indicate they haven't.

I quickly open the browser on my phone, searching for any information about the group. There isn't much, some rants about how someone's son got "mixed up" with them and hasn't come home. An outdated website with a .com address—the last post from six years ago—and a couple meet-up announcements for various groups up and down the East Coast. It doesn't appear the group has spread west at all.

So, they seem legit, if a bit on the small scale. My breathing slowly comes back to normal and my eyelids feel heavy, the weight of the day crashing down on me. I crawl into bed and drift to sleep as the woman's words swirl in my head. *We know it's you.*

······•••••••(❂⁄☉)••••••••······

When I wake, the bed next to me is empty. It discombobulates me at first, not knowing if it's still night time or if it's morning yet and my mom just never slept. I check my watch and remember her saying that she was going to go for a run in the morning. It sounded like a vaguely good idea, and I considered going for one as well—on my own, of course—but sleep felt too good, so I must have turned off my alarm when it beeped about a half-hour before.

I stumble into the bathroom, feeling drunk off too much sleep and too many emotions. I stand in front of the shower, hand hovering over the nozzle when a movement catches my eye.

The fear and panic that was tightening around my heart releases like fingers, one by one, until I feel a weightlessness in my chest. She is more beautiful than I remember, her skin smooth and a few shades darker than mine. Her hair enviously perfect, soft waves without a single strand out of place. This time she is alone, and I am glad it is just her and I again.

"What is happening?" I ask her.

She smiles. "I think you know."

There is a seed of frustration budding at the back of my mind, but the joy! Oh, the joy I feel stifles it, refusing to let it grow.

I try to take a step toward her, wondering if I can reach out and touch her, but my feet won't cooperate.

"Shh," she says, her voice so soft. So perfect. It relaxes me and I forget why I was trying to move at all.

"I got a phone call."

"I know."

Of course she does. She knows everything about me. I know this as if I am inside her mind, thinking her thoughts alongside her.

A knock on the door rips my attention away from her and the spell is broken. I find myself sitting on the floor, covered in a thin film of sweat.

"You about done in there, sweetie?" my mom asks. "I wanted to take a quick shower before we need to leave."

"In a minute!" I call.

I'm guessing my voice didn't betray me because her footsteps move into the other room. I stand and press my face against the cool mirror, taking measured gulps of air to steady myself.

This woman calls me last night, says I am a prophet, and the next morning Mary comes back to me again? What does it mean? What does this all mean?

For now, I am as certain as ever that there is no way in hell I'm getting that surgery.

CHAPTER SEVENTEEN

·············(❋⁄❋)·············

The large screen on the wall holds my MRI scans, slightly more detailed than the CT scan from the hospital, but similar enough. I'd think they'd be burned into my memory after seeing them just once, but it's as if I've never laid eyes on them before. I stare, transfixed at the small, dense mass that has the appearance of sitting in the middle of my forehead, like if I looked at a mirror right now, I'd be able to see it.

Dr. Oppenheimer takes out a metal object that looks like a pen, but uses it exclusively for pointing. Such odd things are created, I think. Someone at some point came along and said, "Well, Dr., I know you have been pointing perfectly well with that pen of yours, but can I interest you in this shiny silver thing? It serves one purpose, but oh boy, it does its job well!"

I'm not sure how I feel about this person that's supposed to be a genius brain surgeon who also seems to be a bit of a gullible man.

Though, really, even if he'd had a pen, I'm still not going to let him within an inch of me holding a blade.

"So, Mr. and Mrs. Albie," the doctor starts. I can see my mom shift out of the corner of my eye, but she doesn't correct him. My father also stays silent.

The doctor continues, basically repeating everything the one in Orlando said and confirming the diagnosis. I wonder why we had to come all the way up here for them to tell us what we already know. He confirms the tumor is slow-growing, but that removal is the best bet. His rate of success is in line with what the Orlando doctors said and what I'd read online. After a few minutes, I tune him out, instead turning my attention to the pictures and plaques on the walls.

There are a number of him shaking hands with people I don't recognize, but imagine are meant to impress visitors. There's also one of him holding the antlers of a large buck, its tongue lulled out the side of its mouth, its eyes unfocused, but maybe I'm projecting because I know the animal is dead.

What a strange thing, to save lives all day, and then spend time off hunting another creature. It seems like it meant something, what, though, I'm not sure.

There's a picture frame on his desk. The back faces us, but I assume it contains a photo of his family. An image of a wife and three kids appears in my head. I lean over to see if I can catch the reflection of it in the window, and lose my balance and tip out of my chair.

I crash and three pairs of eyes turn straight at me. None of them move to help me up, which is made especially annoying since I am supposed to be sick and in a delicate position, or whatever. I right the chair and settle myself back in it, my face burning with embarrassment.

"What is it Stevie? Another one of your," my mom lowers her voice, though everyone can obviously still hear her, "*visions*?"

My mom is slick, I have to give her that. She knows I wasn't about to bring this up with the doctor. Lord knows my dad wouldn't have offered the information, mainly because he wouldn't have thought to until we'd left the appointment and he'd curse under his breath for forgetting. Nope, my mom is on top of it. Of course.

Dr. Oppenheimer leans forward. "Visions?"

I nod.

"How often?"

"They appear to come with her seizures, at least that's what her other doctors said," my mom cuts in. The doctor doesn't even glance at her, eyes only for me.

I shrug. "Pretty much, though I'm not aware that it's during a seizure. It happens usually after someone tells me or I pick myself up off the floor or something."

"I see." He rubs the non-pen along the outline of his lower lip. "And when was your most recent episode?"

For a moment I consider lying, but I know not only would my mom see right through it, I really wouldn't be doing myself any favors anyway. "This morning." I refuse to look at my parents. It's not worth it.

"Well, we can up your anti-seizure medication, and that should lessen them. The visions and seizures can go hand-in-hand."

"And the surgery?" my dad asks. His voice is low and I notice he is gripping his right hand with his left. They are pale in their restriction.

"I can fit you in in two weeks. I'd also suggest doing your first few rounds of chemo here. Then once we see how you're tolerating it, I can release you to finish your treatment at home. This isn't a quick fix per-se, but it should be a successful one."

"And if I don't want to get the surgery?" I know I've spoken the words, but my voice doesn't sound like my own. I keep my eyes laser focused on his.

He tilts his head ever so slightly then looks at my parents. "I don't understand."

"Stevie is under the impression these visions are from God and she thinks He's telling her not to remove the tumor." The sharpness of my mom's voice takes me by surprise. Embarrassed heat forms in my cheeks.

"Well," Dr. Oppenheimer goes on, his voice the same evenness. "These are slow-growing tumors, so there is no immediate risk—"

"Doctor," my dad cuts him off.

"But," Dr. Oppenheimer continues, ignoring him, "as it grows, so will the seizures. Eventually they can intensify, putting you at risk for falls, not to mention physical damage to your internal organs from the trauma. In the end, if the tumor gets large enough, it can push on the area of your brain that controls motor function. Plus, there is always a risk, small as it is, that the tumor can metastasize and get into your blood. Your prognosis gets exponentially worse if that happens. It usually results in death."

"Okay," I say each letter slowly. "But that is a while off, right? Months? Years?"

"Probably," he concedes. "We can manage the seizures, do routine scans, and hopefully catch the moment growth is detected and remove at that point."

"Would my success rate still be pretty close if that was done?"

The chair next to me pushes back and falls as my mom gets to her feet.

"Stevie, cut this shit out." The curse words shock me. I've heard her curse a few times, but usually under her breath, and never in public. "You are sixteen. This really isn't your decision."

I turn to the doctor, who nods.

It feels like a hole's been punched in my chest. The air rushes out as if I'm in a compromised airplane, thousands of feet above the Earth.

"May I use your bathroom?" I get out.

"Down the hall, to the left."

I take measured steps, counting one, two, three, in my head to keep myself from sprinting.

I bypass the door with the woman in a triangle dress and walk straight out of the building. It only takes two rings for Dot to pick up the phone.

"I need your help," I say. "How quickly can you get to Atlanta?"

CHAPTER EIGHTEEN

························

W hen I get back in the doctor's office, it's clear that my parents were unloading on him about all my symptoms and resistance to surgery. Their voices fall silent as I walk into the room. It makes me remember that time I was at a sleepover party in sixth grade with Becky Tremble.

We'd been best friends since second grade, but recently she started hanging out with this newer group of girls. I saw her less and less, but couldn't put my finger on the exact moment she started drifting away from me. I didn't have a ton of friends, I guess you could say I still don't, but her distance was increasingly painful.

When she invited me to her house for the night, I was thrilled. It had been ages since we'd hung out and I hoped this would be a turning point. Was it ever.

I arrived at seven like she said, but the house was already filled with five other girls. I had the sneaking suspicion they had all been told an earlier time to arrive. A stack of paper plates with pizza crust confirmed my suspicions. We watched a movie, the other girls laying scattered around the room haphazardly, like discarded clothing, when I got up to go to the bathroom.

On my way back, I heard Becky's voice in a feigned whisper. There was no way she could have thought I wouldn't have heard her.

"Ugh, my *mom* made me invite her. We used to be friends, but she's just so *weird*." The other girls laughed, but abruptly fell silent as soon as I came back. I counted to a hundred three times before announcing that I didn't feel well and asked to call my mom.

Becky didn't even see me to the door. Her mom patted my shoulder as if I was some stray dog and waved to my mom. For some reason, my mother never asked what happened, just quietly drove us home and made me a cup of tea. It was like she knew. Maybe she did.

I never hung out with Becky again.

Now, standing in the doorway, I get the same radiated heat through my body that I felt standing in the Tremble's narrow hallway. They are making decisions about my life that I had no control over. They are done listening, this much is clear.

Dr. Oppenheimer smiles warmly, his straight teeth betraying nothing, as he hands a stack of papers to my parents.

"Stevie, there are some different medicines I would like you to start taking," he says. "There's a pharmacy on the first floor that can fill them. I know this may all seem overwhelming and confusing, but we really do have your best interest at heart."

I stare straight ahead. Silent protest is my new method of resistance.

"We have your surgery scheduled for next Thursday. You'll need to come back tomorrow to get some bloodwork done and to get new scans of a few different areas. I'll also have the nurse give you final instructions for when you come back. Nothing too bad, you just won't be able to eat after eight p.m. the night before. Think you can handle that?" His voice sounds like an olive branch, asking for a truce.

I shrug. He can make all the plans he wants.

After finishing up with the receptionist and stopping at the pharmacy, we walk to the car. My mom hands me the bag of pills and I take them without hesitation. Twenty minutes. I just have to make it twenty more minutes.

Once we get back in our hotel room, I excuse myself to lay down for a bit. No one objects.

After I shut the door behind me, I scramble around the room. I throw my small tote bag on the bed and begin stuffing it with items. If I bring my entire duffle, that'll be suspicious, but I think I can get away with the small tote.

I throw in a few pairs of underwear, a t-shirt, and a pair of shorts. A few toiletries, a pair of flip-flops, and my wallet and I'm ready to go. I glance back and see Al, sitting in the middle of the pillows, half-tucked under the covers by the housekeeping staff. I hesitate for only a moment before stuffing him into my bag with a quick kiss on his forehead and an apology as I smash him in, zippering a small tuff of hair as I close it up again.

I bump into the plastic bag next to me and medicine rattles inside, a reminder there's something wrong with me.

And that I'm not sure what I am going to do about it.

After a quick internal debate, I decide to throw the pill bottle in my bag. Sitting on the edge of the bed, my chest heaves as if I've just sprinted a mile. I lift my phone to check the time and find it shaking. It takes me a moment to realize that it's my hand.

It bings. An unfamiliar number flashes across my screen.

Here.

I fill my lungs with air, letting it release through my nose while counting to ten. I've just gotten to my feet when a knock sounds, causing me to jump and my heart to race even faster.

"Stevie, your dad and I are going to go for a walk. Is that okay?" my mom's voice sounds strange, as if she's speaking through water.

"Fine," I say with an imitation of grogginess to my voice.

Once the door shuts, I frantically throw my remaining items in my duffle—not needing to hide the fact that I'm leaving anymore—and turn to run out of the room. At the last minute I decide to scribble a quick note on the hotel-provided paper. Pen hovering, I'm not sure what to write. Finally, I just say the first thing that comes to my mind: *I'm sorry, but I just can't do this*.

The door to our room makes me jump when it auto-slams behind me. I swipe my hands along my pockets automatically checking for a key, and then remind myself it doesn't matter. I'm not coming back here. When the elevator doors open, for a split second I have the sickening sensation that maybe my parents are still in the lobby and will catch me.

As each numbered light above my head illuminates with my descent, my heart rate increases. The doors slide open and I hesitate, peering around the corner like a shy cat, but the hall is thankfully vacant.

I repeat my peek around each corner before I move on. Briskly moving through the lobby, I stare straight ahead, not making eye contact with the few people waiting at the check-in desk. The automatic doors open in front of me and I step out, looking down either side of the street as I move onto the sidewalk. No one.

A green car, exactly like the woman described, pulls into the covered parking area outside the front doors.

What in holy hell are you doing? my brain screams at me.

This is the wrong decision. I know it in every fiber of my being. The note I hastily scribbled on hotel paper will do nothing to ease my parents' fears. When the police review the security footage and see me willingly get into the car, it will break my mom's heart all over again.

This is a mistake. I know it before I even make it.

But I get into the car anyway.

CHAPTER NINETEEN

•••••••••(e/o)•••••••••

T he woman in the front seat turns around and introduces herself as Gertie.

She gestures to the passenger seat. "And this is Nancy."

Nancy awkwardly leans around to shake my hand, but because
of the angle she more so just takes it and squeezes a bit.

The car smells like fast food and stale cigarettes, though I see
evidence of neither. I lower the window a crack to air it out, but
I have a feeling it's permeated into the fabric of the seats and
it's probably a losing battle.

I feel a vibration in my pocket and curse inwardly. Jorge's
name pops up on the screen and I breathe a sigh of relief. My
absence hasn't yet been noted. Of course, I know I'll get caught,
hell, I half expect to be pulled over by a cop at any moment and
dragged back to the hotel. But there is a small ounce of relief
knowing I have a bit more time. My thumb hovers over the green
and red icons.

Making a decision, I press my thumb to the side of my phone
until it shuts off. They will fi nd me, I know, but I'm not ready
for that yet.

Gertie calls something back to me and I have to roll the
window up to hear. The smells waft in again and I try to breath in
and out through my mouth.

I lean forward. "I'm sorry, what?"

Nancy laughs, which I'm surprised to hear is more of a childish
cackle. Both Gertie and Nancy look to be about my grandmother's
age. They are all softness and rounded edges. Exactly the two
people I'd pick to make a scared girl feel less apprehensive about
running away with strangers.

The enormity of it hits me.

I've run away.

"You feeling okay, sweetie?" Nancy asks.

I nod, blinking hard against the tears forming.

"You don't have to talk or say anything you don't want to say," Gertie calls back. The woman shifts forward. I've got a million questions I want to ask, but in this moment, I'm so tired, I lean back and shut my eyes.

⋯⋯⋯⋯⋯⋯⋯

I must have fallen asleep, because the next thing I know, the car slows. For a second, a jolt of fear courses through me. I look behind us, expecting to see the flashing lights of a cop car ready to take me back.

Nothing. Just a line of normal-looking cars following us off the highway.

We pull into a rest stop to use the bathroom and grab a late lunch. The ladies buy me food and I didn't realize how ravenous I was until the smell of pizza hits my nostrils. I'm halfway through scarfing down a slice when I look up at the two faces staring at me.

No one, not even my parents at their most proud, have looked at me the way these ladies do. Their eyes are soft and appear to be on the brink of spilling tears, their lips in a straight line with small upturns at the corners. In short, they look enthralled with me.

I double check to make sure I haven't spilled pizza sauce on my chin.

"So," my voice trails. I think these are the first words I've spoken in hours. "What's the plan?"

I'm an idiot, I know. I get into a car with strangers and am just now asking where they are taking me. To some murder house for all I know. I look around the rest stop, there's only a few people here, but enough that if I'm in trouble, I can scream for help.

Gertie smiles broadly, showing that she has one lower tooth missing. It makes me rub my tongue against mine. "We're part of the Georgia chapter of The Church of the Eye."

"We're driving you to the state line where someone from our Florida chapter will take you the rest of the way," Nancy jumps in.

"Oh, so you won't be coming the whole way with me?" I'm not sure if this is disappointing or a relief. They seem like nice enough people, but something is just a little off about them. Maybe it's their eagerness that makes me uneasy. But at the same time, what strangers will I be trading them in for?

Nancy cackles. "Oh, no, we wish! But Luke said it would be best for us not to, um..." she trails as if unsure of what words to use.

"The, um..." Gertie starts, but also breaks off.

It dawns on me. "State lines," I say quietly.

They nod slowly. "We believe in this cause. We believe in this movement," Gertie says, her voice strained with the hope that I will believe her.

"But our legal counsel—" Nancy starts and I hold up my hand.

"I understand." Which was partially true, but really, I just want this uncomfortable conversation to end. It's my first hint that what I am doing is breaking laws. I'm not sure if I would really get in trouble, but those helping me can. Is it worth it? And more importantly, why the hell do these people think it is? I'm a stranger to them. They maybe saw a news story about me, but really, what is making them help me? My online searches yielded little information about the group, much less about their teachings and doctrine, but the way these two women look at me, it's clear they think I'm special. But why? It's as if I'm a god myself.

It's not an all-together bad feeling, I have to admit.

We clean up our trays and head back to the car. I press the button on the side of my phone until the screen illuminates. It searches for service for a few seconds before it starts making a series of beeps and noises. Text messages flash along with voicemail and missed call alerts. I switch off my location icon, just in case. My thumb hovers over the message icon with a red "31" to the right of it when another one pops up on my screen.

Call us this instant! From my dad's number. It's too much. I turn my phone off again and buckle my seat belt.

CHAPTER TWENTY

·············(⚬⁄͜⚬)············

A short while later we turn off the highway, the *Welcome to Florida* sign visible in the distance, and into a welcome center. It's a small building that mostly houses brochures, and I wonder why the tri-fold pamphlets are still made.

I thumb one with a picture of a gator on the front and some air boats.

Do people still travel to a new city with no plans, see a picture of a manatee, and go, "Ah! *Now* we know what we'll be doing on this vacation!"

Three women in matching green shirts and khaki pants walk toward us, smiles plastered on their faces. They embrace Gertie and Nancy before introducing themselves. Angelic has skin paler than mine and brown curly hair, Jackie is dark skinned with a short, black bob, and Abby—who looks about my age—is also dark skinned, but with purple and pink hair. It sticks out at crazy angles and I want to ask her a million questions about it, but I just hold out my hand and say my name.

Angelic bypasses my palm and pulls me in for a hug. Taking this as consent, Jackie and Abby do the same. Now that the precedent is set, Gertie and Nancy embrace me as they say goodbye. I've never been much of a hugger. I don't really understand why encircling arms and pressing chests to one another is a thing. Especially with strangers.

But I play along and thank Gertie and Nancy again for lunch and for taking such good care of me. I sling my bag over my shoulder and half-smile to them, hopefully indicating that this is the most they are going to get out of me. They take the hint and turn to walk away. I have mixed feelings when I see Gertie wiping at her eyes as they exit the center.

"We're parked through here," Angelic says, gesturing to a door on the opposite side of the round room. Abby walks next to me and bounces with each step, as if she's fighting the urge to ask me a million questions. If these women are anything like the adults in my life, Abby would have been coached prior to meeting me. I'm sure something along the lines of *don't ask too many questions, let her settle in first, it's rude to bombard someone you just met.*

I may not be touchy-feely, but I am inquisitive—or nosey as my mom calls it—so I've had these pointers said to me my whole life. I never really understood the need, but now on what I'm sure would be the receiving end of twenty-questions, I can appreciate wanting to be left alone.

Jackie gets in the passenger seat as Angelic gets behind the wheel. Abby and I sit in the back. Apparently, the walk from the welcome center to the car is all she can take.

Abby takes a deep breath and launches into her questions.

"How was Atlanta? Were Gertie and Nancy nice? I've never met someone from another region before. They seemed really nice. Was it a long drive? What did you guys talk about? What did the doctors say? How are you feeling?"

She's speaking in such rapid succession, there's no way I can answer them all. She wants to know *everything*. Heck, I don't even know how I'm feeling. When she stops to catch her breath, Jackie turns and quietly says her name. It's all that's needed, and the questions stop.

We drive for about an hour when it happens. One second I'm staring out the window and the next this warmth spreads through my body. For a split second, I realize I missed a dose of my medicine, but then I'm pulled under.

I'm still in the car, but Mary is driving now, not Angelic. Jackie has disappeared and Abby is replaced by the same young version of Jesus I saw the first time. I smile at Him and He returns the gesture.

"This is a long trip you're on," He says, and I'm not sure if He means from Atlanta or something bigger. I want to ask Him, but

I'm so warm and relaxed, I can't seem to talk. I lay my head back against the seat and just stare at them.

Mary turns to me and I want to tell her to look back at the road, but then a new calm comes over me. Of course she has this handled. I needn't worry.

"What will happen when we get there?" I manage to mutter.

"You worry too much," Jesus says.

"Please, just tell me," I beg.

"What needs to happen," Mary says. I believe her. "Stevie, you need to trust. Can you do that for me?"

I nod, surprised she knows my name. This is the first time she's used it and it makes me feel even more special. *She* knows who *I* am.

I look out the window and press my forehead against it, the coolness of the glass feels good against my skin. The sun heats my face and I wonder if I'll get burnt. My mom will yell at me for not putting on sunscreen. I always forget.

Awareness comes in ticks. A hand on my hand. Fingertips on my shoulder and neck. Soft breath that tickles my cheek.

I turn and am shocked to see not Mary's face, but Jackie's pressed close to mine. She is talking in a low voice, but I can hear the worry in it. It takes me a moment to realize she's saying my name, over and over.

"What?" I ask her.

"Oh, good. We weren't sure what happened. Abby said you slumped funny in your seat, so we pulled over, but we hadn't been able to get you to respond. Was it a seizure?"

I must have looked at her confused because Angelic said that Jackie is a nurse. I nod, but carefully, afraid my brain may fall out if I move it too quickly. My post-seizure feeling is strange, like a tingle in my body, and I worry that parts of me will fall off if I use them too fast.

You worry too much.

His words replay in my ears.

"Did you have another vision?" Abby asks. Neither woman shushes her. I hesitate, but nod. The air in the car instantly shifts.

CHAPTER TWENTY-ONE

t takes me a few minutes to regain my composure. The car comes back into focus. Angelic is again in the driver's seat, not Mary. No, it was never really Mary driving. I take a breath, steady myself, and open my mouth. But once the words form, it's not their questions I answer, but my own I ask.

"I have a few things I need answered. So, what's the deal?"

They look at me as if the words I'm speaking are in some foreign tongue. I roll them around in my mouth, make sure I am forming them correctly and whatever episode I just had hasn't affected my speech, but no, I am speaking clear, normal words.

"Deal?" Abby pinches her eyebrows together in confusion.

"I did some research about your group online, but there wasn't a whole lot I could find on the specifics."

"We like people to come meet us in person," Angelic says.

"It helps if we can get an idea of what they're searching for, and see if we can provide them the answers," Jackie adds.

"So where do I fit in? What answers am I looking for?"

Abby laughs. "Um, you *are* the answer!"

"Our leader, Luke, will explain this much better than we can, so I don't want to confuse you with any conflicting information," Angelic starts. "But in our teachings, a prophecy says someone will come to us, most likely in the form of a young woman, with a direct link to God. That person will help us walk in His light and find the most direct path to The After when the end-of-days are upon us."

"The signs have been building for months," Abby says, bouncing a little with nervous energy and excitement. "The white birds, the dark clouds, the trees."

"Birds? Trees? I don't understand." Their words swirl in my head like leaves picked up by the wind.

"The Leader. He will explain everything." Angelic smiles, putting a clear end to the conversation. "Do you feel all right to get back on the road?"

I nod and off we go.

········••••◄(●⁄◌)►•••••·······

It's late when we arrive, jostling down an unpaved road riddled with potholes. I fight to keep my body straight, but end up crashing my shoulder and head into my window twice. You'd think with all the roller coasters I've ridden in my life, this would be a cakewalk, but by the time we pull into a grass lot, my stomach is queasy.

Bed.

All I want to do is find a soft bed and crawl into it. The enormity of what I've done hits me as I get out of the car and breathe in the warm, fresh air. *My parents are going to kill me.*

How did I not think this through? Was it really something we couldn't have work out? But I think back to the hushed conversation my mom and dad had in the hotel room. No. I had no real say in the matter. They were going to force me to go to the hospital and let some guy cut into my brain, curing me, sure, but at what cost?

Before I can stop her, Abby grabs my bag and walks toward some darkened buildings with it. It isn't terribly late, a little after nine, but there are only about a half-dozen lights I can see around the entire place. They cast weak shadows, making the trees appear gnarled like they're straight out of a scary movie. One window on the far right is illuminated, but other than a couple of highlighted walkways, the place looks deserted.

Fear makes the breath catch in the middle of my throat. What if this isn't the inclusive place I was imaging? Maybe there was a reason I found little information online, maybe this isn't really *real*. Oh gosh. Am I going to be made into a Lifetime TV movie where it turns out I am kidnapped and sold as some kind of sex slave? And I willingly went, the audience at home yelling at the television the whole time at my stupidity?

I look around, deciding on where I should run, but I only see the forms of non-descript buildings, backlit with flood lights, and trees. Should I try to escape? Is escape even the right word, or just slip away and call for an Uber? I could follow the driveway, but they'd surely stop me before I made it to the main road. And my bag. They took my bag. I casually pat my pockets. At least my cell is still there. Worst case, I can call for help and pray someone gets to me before anything bad happens.

Angelic and Jackie move forward, but I stand in place, my fingers still lightly touching the door handle of the car.

"Awfully dark and quiet around here," I say, trying to bait them into confessing their plans. It's a long shot, but I've seen it work on Investigation Discovery shows.

Jackie looks around as if she just noticed. "Oh, yeah. We go to bed early here. Lights out at eight thirty."

I nod. This may be reasonable.

"Won't you get in trouble then for being out?"

Angelic shakes her head. "Oh, it's not like that. I mean, there are rules, I guess, but it's not like they'd lock you up for being out of bed late. Breakfast and morning worship starts at five thirty and while it's encouraged for you to go to bed early to ensure a proper amount of sleep, no one forces you to. But most people do."

Getting up at five thirty sounds like its own version of torture, but I keep that thought to myself.

"So where are we going?" I still haven't let go of the handle. I'm not sure what I think will happen when I do—it's not like I could use it as a weapon or anything—but I'm still reluctant to move my fingers.

"Abby is taking your bag to your room and making sure it's all set up for you. You're going to meet Mr. Ackerman. He'll go over some things with you before bed." Angelic nods as she says the last word, putting finality to the conversation.

Because I'm not sure what else to do, I let go of the car door, step forward, and follow them toward the one glowing light.

The light in the office hurts my eyes and I have to raise my hand to shield them until they adjust. Wood paneling covers every inch of the space, including the ceiling. It makes it feel somewhat tomb-like. A man in a well-fi tted navy suit sits at a small desk in the cluttered space. Papers form walls around him. Deep purple rings hang under his eyes and I wonder if they are from years of stress, or from me. I hope the former.

As soon as we enter, he springs to his feet. For some reason I expect him to be slow-moving, as if the offi ce has made him a part of it. Maybe I am also the cause of the haphazardness around here.

He reaches out his hand to me—I'm relieved he doesn't try to hug me—and introduces himself. "I am Kenneth Ackerman, legal counsel to the church, and you must be Stevie. It is an immense pleasure to meet you. I hope the drive wasn't too tiring. I need a few minutes of your time before you head to bed. Is that all right?"

Legal counsel? The uneasiness in my stomach returns. I nod, though wonder if I really have a choice in the matter. "What do you need from me?" I hate how small my voice sounds. Assertiveness has never been my strong point, and this experience is truly testing any amount I possess.

I've always been a back-of-the-class kind of girl. Trying not to make too much noise or have too much personality, just blend in. Life is easier that way I fi nd. Sure, I have friends and get along with people, I'm not totally socially inept, but being the center of attention this is probably my reality change.

He moves back to his desk and pulls out a blue folder then removes several papers. There are dozens of similar looking folders all over and I wonder how he keeps it all straight. Maybe organized chaos is just how this guy rolls.

"All right, Stevie, first thing's first. I know we have a lot of information to get through in a short period of time and it will be difficult to process, but there are legal issues we need to resolve as quickly as possible."

"Okay," I say, but have no idea what he is talking about.

The panic feeling rises in my chest again and I take the seat he offers me across from his own. I turn to look at Angelic and Jackie, but they are gone, the doorway a black hole into the night. How did I not notice them leaving? I take a deep breath. There is no reason for anyone here to murder me. Sure, no one knows where I am, my cell phone is turned off, and they took all my stuff, but what would they benefit from spending all the time and money to bring me here just to off me? And a lawyer? If anyone is going to kill me, it's certainly not going to be a lawyer, right?

Yes. I am fine. Not dying today.

"So, there are all sorts of laws pertaining to the custody of minors, as well as moving minors across state lines."

"Yeah," I interrupt. "Gertie mentioned that was why they couldn't take me all the way here."

"Exactly!"

His reaction's as if I've solved some great mathematic mystery, like I had some higher understanding most people don't. It's strange, but a compliment I decide to take. Maybe I am a legal genius. Who knows?

"And these papers are supposed to help with that?"

A smile breaks out on his face, erasing some of the tiredness from his eyes. "Yes, these papers here are statements of intent. Basically, you're saying you willingly left where you were and are staying here under your free will."

"Okay…" I trail. This isn't what I was expecting. I trek all the way here, and have to sign papers? Seems anticlimactic.

"And this second paper is the application for medical emancipation."

Chapter Twenty-two

A funny sensation bubbles up deep in my gut. "Medical emancipation?"

"Stevie, what you want..." He moves to sit in the chair next to me. "...declining or postponing medical treatment, requires legal action. That is what we are willing to provide for you, what *I* am willing to provide for you. As of right now, your parents have control over your medical care. Whether it's in line with what you want or not, that doesn't matter. What they say goes, unless..." He taps the papers in my hand. "...this starts the process to revert that control to you. We'll apply with the courts, there will be a trial—"

"Trial?" I cut him off. Now my head is spinning along with my stomach.

He leans toward me and lowers his voice like he doesn't want anyone else to hear what he's about to say. "This is not something to take lightly, and I know this is a lot of information in a short amount of time, but we really need to make a move on this if we're going to be successful. We need to establish your wishes and get the ball rolling. That in itself will give you some protections, albeit temporarily. It will at least put a medical stay on any procedures until we can get in front of a judge."

"And then what?"

"Well, we have to present a case. Show you are of sound mind," he stops, a wash of embarrassment over his choice of words.

"Funny, since my mind is kinda the problem." My joke falls flat and I laugh to break the tension.

He humors me with a half smile. "Once we prove you are what is called a 'mature minor,' then we make a case to have our leader, Luke, become a limited guardian for you."

"Why?" Maybe I wasn't a legal genius after all.

"Because of your age, the court most likely won't allow you to have full emancipation rights. You have a better chance to name someone else to be your... mentor."

My hand moves to the paper, but hesitates.

"What will happen to my parents?" The question sounds childish as I ask it, but I need to know.

"This doesn't change their legal status as your parents. Nothing will change in your relationship unless you want it to. All this does is say you don't agree with the medical care they want for you and you think you're mature enough to make those decisions for yourself."

I hover for a moment, an image of my mom, dad, and stepdad pop into my head. I don't know how else to make them understand and stop this train heading in the wrong direction. My rest-stop dinner bubbles in my stomach. I lock eyes with Mr. Ackerman, not blinking until he meets my gaze with the same steady intensity.

"They still will be my parents, right?"

"Always."

I lean down and sign the papers. I know it will hurt them. It's a lie to say our relationship won't change, I know that as well, but every cell in my body is telling me not to get the surgery.

This will crush them, but I do it anyway.

········•••••••◄❁⁄❁►•••••••········

I feel different when I leave his office as if severing legal ties cut actual strings tying myself to my parents. Jackie is standing outside and walks me to my room. It's almost ten when she leaves me there.

The room is tiny, about half the size of mine at home, with blank walls and a single window above the bed. My bag is on a twin bed with white sheets, a single side table is to the left and there is a small three-drawer dresser on one side of the room. There isn't an attached bathroom, but it's right next door, so that's not too bad.

I take the few things out of my duffle and place them in the dresser. I pull my phone out and hesitate, but then toss it back in the bag.

I move to put my bag under the bed and something rolls out of the side pocket. It bounces against the wall and stops by my feet with a rattle.

My pills.

I try to remember the last time I took a dose. The restaurant I think? I pick them up and pause. There's a bottle of water on the side table. Do I continue? Swallow these pills that take away the visions, or give them up entirely?

Heck, no one is forcing me to take them now. No one's watching. My parents and doctors aren't here.

I hold the white rectangle in my palm. In a single motion, I place the pill in my mouth and take a swig of water.

The small step of signing the papers was enough for today. I'll decide what's next later.

CHAPTER TWENTY-THREE

········•••◦(✪╱✿)◦•••········

When my eyes open, confusion is my first thought. I am in a room, but it's not *my* room. The dark mounds of furniture are in the wrong place and while the bed is comfortable, it's smaller than mine and not quite as soft. The sheets are well-worn and scratchy. Hotel? Right, I went to Atlanta. But no, this isn't the hotel room.

You ran away.

The memories penetrate my half-awake state and pull me the rest of the way to consciousness. I roll over and hit my phone to see the time, turning it on in the process. The screen lights the room blue. It's quarter after three.

At first, as the phone is warming up, I think maybe everyone's calmed down as it stays silent, just the original thirty-one texts appearing on the screen. Then the new notifications start. Pings sound like cannon fire and I rush to silence it. After a few moments, the vibrations stop and I assess the damage.

Sixteen new missed calls. Ten from my mom, four from my dad, and two from Jorge. And one hundred seven text messages. There are a few random ones, but the majority are from my parents and Jorge.

Stevie, where are you?
OK, honey, I know you are upset, but you need to call us.
Stevie! Stop ignoring us.
Call us back immediately young lady.
Babe, what's going on? Call me.
Stevie, you are scaring us, please call us back.
Babe, call your mom. Your parents are freaking out.

They increase in intensity, and by the last few, it's clear they've contacted Jorge to find out where I am. The voicemail icon also shows at the top of my screen, but I chicken out and delete the notification.

Shouldn't this be an indication what I'm doing is wrong? I mean, I've *never* done something I feel ashamed to face my parents about, or hell, even my boyfriend about. Sure, I've done dumb things, failed tests, whatever, but part of me never wants to talk to them again. To never face this betrayal, because I know that's what this is.

My chest tightens when I think about the paperwork I signed. I'm not sure how long it will take, but pretty soon my parents will have a courier come to their door and present them with papers. Do they say "you've been served" like in the movies? Their hearts will break and I won't even be there to explain myself. I'm too chicken-shit to explain myself now.

I thumb through my contacts and press the green phone button.

Jorge answers on the first ring despite the late hour.

"Stevie?!" His tone is both a question and a shout of relief.

"Hey, yeah."

"What the hell is going on? Your parents are freaking out. Did you run away? Tell me what the hell is happening."

The stress of the last few hours builds until it pours out my eyes in liquid form.

"Stevie? Are you okay? Is someone hurting you?"

"I can't get the surgery." It's too simplistic, but that's all I've got for right now. I sniff and wipe my nose on my sleeve.

"The surgery? Oh shit, Stevie. Seriously? Your parents said you got into some strange fucking car. You did that because of a surgery? What kind of bullshit is that? That's not you."

His language shocks me. Jorge almost never curses, convinced his grandmother will appear out of nowhere and catch him in the act.

"I just…" What? What answer do I have for him? "Listen, they were going to force me to get brain surgery. *Brain surgery*."

"Because you have a tumor. Because there is cancer *in your brain*, and that's how you get it out. I get you're scared. You think

I'm not freaking terrified? I am, but you have to get this surgery. You're going to die if you don't."

It is a sickening realization to know the strangers surrounding me in this compound are the only ones on my side.

"Jorge—" I start but he cuts me off.

"You have to go home. You have to call your parents, tell them where you are, shit, tell *me* where you are and I'll come pick you up. Running away isn't going to solve anything."

"I filed papers to be medically emancipated." The words fall out before I can think. The silence that meets me on the other end is so strong, I pull the phone away from my face to make sure he's still there. The seconds tick by on the counter. Twenty-two before he says something.

"Stevie," he speaks in a low voice, as if I'm a spooked horse. "A lot is happening right now. You got diagnosed and whisked away to doctors, maybe it was too quick. Let me talk to your parents. Let me get them to agree to back off for a bit. Just tell me where you are."

"They aren't going to change their minds, Jorge."

"What is so important—"

I cut him off. "I *see* them."

"Is this about the visions you think you're having?"

"I am having them. They're real." I don't hide the defensiveness from my voice.

He sighs on the other end. "Of course you think they're real, they're happening in your head, but they aren't *real* real. It's the tumor. It's making you see these things."

I shake my head even though I know he can't see me. "No, that's not true. The tumor is just a window. It's letting me see what's real for the first time. There are people here, a whole community of people, who believe me."

"Stevie, tell me where you are."

"Let my parents know I'm okay. They'll be hearing from me soon." I hang up and turn my phone off, as lost and alone as ever.

CHAPTER TWENTY-FOUR

A tapping at my door wakes me. After my conversation with Jorge, it took me a while to fall back asleep and now my eyes feel itchy with tiredness. I have so many emotions running through me. Hurt, anger, and sadness at his not understanding. And right under the surface, fear.

A deep fear underlies everything else I'm going through. At what will happen, to me, my parents, the tumor. About the visions, fear about them stopping, and an apprehension on meeting this leader guy today.

The knock grows louder and I pull myself from the bed to answer it, tucking Al under the covers. I'm not sure why his presence embarrasses me, but after a quick apology, I shove him out of sight before getting the door.

Abby has a bright smile that doesn't match the early hour. "You've got about ten minutes before first service," she says then chews at her lower lip. "I've been trying to wake you for a while."

"Oh, sorry about that. I didn't get much sleep and I've never been much of a morning person."

"Don't worry, we'll fix that and get you on board in no time. Bathroom is to the left, I'll come back to get you in five and we can walk together."

I nod, but I'm not really sure why I have to follow their schedule, especially since I just got here. Not that I one hundred percent knew what to expect arriving here, but early morning wake-ups certainly isn't it.

I guess I should go along with it for now at least.

The hallways are empty, and I rush to use the bathroom and brush my teeth before tossing some clothes on. True to her word, Abby is back in exactly five minutes. She chats a bit as we walk, something about scheduling and the geography of the structures we pass, but her words don't register in my brain. I'm still playing over the phone call last night and the meeting with Mr. Ackerman.

We exit our building and go across the courtyard. It's still too dark to get a good idea of the layout of this place, but we are heading in yet another new direction, away from Mr. Ackerman's office as well as our dorms, as Abby calls them. The edges of the sky are a burnt orange and I hope the next time I'm outside I'll be able to see more.

We go through a small arched path and come upon an illuminated building. It's simple, one story tall with neat rows of windows, and smells freshly painted. The newness of this place seems odd to me. Most of the structures we pass appear almost just-built. Save for Mr. Ackerman's office building, it's like they've suddenly expanded.

When we walk inside, I can't help but notice how the new morning light floods in from each angle. From outside some of the windows appeared dully colored, but from this side they sparkle with rich blues, reds, greens, and yellows. They cast rainbow-colored beams along sections of the floor and the people sitting around tables as the sun races up the horizon.

It's really breathtaking.

People shuffle in around us speaking in low voices. I'm not sure what it is about the stillness of the dawn that makes you want to whisper, but I do the same thing when I lean over to ask Abby a question.

"So, this is your meeting room?"

She laughs. "Have you not been listening to anything I've said?"

"Sorry, I'm not much of a morning person."

"I think we established that. It's our meeting and eating place. We like to multi-task. Our first service in the morning is during breakfast, nourishing mind and body."

She says this last sentence in a tone that makes me think she's repeating the line from someone else.

The room is dimly lit, I guess to not complete with the stained-glass sunrise. The smell of eggs and bacon fills my nostrils and my stomach growls in a Pavlovian response to the food. We get plates and fill them sky-high, Abby giggling as we go. A middle-aged man and woman narrow their eyes at us, but Abby doesn't seem to notice. From the looks we get from some of the other adults, I imagine talking this much is frowned upon, but no one says anything. I make a mental note though to be a bit more reserved at lunch.

A woman comes up to me, a bright smile on her face. She is petite and wearing head-to-toe animal print. Her hair jets in every direction and something tells me this is intentional.

"Stevie!" Her voice sounds familiar, but I can't quite place it.

"Umm, hi?"

"It's me, Dot. We spoke on the phone."

The wheels slowly click into place and I have to adjust the mental image of who I thought she was with this person standing in front of me. She goes to hug me, but my tray gets in the way, so it turns into a more awkward shoulder squeeze.

"Hi, yeah, thank you," I say.

"I'll let you get something to eat before we get started, but I just wanted to introduce myself in person and let you know how happy we are you're here!"

She turns and walks away. I smile at Abby and shrug my shoulders.

"She's the one who called me when I was in Atlanta," I explain.

"Oh, don't worry, we all know. It was a really big deal, plus," Abby leans forward and lowers her voice, "Dot relayed the story about a million times."

Abby winks and puts her tray on a table, gesturing for me to take the seat next to her. "So you can see the screens better."

"Screens?" I gaze around as I shovel some of the best eggs I've ever had into my mouth and notice two large projection screens set to either side of the stage.

People murmur and look at us, but thankfully no one else comes over to say anything. I may have food in my belly, but I'm still not really awake enough to interact with strangers yet.

I am surprised Abby's mom and dad don't come sit with us. Maybe they are somewhere else? I actually wouldn't mind meeting them. I'm curious what kind of family would choose to all live in a commune of sorts.

"So where are your parents?" I ask.

Her eyes drop from mine to the table. "Died."

"Oh my gosh, I am so sorry." I feel terrible and wish I had something better to say to make up for my snafu.

"No, it's okay. It was a long time ago. I came to live here with my Aunt Jackie after it happened." She smiles and shovels a forkfull of eggs into her mouth.

Ah, so that's why Abby came along on the car trip. I was wondering what her connection to the other two ladies was, other than them all being part of the same…what? Group? Cult? The internet had a bunch of different terms for the organization, not all kind. But looking around at the people seated here, they all looked happy. It was not even freaking six in the morning. As far as I could tell, they were all well-fed and no one had bruises or anything, at least no injuries visible, to indicate something sinister was going on. But I also know there are few religious organizations, legitimate ones at least, that have its members live together in one central place. Usually you just went to worship once a week or so. Sure, there were retreats and stuff, but I didn't know something as long-term as this.

Did that make this more or less legitimate than my own religious upbringing?

I wonder what brought all these people together. Why they decided living in this manner was the best way to express their religion. Why it demanded such a complete dedication.

A few cheers break out, stopping my internal dialogue. I look up and for the first time notice there's a stage at the far end of the room. A thirty-something looking man strides up to a wooden podium. There's a placard in front of it showing a cross with different colored light beams surrounding it and the words "Church of the Eye." There's a shape in the middle of the cross I can't make out clearly, but I can guess it's probably an eyeball.

On either side of the stage, the screens light up with an image of the man. It isn't that deep of a room, and there are maybe a hundred fifty people sitting in it, but the screens do help me see that, yes, a single eye is placed right where the points of the cross met. The man smiles at the group.

I am transfixed.

Okay, so I'm a teenager, whatever. Way, way, way too young for this guy, I know that, but holy cow is he attractive. His eyes are deep ocean blue, his hair dirty blond, and to top it all off, of course he is fit, wearing a purple button up shirt that looks like it was made just for him. Before he even speaks, part of me knows how someone like this could be their leader.

He reaches out his arms, silencing the clapping and whoops from the crowd below. The clock above his head reads five fifty-five and I'm suddenly wide awake.

"My dear, dear brothers and sisters," he says, his smile now showing both rows of perfect white teeth. I laugh a puff of air. Where did they get this guy? Some Insta-Model account?

"As many of you know, we have a new member in our group."

I wonder if he means member like, member of the human race, or follower of whatever this is. Because I'm not quite ready to claim I am part of the latter camp.

"I think this is a great time to talk about how we came to be such a strong and powerful movement." A smatter of claps rings out as he talks, but he silences them again with a raised hand. "Fifty years ago, our one and only prophet Jacob had a vision that he needed to tell those in his church, but his pastor did not believe him. Did not believe that he, a simple man, could have had such a communication with God."

As I look around, people are shaking their heads. They all stare forward as if this is the first time they've heard this story and are completely surprised by it.

"But Jacob knew, *knew*, that it was real. He had truly been spoken to. And several of his friends and family also knew that he'd been chosen for this message. They moved to this very property which had been gifted to Jacob by a devoted follower and he continued to build on his message. They were green before green didn't mean a color. They were sustainable before that was a thing. They were committed to saving the planet before people knew how badly the planet needed to be saved."

"They knew!" someone shouts.

The leader laughs. "Yes! Yes, they *knew*! They knew because God told Jacob that first he needed to treat the earth better, then get others to treat the earth better, and if they did that, they would be rewarded with more information on how to reach The After.

"And you, all of you, have continued his legacy. You have traveled and brought his message with you. When he was called home to be with the Lord, did his message die with him?"

"No!" the voices around me cry out.

"No," the leader echoes, "it got stronger! Our commitment has not waned. And he told us what God told him. If we were strong and true and good shepherds, we would be rewarded. God would send another prophet for us, to guide us, to bring us on our final journey."

My breathing stops.

"This person, this *girl*, would continue with Jacob's teachings and enable us to fulfill all of God's wishes, and with her, the final days would come, but we would not be afraid."

"There's no need to be afraid!" a voice shouts to my left.

"No need," the leader repeats. "Because she would show us. She would save us."

He pauses and opens his arms up again. The entire room turns to face me. "Stevie, we've been waiting for you."

CHAPTER TWENTY-FIVE

················(C/O)··············

T he rest of the day passes in a blur. Abby chaperones me around
the grounds, now finally fully visible. It's a huge swath of land
with the meeting hall, living spaces, and offices toward the
front of the property. Lines of trees appear to go for miles,
fencing the whole thing in. At the back is acres of farmland
plus some smaller raised beds at the rear of the hall. Chicken
coops and pens with goats and geese flank the side. There's
also a sort of outdoor amphitheater which, despite the heat, is fi
lled with people in Bible study.

We sit for a few moments, but just like each place we've
stopped at, soon people are barraging me with questions. She
acts almost like a bodyguard, apologizing and telling them we are
needed someplace else.

I'm immensely grateful.

We sit in one of the side gardens helping to pick lettuce for
lunch that day, when a man comes up to me and plops on the
ground. Abby smiles at him, but doesn't introduce us.

"Stevie," he says as if we're long friends.

I look at him, but say nothing, wondering if this is going to be
a lecture on properly picking produce or another series of questions from the residents about what I am going to teach them.
Which frankly, I am having trouble putting into words.

He doesn't say any more and soon gets up to move to a far
corner of the garden.

Just when I think I may be left alone, the woman in the row
behind us calls out to me.

"So, what happens when God comes to you?" she asks. "Are you able to ask Him things, get answers to your questions?"

I look around and see people moving toward me.

"Next time it happens," a man calls over her shoulder. "Can you ask how my mother is? She passed recently. I need to know she is all right." Tears swell in his eyes and another woman places a hand on his shoulder.

I'm like a deer in headlights.

"I…" is all I manage to say.

"Have they told you about the afterlife?"

"How will you know it's the end of days?"

"When will they visit you again?"

"I have a bank loan that's in default and I've been praying, but it doesn't seem to be helping. Can you ask what else I should do?"

"All right everyone," Abby interjects, making a point to check her watch. "We are on a tight schedule."

She pulls my arm and drags me up and away from the group, my mind reeling. We march right to the edge of garden, sparse with people. We settle next to the guy from before and I brace myself as he starts gently pulling romaine from the ground and brushing off the dirt.

"I bet this is all a little overwhelming," he says, eyes still fixed on his task.

"You can say that again."

A crane flies by us, voice crackling as it calls to no other birds in sight.

"A crane," Abby whispers.

"I see it," the man says.

I do too, but apparently, I'm supposed to *feel* something about seeing it. Really, I don't feel anything, except the fact I'm not a big fan of cranes and their crazy voices.

"Birds are very important in our teachings," the man says, finally turning to look at me. I put down my lettuce and shift my weight to face him.

"There haven't been any birds in my visions," I admit.

"I don't think we expect there to be. Those visions are for you. Then you can interpret and share with us. The birds, they are for us. They symbolize our connection with the heavens. A creature bound to earth, yet can soar and touch God. Amazing beings, if you really think about it. It was a bird that let Noah know his journey was coming to an end. We think they will be there for us in the same way, when the time is right."

I nod, but this sounds like gibberish. Sure, some birds are cool. Eagles? Yup. Swans? Okay. Pigeons? Not so much.

"I know coming here couldn't have been easy for you," he continues, "but what has brought you to us, will ensure that you stay safe." He smiles. "All you need to do is speak your truth. And we will do our best to listen."

He nods to Abby, gathers his vegetables, and leaves us. My head swirls as the crane's noise fades into the distance.

CHAPTER TWENTY-SIX

···········•••••◦◦◦•••••···········

The shoelaces on my right sneaker click rhythmically on the linoleum floor as I swing my legs back and forth in the tall chair. I should tie it, but I'm enjoying the sound.

The leader, who's name I learn is Luke, asked me to come to his office. The space is slightly larger than Mr. Ackerman's, but more densely populated with chairs, tables, and books, making it feel more cramped. The walls are covered—literally I can't find even a postcard-sized blank space—with posters, news clippings, and scraps of paper. The choice of some is obvious, Bible quotes or stories about members of different churches and even a write-up of The Church of the Eye, but others don't make a lot of sense.

A story about land conservation. Another about a new tax collector in the area. One about farming with cows. Maybe they are going to add more livestock to the back land?

One of the short walls has bookcases stuffed with knick-knacks and framed photographs. I look back, but the door is still shut. He left to get us coffee, and I fight the urge to poke and prod through all the shelves.

I stand and move toward his desk. There's a mess of papers covering most of it, a small corner bare, and I wonder what level of effort it took to leave this one part blank. I lean over the stacks to get a closer look at the papers. Some I recognize as credit card statements and one with IRS letterhead. I glance back at the door before leaning over to read what I can beneath the rubble of other papers.

not considered a recognized religious sect

exemption wouldn't apply

Land dues are as follows

The lines are in fragments, and while I can assume the gist, I want to know for sure. My hand hovers over the papers to lift some up when I hear a noise behind me and race back to my seat. My heart feels like it is going to crack through my ribs as he walks back in.

He hands me the steaming cup, leaving the office door open behind him.

"Stevie, thank you for coming to meet me. I know Abby had some activities planned for you two, so I won't keep you long."

I take a sip. The coffee is laden with sugar and cream. Just how I like it.

I'd been sneaking sips of my mom's coffee ever since I was little. About a year ago, I started pouring myself cups from the pot on the counter. She shook her head and told me to keep it to a single mug a day. I mostly listened.

"Mmm, thanks," I say.

"I hope you're settling in all right. I know nothing can feel like home but home, but is there anything else you need?"

"No, everyone has been wonderful. This place..." my voice trails as I struggle to put it into words. I love that everyone works for a common good. The people here seem kind, even if a little too eager for my presence. The land expands in every direction where you can almost forget for a moment that a whole world exists out there. It both helps me focus and distracts me.

"Pretty special?"

I nod.

"I wanted to see if you had any further questions after my sermon yesterday morning. While everyone does love to hear our origin story, that was meant mainly to give you an introduction to our teachings."

I hesitate, turning to put the cup on the small island of free space on the desk between us. It has old coffee rings on it and a slash of black permanent marker. I wonder why an attempt to clean the spots hasn't been made. But then looking at the rest of the room I guess it's pretty clear there's no cleaning staff tidying up his office. I try to put my cup directly in one of the old rings, but it's just a bit smaller.

"I just…" I start, not really sure how to continue.

"This is a safe space. I'm not going to be upset about anything you tell me. Please, speak freely."

"I don't know where I fit in. Yes, I've been getting visions, but they haven't really told me anything. I'm not sure how I'm going to help you."

His smile is broad and warm, intoxicating. A flutter forms in my stomach that I promptly push away. "That, Stevie, is something for me to worry about, not you. We are a community here. Do you know what that words means, really means? Community?"

"A group of people?"

"Yes, but a group of people that share something in common. For us, it's faith. We share the same faith. And that faith speaks of a visionary. It doesn't say the person also has to be an interpreter. That is what your community is for. We can't be tasked with having to do everything—that is a burden too great for any one person. God knows that. That's why He gives us each other. If people could do it all on their own, lead full lives that led them to heaven, He would have had no need to make Eve. But He knew we needed each other."

"So, you will interpret what I see?" I ask.

"Me, everyone, anyone. People have different strengths, and we pride ourselves in highlighting and cultivating those strengths. We have a few people who are more well-versed in our teachings, myself included. When the time is right, we will all work together. Maybe," he pauses, hope on the tip of his tongue, "we can get to a point where our discussions will allow you to have different conversations with the entities that visit you. Together, we can figure this out."

It still seems a bit pie-in-the-sky, but I am glad the pressure is off me to try to figure it all out.

"Stevie, this is an incredible thing happening to you. Not everyone may see it that way. It sounds like your parents may feel differently?" His words are gentle, no accusation in them.

I huff. "Yeah, they definitely feel different. They think the visions are just because of the tumor. Which, maybe they are, but my parents don't think they can also be real."

He nods. "Changing perceptions is a tough thing for people. It even happens here, those who struggle with following even if they want to follow. They are used to religion teaching them one thing, and when an alternative is offered, they fight against it. They don't want to change or admit that maybe something they believed, something that was *taught* to them, could be inaccurate."

"Like what?" I ask.

"That God exists only in the past and the future. There is no place for Him in the present other than to read the old texts and to wait for revelations. We don't believe that. I don't think you do either. And together…" he leans forward over the desk, "…we are going to make other people realize it, you and I."

I nod back. I *am* the person he was talking about. I am struggling with believing, but looking into his eyes, so full of conviction and truth, I find even if I don't believe, not quite yet, I feel the inexplicable pull to want to.

His eyes stare straight through me and I am unable to look away. "Stevie, you are going to change the world."

Chapter Twenty-Seven

········•••(☙❦☙)•••········

When we head out of Luke's office, Abby is waiting for me. A line of people in the same matching khakis and green shirts the crew that picked me up were wearing load a pickup truck with crates at the edge of the garden. I watch as they pass the crates from person to person in a line. An image of ants pops into my head as they snake around and out of my view.

"What's going on?" I ask.

Luke's expression lights up. "Every month we set up at one of the farmer's markets and deliver free food to the homeless."

"Really?"

"It's pretty awesome," Abby says. "They don't really have access to fresh vegetables and fruit, so we set aside some of our harvest and bring it to them."

"Would you two like to come?" Luke asks.

Abby agrees without hesitation and I nod.

"You are going to *love* it," she tells me. Luke leaves us to help, the truck bed sinking lower and lower on its back wheels as the weight of the crates increases.

"Here, let's get changed real quick. I have an extra outfit you can borrow," Abby says.

"Changed?"

"We try to match when we go out. That way it's easier for people to find us if they need help. Works for cops and the theme parks." She laughs and shrugs. "Why not us, too?"

When we get back, clad in our own light pants and green tops, the truck is packed to a near-dangerous level with crates.

An image of smashed fruit spilled across the highway enters my mind, but I push it away.

"And people don't mind that you give away all this food?" I whisper to Abby.

"Oh, I mean, I don't think they like it, but we set up at the edges, so we aren't really part of the market. And, well, it's a bit complicated, but we have to split up. I've only done it once, but we split up, half staying with the food and the other half walk the area to where the homeless live. We give them all quarters which they exchange for food."

I shake my head. "I don't get it."

"Ugh, it's really annoying, but the city passed some crazy law where you aren't allowed to feed people for free, so it's how we get around it. So technically we don't give it away since they buy it, but we don't tell them it's our money." She winks at me.

Forty minutes later, we exit the passenger van with ten other members of the church. Luke and another man move to unload a table and a pop-up tent, the sun and eye logo protruding from each of its four vinyl peaks.

Wordlessly the ant line forms again and the crates are unpacked in reverse fashion. When one is passed to me, I struggle under the weight, not expecting it to be so laden with food.

"This is a lot of food," I whisper to Abby as I struggle to hand it off to her.

"Right, they will be so happy."

I can't help but think how many people this will feed at the compound and wonder if they really produce enough food to be without so much of it.

Once the crates are set up, a few of the older members speak with Luke briefly before moving down the road, the clinking of coins in their pockets making them sound like they're wearing jingle bells.

"Now what?" I ask.

Luke hands me a plastic bag. "We redistribute."

The man I met earlier from the garden shows me how much of each item goes into the bags and quickly the crates empty. We've got probably fifty bags set up on the table. It creeks under the weight of it all, but holds steady.

Men and women in filthy clothes form a line on the other side of the table. One presses a quarter into my hand. Her nails are long and brown with dirt embedded under them. I pass the bag over and her arm shakes while holding it. I place a hand under the bag, helping to share some of the load. She nods and steps back, stumbling a bit before shuffling away.

This continues for about ten more minutes before a man and two women walk by.

"You know, there are programs for them," the man calls out.

"You're not really doing them any favors," the taller woman says.

"Plus, you're breaking the law," the other says as they stride by, eyes narrowed in our direction.

Their words shock me. Who cares what we do? How does helping someone take anything away from those three?

I look over to Luke and he shrugs as if to say this happens all the time. A few moments later, I hear a few more people speaking a little too loudly.

"That's the crazy cult again. I'm not sure why they have to come here. My aunt says it scares off the customers since her booth is the closest to them. I'm all for helping people, but not when it hurts others." The girl makes a tisk noise in the back of her throat as her friends shake their heads.

I move closer to Luke as he hands out the last two bags. "They hate us."

"No," Luke says. "They hate themselves. But we can help them. They need us to show them our love."

"How can you love them? How can you love that wickedness in their hearts? We're helping people and they're shitting on it."

He shakes his head at my language, but doesn't tell me to tone it down. "None of us are perfect, Stevie." He places a hand on my shoulder and a shiver runs down my spine. "But if we can't be an example, if we can't be better, how can we expect anyone else to be?"

············•••••◖◗•••••············

The weight of the day crushes me when I lay down in my bed that night. Questions swirl in my head as I wrestle with what the last few days mean to me.

I was happily going through my life when out of nowhere I start seeing religious visions then find out I have a brain tumor. And if that wasn't enough, I'm now living in a compound filled with people who think I am their salvation, the key to the next life. And I'm not sure how I feel about any of it.

As if hearing my calls for help, the blissful warmth of Mary's arrival washes over me like a wave, turning the blackness of the room light and airy. I sit up, all pain and stiffness removed. I smile at her, but she doesn't return the gesture.

She sits in a red chair like a wound slashed across the pristine whiteness surrounding it. I want to look down and check if I'm still in bed, but I can't take my eyes off her even for a second, terrified she's angry with me.

"I'm scared," I say. "I'm not sure if I'm cut out for this."

"Do you trust us? Me?" she asks. Her face is so serious, no hint of the motherly softness I'm used to. It makes me unsure of myself.

"I want to, but I'm not sure I can trust myself." I rub my fingers across my face and press my palms into my eyes. The realness of it comforts me. When I lower them, I'm startled when she's directly in front of me. Still in the chair, but moved silently closer.

"What can't you trust?"

The relief of having an actual conversation with her feels like salvation in it of itself.

I open my arms wide. "This. All of it. You. Me here. These people. Two weeks ago I was nobody."

"You were never nobody."

"You know what I mean," I say.

"I do. But what makes you think this wasn't the plan the whole time? You may be scared, but we aren't. You may not trust, but we do."

We sit in silence for a moment before I can't take it anymore. The normal calm she brings me is lacking this time. It allows the anger to flare up.

"You say you trust me, but tell me the truth! Tell me why you're here, what this is all for! We're just going in endless circles. I'm not learning anything. I'm not *doing* anything," I'm practically yelling by the end of my speech.

"Are you not?" Her voice floats, each word taking a small piece of her away until all that's left is the echo of her words and the red chair until it melts into the floor, washing the white in color until the darkness replaces it.

Hot tears fight their way out of my eyes. I want to take the words back, apologize for yelling at her. She didn't deserve that. Here she is, trying to help me, trying to bring me a wonderful gift, and I practically spit in her face.

I'll apologize as soon as she comes back to me.

If she comes back.

Chapter Twenty-Eight

•••••••••••◄(ℰ ℴ ℊ)►•••••••••••

My head is on fire with pain. As if the absence of her has doubled up the effects of the headache. I don't remember having one all day, come to think of it, and now I guess I'm paying for that freedom.

I struggle to open the pill bottle in my nightstand and swallow a few of the white pills with one slug of water. I squeeze my eyes shut against the pain, waiting for the relief of the meds to flood into my veins. It takes ten minutes before I'm able to relax again, the edge taken off.

My room is cloaked in darkness, only bits of moonlight helping to throw shadows around like discarded clothing. I automatically pick up my phone to check the time, but remember I've had it off. After the day I've had, I'm longing to talk to Jorge and share all the craziness that's happened.

I turn the phone on, ignoring all the messages, and call him as soon as the weak single-service bar fills.

"Stevie," his voice is full of relief.

"Hey."

"Your parents—"

"I wanted to talk."

"Yeah, yeah of course." There is a strain in his voice, like he's fighting the urge to yell or something. "How are you? Not sacrificed or anything yet?" he asks.

I know it's a joke, but for some reason it kind of hurts. "No, I'm fine. Seriously. This place…" I let out a deep exhale.

"The place that is suing your parents?"

My heart falls. "Is that what they told you? So, what, you're like, chatting with my parents now?"

"Stevie, we talk like a million times a day trying to figure out where the hell you are and how to get you back. They got a certified letter from some weird company and can't seem to track down who and what owns it. They were hoping you'd called me."

"What did you say to them?" I can tell there is an edge to my voice, but my panic is rising.

He sighs. "Nothing, really. Just that you called and said you were okay but hung up before I was able to get any information from you."

I relax a little. "Thanks."

"I mean, really though, that *is* about all I know. Where are you? Please, I promise I won't tell them. I won't even come get you unless you want me to. Maybe I can visit? Just tell me where you are."

"I can't. Look, just know I'm safe and I'm where I'm supposed to be."

"How do you know that? The visions? Are they telling you things? Telling you to do things?"

I don't appreciate his tone. "Are you making fun of me?" I ask.

"No, no, I don't know. Stevie, look, I'm just trying to figure this out. A few days ago, you were laying in a hospital bed calling me to say you have a brain tumor. Then you tell me about how you're seeing visions of God. Then you run away and won't tell me where you are. I'm just confused and a bit hurt. Why can't you trust me?"

"It's not about trust. I just, okay, these people like really try to help people. So today, we went and handed out dozens of meals to the homeless. And people were harassing us. Literally yelling at us."

"Stevie, you can help the homeless anywhere. Nothing is stopping you. Our own church does mission work like that. Volunteer at the food bank."

"No, you don't understand." I struggle to find the words. This is different. I know that, but *how*?

"Come home. I'll take you to a shelter. I'll go with you and you know how lazy I am." He laughs, trying to pull a similar noise out of me. I don't give in.

"You don't understand."

"I'm trying."

"I gotta go."

"Stevie—"

His voice cuts off as I hang up and turn off my phone. Anger builds in me, but I'm not sure why.

Chapter Twenty-Nine

•••••••••◖◗•••••••••

My sleep is fitful and I finally give up on it around four. I pad to the bathroom and decide to just suck it up and get ready for the day. In some small way, I think my mom would be thrilled I'm willingly getting out of bed in general, much less before dawn.

I step out of the building and my eyes struggle to adjust to the dark surroundings. I stare up at the sky and see every star ever created. The heavens are littered with them, not a single space unlit by even a tiny pin-prick. I stare up at the past, at the burning balls of light, and think of all those who came before me.

I stare until I get a crick in my neck.

My head feels as clear as the morning air, which is unseasonably cool for this time of year. I'm used to my hair instantly frizzing as soon as I walk outside. If four in the morning is always like this, I could get used to waking up this early just to enjoy it.

I walk toward the chicken coops and lean against the wiring surrounding their enclosure, twisting my fingers in the honeycomb pattern. The hens make soft noises, but remain motionless. The sun hasn't yet pulled them toward activity, the rustling of sleep the only indication they aren't stuffed animals.

The gardens are illuminated by the moon and they pull me to them. It takes a bit for my eyes to adjust to the empty rows between the crops and I take cautious steps to move away from the buildings. What little light was on fades away as I go deeper to the middle of the field. Most of the stars are gone, fled to other places in the universe while I walked. Only a few remain, like pieces of leftover glitter no matter how much I try to clean it all up.

I reach my arms out and stand still with my eyes shut, a scared scarecrow in the middle of a peaceful place, terrified to my core.

How am I going to do this? I think back to my conversation with Mary last night, embarrassment flooding my emotions again. I feel terrible for how I treated her. Hopefully she'll come back soon so I can apologize. Then I remember my talk with Jorge and the feelings in me swirl and mix again.

I open my eyes to the heavens, a soft breeze rustling the lettuces growing around me. The silence of the world makes phantom noises echo in my ears and helps clear my mind.

I could live here. This could be my home. I could grow food here, go to school, learn about myself and this place.

And lead, a voice says quietly.

I picture myself standing next to Luke, arms raised in prayer, putting my visions into words. Repeating what's said to me. Hearing the interpretations. The prospect of all that responsibility both excites and nauseates me.

I've never been so important, so needed, so wanted. This is a place where I could belong, where the mundane day-to-day of my current life could slip away to more purpose. But how? I can't make the visions come, and I worry I may have jeopardized them all together.

I shut my eyes tight, willing the warm sensation that indicates the arrival of Mary to come. A shiver runs through me with the next wind gust. I open my eyes, the soft orange of the sun beginning to warm the horizon. I hear a bird call in the distance, welcoming the day. I smile, thinking to Abby's declaration of how birds are associated with me.

I want to believe her. I want to believe in all of this, but especially, in me.

CHAPTER THIRTY

...........•••••••(◦⁄◦)••••••...........

I sit in the back seat of a giant old car as Luke chats with Mr. Ackerman in the front. I rhythmically twist the ring on my thumb as we bounce down the dirt road. It's only been two days since our trip to the farmer's market, but when we immerge from the woods and turn onto the road, it looks like a different world to me. The compound is so removed from the rest of the surrounding area, I almost forget it's still spinning along. Now, I'm not saying I'm enjoying the early mornings or anything, but there is something to be said for the simplicity of it all.

The only TV is in the main common room where meals and services are held. Each night, people gather to watch a show or movie. I'm not sure how they decide, maybe they take turns on who gets to pick from the old stack of donated DVDs?

It's been a strange adjustment not being connected all the time. Phones aren't allowed in most places, so I tend to leave mine in my room. Not that I really need it anyway. I've ignored all the texts and haven't spoken to Jorge since I called him the other night.

Someone was nice enough to give me a watch—I never had much need for one since my phone always told me. Stuff's not strict per-se here, but people do tend to follow the rules and be places when they're supposed to be. Since they're putting me up for free and giving me legal counsel, I fi gure I should probably follow along.

But what doesn't take long to figure out, is the power of Luke.

Whoever this Jacob guy was, he chose well for his successor. There's this strange thing that happens when Luke enters a room:

you can *feel* it before you realize it's happening. It's like the molecules in the air change, adding an electric charge.

After lunch yesterday, he was surrounded by a group of elementary school-aged children. I was astounded that he knew each and every one of their names.

"Ricky, are you ready for your math test?" A small boy nodded.

"And Nicole, did you get your art project completed?"

"Yes, sir," the girl answered.

Catching the eye of a man about to leave, he called over to him. "Greg, you feeling better?"

"Oh, yes, thank you. Think that tea did the trick!"

"Always does!" Luke said.

That night I even heard him ask a man delivering some boxes how his children were.

I suppose it's a little thing, and maybe I'm only picking up on it because I'm new and trying to take everything in, but it's just one more thing that gives him credibility. Whether he's doing it consciously or not, it's an effective tool to get people to do what's asked of him. Anything to have that smile fall upon them.

He asks for volunteers and every able body throws itself into the air. I even find myself getting wrapped into wanting to please him, but I stop myself from saying, "I'll help clean the cobwebs from the old barn." Just the thought of it makes my skin itch.

But I try to do my part when I can, cleaning up after dinner and helping in the garden. My life skills are minimal. This is clearly proving how unprepared I am for any sort of apocalypse that will revert humans back to a pre-technology era, but I'm trying. Any effort though seems appreciated by everyone. Sharing, whether physical items or words, appears as ingrained in their minds as God is.

When it was announced the previous evening I needed something to wear to court today, women were literally offering me the clothes off their backs. Luckily, Abby is about the same size as me and had a calf-length skirt and button up top that fit well enough to work. It's a bit itchy and isn't particularly flattering, but I didn't dare speak badly of it. She told anyone who would listen that she was able to provide me with my court outfit.

If pride is a sin, they seem to gloss over that one here.

"Hey, you awake back there?" Mr. Ackerman's voice pulls my attention to the front seat.

"Sorry, what?"

Luke laughs. "We've been speaking to you for the last few minutes."

My cheeks go hot. "I'm so sorry. I must have been daydreaming."

"Just a daydream?" Luke's voice is an octave higher than normal, laced with hope.

I shrug my shoulders and nod. So far, I've been good about taking my pills, which seems to have stopped the visions. Tonight though, I'm considering missing a dose. I *need* to see Mary and make sure she is still willing to come to me, that I haven't chased her away.

A strong desire to take Al out of my bag and rub his ears pulls at me, but I ignore it. I already feel like enough of a child, I don't need to take out my stuffed animal to really hit the nail on the head. I play with my ring instead.

"We were just discussing the protocol for when we get to the courthouse," Mr. Ackerman chimes in. We went over it last night, but it makes me feel better that they are being thorough in preparing me. "When we get to the courthouse, we'll have to go through security."

"Security?" Nothing was mentioned before about that.

"It's very routine," he says. "Just metal detectors, won't take very long. Then we'll be in Courtroom ten-b with Judge White. We'll have to sit outside until they call us in. There are other matters the judge is dealing with this morning, not just us."

"And my parents?" I've been too afraid to ask this question before and they haven't brought it up on their own.

"They will be there," Luke says. He turns, giving unblinking reassurance. "But it is entirely up to you what level of interaction you wish to have with them."

I don't know the answer to that. A realization hits me. What if they don't want to see *me*?

We park and walk to the front of a complex of three buildings, heading toward the tallest one in the center. I've seen it my whole life, but had no need to go inside. As soon as we go through the doors, rows of metal detectors loom over the polished lobby. I'm glad the lawyer warned me, the sheer number of cops and other people would have been overwhelming.

We get through without incident and head to the elevators. A screen directs us to which one we need, and we wait. I scan the growing crowd, but I don't see my parents among the faces. Sweat gathers along my hairline and under my arms. I wonder if I'm going to pass out.

We ride the elevator up, just the three of us, and my stomach lurches slightly as we are catapulted upward. If I wasn't so terrified, I may have let out a laugh at the sensation, one I typically relish at the theme parks. Now, it just adds to my nausea.

The elevator puts us out in the middle of the floor and we turn toward the sign for our courtroom. In the far corner, my parents speak with a man and woman dressed in suits. My mom looks up, sees me, and leaps up.

She pushes by Mr. Ackerman and throws her arms around me. She shakes and trembles with sobs.

"Mom, Mom, it's okay." I pat her back, unable to extract my arms to do anything else.

My dad and stepdad follow close behind, the lawyers still in the corner. Mr. Ackerman and Luke step to the side. Luke makes eye contact with me, asking if I am okay. I nod into my mom's neck.

"Please don't do this," she whispers into my ear and pulls back to look at me.

Her eyes look puffier than this crying spell could have accounted for. I feel a hole being punched in my heart at the pain I've caused them. That I *am* causing them. My stepdad puts a hand on her shoulder and she lets go, allowing my dad a chance to hug me. He's wordless, which I think may be worse.

"I'm sorry," my words feel small and empty, but I'm not sure what else to say.

"Then you don't have to do this," my mom says. I shake my head.

"I think it's time to go in," Mr. Ackerman says, putting an end to the awkward reunion.

Luke extends his arm, creating a small space for me to walk through. My dad gives him a look that is both questioning and angry. Basically, "who the hell are you and what are you doing with my daughter?" I almost introduce them, but figure that'll be taken care of in the courtroom. I guess all of this will.

The courtroom is all mahogany and burlap, like it's trying to look hard and soft at the same time. A uniformed officer opens a saloon-style door and we pass through, taking the table to the right of the room. My parents and their lawyer take the spot on the left, my stepdad sitting in the first row behind them. An empty jury box is to the right, twelve vacant chairs ominously judging the proceedings.

There are people sitting on a high platform to the left and I wonder who they are. None wear black robes or look particularly interested in our arrival. The man who ushered us in announces the judge and asks us to stand, which we already are, but I guess he has to say it anyway.

Judge White looks to be about my father's age, his dark hair graying at the temples. His robe looks official, but about a size too big, making him look slightly comical. He asks us to take a seat and I do as I'm told, but Mr. Ackerman stays standing.

"Today in docket number," the judge pauses and looks down at his paper, "five four six two, the petitioner, Stevie Albie, is asking for medical emancipation from her legal guardians, Veronica Laurel and Edward Albie. Who is here for the petitioner?"

"Kenneth Ackerman."

"And for Mrs. Laurel and Mr. Albie?"

"Wendy Kwong," the female lawyer says, half standing before returning to her seat.

"You may proceed."

Mr. Ackerman comes to a podium in the middle of the room with several papers in his hand.

"Judge White, I have today several petitions signed by Miss Albie. They include a request for medical emancipation, a request for granting of status to a minor, and a request of change in limited guardianship made on behalf of Lucas Gaines."

"Please bring these documents to the clerk," the judge says, gesturing with his hand to the man sitting at the right of him. In front, a woman is typing in a strange manner over a truncated keyboard. The court reporter, I assume.

Mr. Ackerman brings the clerk the papers and sits back down. The whole process seems simple, and appears to be going exactly how he told me it would, but my throat still feels tight and dry. After looking over the papers, the clerk hands them to the judge and he takes a moment to look at them.

"Do you have anything to add, Ms. Kwong?"

She stands and also has a few papers in her hands. This I wasn't expecting and I turn to Mr. Ackerman to ask him what they may be, but Luke puts a hand on my wrist. He shakes his head. My questions will have to wait.

"We do, Your Honor." She taps the papers on the podium even though they already appear in perfectly straight order. "We have counter applications requesting the immediate return of the minor, Stevie Albie, and a cease and desist letter for any future interaction between said minor and the group, which calls itself the Church of the Eye, plus its leader Lucas Gaines. In addition, Mr. Albie and Mrs. Laurel request a court order for treatment be requested to ensure proper treatment of the minor, Stevie Albie, as directed by her doctors."

I can't breathe. They can counter what I am requesting? Mr. Ackerman didn't say anything about this. And on top of that, they can legally *force* me to get treatment? How is that right? How can they do that?

I open and close my mouth like a beached fish gasping for air. My fingers tighten on Mr. Ackerman's arm, but he makes no move to look at me. No. This can't be happening. Could what I'm doing possibly make my situation even worse? Mr. Ackerman made it seem like this was a simple proceeding—we'd get in, the judge would sign the paperwork, and I'd be protected. My breakfast sits like a lead ball in my stomach and I'm afraid I might throw it all up.

The judge again motions for the papers to be brought to the clerk who looks them over then hands them to him.

I try to catch my parent's eyes, but they stare straight ahead. I want to scream at them to look at me. Stop this! Let me make my own decisions. Don't force me into this. I know an outburst won't help my case, so I sit uncomfortably silent.

After a few moments, the judge looks up. Both Ms. Kwong and Mr. Ackerman stand, he gestures for me to do the same. I'm not sure if my legs will hold my weight, so I push up using my hands as support on the table.

"I have read the petitions of both sides and have determined that further information is needed."

Wait, what?

"I will set a hearing date for two weeks from now due to the sensitive nature of the matter," he continues. "Will this be enough time for both sides to gather any additional information needed?"

"Yes, Your Honor," both attorneys say in unison. It's as if they've practiced this charade a million times.

"Good. Then we will meet back here on the last Monday of the month."

"Your Honor?" Ms. Kwong asks.

"Yes?"

"As for the first two counter petitions?"

"At this time, the court grants custody of the minor back to her legal guardians. While the court does not bar communication with the group known as the Church of the Eye, the court will agree to supervised visits between any willing members and the minor. These visits will take place at a neutral location determined by the supervisor, taking into account distance for both parties, as well as coordinate the dates and times of said meeting. Further, the court also requests that new medical information is gathered on the progress of the minor's illness as well as a mental health evaluation by a court-appointed counselor. Does this satisfy the petitioners at this time?"

My mind is whirling as he talks. I try to process his words but they feel all jumbled in my brain.

"It does, Your Honor," Ms. Kwong says. My mother tugs on the woman's sleeve, but she shakes her head the slightest amount.

"Yes, Your Honor," Mr. Ackerman says.

I don't move. My brain is spinning with information that I only half understand. So, I have to live with my parents? And I need some shrink to talk to me? And if I want to see anyone from the Church, I need a chaperone?

So, did I win?

"The matter is settled until the date as set. If any additional information comes to light or violations of the order are made, those will be handled in a separate proceeding. We are adjourned." He bangs a gavel just like they do in the movies on his table. The officer asks us to stand and the judge leaves us all to sort out what the hell just happened.

CHAPTER THIRTY-ONE

"So?" I turn to Mr. Akerman. "Is this good?"

"Well, it isn't bad," he says.

"Kenneth, I wasn't aware this was an outcome that could happen today," Luke says, his jaw clenched as he talks.

You and me both, buddy.

"It isn't necessarily what we were hoping for, but it isn't all bad. The judge had an option to throw out the entire petition and side with you parents, reverting all control back to them. That hasn't happened. That's a good thing."

"But I still have to go back with them?" I look over and they are huddled around their own attorneys, probably asking the same questions I am.

"Yes, you do, but without any requirement for treatment, which is a victory, Stevie. It means the judge is willing to hear your case in a fair and impartial manner. So, now we have to make a case of it."

"A case?" Luke asks.

"We will have experts testify, you both will probably also have to speak to the judge."

"And a jury decides my fate?" I ask, glancing at the empty chairs to my right.

"Not in family court," he continues. "Here we go in front of the judge and he makes the final decision. In the meantime, you can still be in touch with us, which is a victory in and of itself. He didn't have to do that. We're going to find our own specialist in Atlanta and get you rescanned, which I think can also work in your favor as these are typically slow-growing tumors. And you'll have to speak with a counselor."

"About what?" I can hear the defensiveness in my voice.

"Stevie," he says my name like I'm a child. I guess maybe I still am. "This is a very big decision you're making. That we all are making." He looks pointedly at Luke. "The courts, everyone, wants to make sure this is the right thing for you. That's what we're all here for."

"Shouldn't I be the one who knows the answer to that?" I feel prickles at the back of my eyes. It's all so frustrating and unfair.

"Maybe, but that's what everyone here, your parents included, are trying to figure out. And we will. We'll get the information we need, present what we've gathered, and a decision will be made. For better or for worse, in two weeks, you'll know."

For better or for worse.

I nod and thank them for their time and help. Both men embrace me, and I let them. I turn and walk toward my parents, who are trying to dampen broad smiles. They are pleased, but trying not to rub it in my face. I sort of appreciate it, but I sort of hate it, too.

"Honey," my mom says, "let's go home."

She touches my arm the way she has a million times. A small part of me hopes that maybe this will be all right. Maybe what I've done hasn't ruined us. We can have a calm conversation that will end with me convincing them to drop all of this and allow me to gain control.

We walk out of the courthouse and news reporters stand in the courtyard. They shout questions at me as cameras are trained on my face.

"Stevie, is it true you're trying to get emancipated from your parents?"

"Mrs. Albie, why don't you believe your daughter? Do you consider yourself a religious person?"

"Mr. Albie, how does it feel that this cult has tried to make your daughter their leader?"

The questions come so quickly, I'm unable to pin-point who is saying what. Mr. Ackerman pushes ahead of us, telling the reporters none of us have any comments and ushering us to the parking lot. He holds them back, saying something about privacy rights, as I get in the car.

"Wonder who told them about our case." My stepdad says.

"I'm sure your new friends," my mom calls back to me. The comment hurts, but I don't say anything, hoping she isn't right.

CHAPTER THIRTY-TWO

I clutch my bag as I make my way up the drive to the front door. My mom and stepdad walk a beat behind me, my dad already heading to the airport to go home. Our goodbye was quick from all the confusion of the reporters. He'll be back for the trial, but has things in Nashville to take care of before then.

Part of me wants to accuse him of leaving again, to say something hurtful and biting and make him have a small amount of the pain I have, but I can't bring myself to do it. I know he doesn't want to leave.

I struggle to readjust the duffle. I didn't want to bring it to the courthouse, but Mr. Ackerman insisted.

"Just in case," he said, but it was so light, so casual, I still don't think I'll need it. I feel betrayed by him as well. From the look on Luke's face as we were leaving the courtroom, I think our feelings are mutual.

In all of this, he's the only one who hasn't deceived me today. Even my parents, what was with that counter petition? Why couldn't they just let the judge rule on what we asked? Why did they have to come back twice as hard, to force my hand in the matter even more?

What does it say that Luke, this relative stranger, seems to be the only one in my corner? I clutch my bag harder in frustration. Screaming right now would probably be frowned upon. Probably something I'd have to tell the head doctor.

Mom's relief and happiness at seeing me vanishes when we get in the kitchen. She slams her purse on the counter, Chapstick and pens spilling in every direction. My stepdad walks up to her, but she points a hand out, stopping him.

"No, I need to say this." Fire smolders in her eyes. Even that time Stacey and I skipped school and stole those shirts from the mall didn't get me a look like this. If I didn't know how much she loves me, I would say it was pure hatred staring back.

"You can NEVER, and I mean absolutely never, pull a stunt like this again."

My stepdad starts, "Veronica—"

"Not now." She cuts him off and takes three giant steps to be face-to-face with me, her finger pointed millimeters from my nose. My mom is about two inches shorter than I am, so in any other situation this would probably be comical, but I don't dare laugh.

"I know," I say, a small peace offering. It's all I have in me.

"No, you don't know. You don't know what it's like to create a life—to physically carry another human being inside you, to birth it, raise it, and see it get a death sentence from a doctor that can be fixed, but that fix be denied. More than denied. To run away and leave us in a city where your father and I didn't know where you were. To go crazy with worry until we saw you on the security cameras GET INTO A CAR! A fucking car, Stevie." She turns, her anger making it impossible for her to stay in one place.

I can feel my body fold in on itself and try to roll into a small ball, hoping she'll take some mercy on me.

She takes a breath, places her hands on the countertop in the kitchen, and addresses it, not me.

"Here's what we're going to do. You are going to get retested, speak to the counselor, and come home. You will not leave here unless you're going to one of those two places. In two weeks, we go back to the courts, and this matter will be behind us."

I want to mention the visits, but decide this is the wrong time. Probably also not good to ask about Jorge or my friends either. I don't nod, both because I don't agree to what she's saying and because I don't want to give her any indication I may, in some small way, go along with her plan.

"Can I go to my room?" I ask.

"Please."

122

I turn on the spot, fighting the urge to slam my door. I don't want to give them fuel to the fire of me being an out-of-control child. I lay down in bed, my breathing slowly coming back to normal.

I think back to that day at the mall two years ago when Stacey and I left school and hopped on a bus. She'd wanted to get this shirt her mother forbade her to wear because of the thinly veiled sexual innuendo on it. We'd just had study hall left, and Mr. Chapman never seemed to take attendance.

We doubted he'd even noticed we didn't show up.

My heart raced as we walked the short distance from school and waited for the fuchsia-colored bus. Stacey held my hand, probably just as much to steady her own nerves as mine. Neither of us spoke. I half expected the bus driver to shake his head and tell us to get back to class, but he let us on. A short while later, we were strolling down the polished floors of the mall. We had exactly thirty minutes to shop and catch the return bus back to make it before the final bell.

We were rebels, but we had limits.

Actually, we weren't rebels at all.

I'd never so much as copied a friend's homework before, much less leave campus during school hours. I'm not sure what made me agree. Maybe the pleading look on her face? Perhaps the newness of our friendship made me take risks I normally wouldn't.

I followed her from one dumb decision to the next. Out of class. Out of school. On that bus. In that store. Into the dressing room. Agreed to put the shirt on and then layer my shirt over it, not noticing the small plastic tab at the bottom. I was so stressed about getting caught, the rub of the security tag against my skin didn't send up any red flags.

But the store alarm certainly did.

Stacey looked stricken as the clerk grabbed my arm and called for security. I could see the momentary pause in decision making in her eyes. Bolt? Or stay?

She stayed. There was something about that action, even though she was the catalyst for the whole damn thing anyway, that tied us together.

Our moms came and picked us up, Stacey and I slathered in shame. My mom was silently furious and told me I couldn't hang out with Stacey anymore. I was on my best behavior for a while after that, and save for a joke or two from my stepdad when I went to the mall, we never talked about it. My mom eventually relented and Stacey became a fixture in my life, our past indiscretion forgiven.

I had a feeling I wouldn't be that lucky this time around.

CHAPTER THIRTY-THREE

••••••••••••《♧⁄♾》••••••••••••

I blink and she appears.

Mary is holding the hand of a small child dressed in plain white clothing and I can't tell if it's a boy or a girl. The child looks at me with a half-smile, but doesn't say anything.

My body gets the familiar tingle and warmth that happens when she appears. I am so relieved to see her, it's been several days and I was worried the whole time my frustration during our last visit pushed her away.

Oh, how I've missed her. Each time she leaves, I forget what this feeling is, but when she returns, it's like an old friend.

Oh yes, you, I remember you.

I get up and walk with them, the room white-on-white-on-white and I'm afraid I may step off into some unseen abyss. I let Mary go a half-step in front of me, fi guring she will know the way. Allowing her to erase my fear.

After we've gone a short way, I stop, needing to speak and wishing the child wasn't here. It feels wrong, this unknown observer. I want Mary alone, all to myself.

"I'm sorry," I say. As I talk, the letters appear in the air, black against the white. They turn to gray and float away in pieces, like dandelion seeds in the windless space.

When she speaks, no words form. "There is nothing to be sorry about."

"But before..." I say.

She smiles. "There is only now."

"I am lost." The words are the most truth I've spoken in days.

"You know your heart."

"But, what if I don't."

Her smile is warm. The child stays expressionless.

"I can't give this up. This is too important," I say, the letters wrapping around us, the gray acting like a string tying us together until they fade.

She smiles again. She knows. She doesn't want this to go away either. I can feel it from her. She needs me and I need her. But this child, what is it doing here? I want to take its hand away from her and hold hers myself. I wonder if the child is solid, if I can push it away.

As if reading my mind—maybe it can—the child takes a step back and hides behind Mary. If she wasn't looking, I'd stick my tongue out at it.

I want to ask her what it's doing here. I don't recognize it, like I have with the younger version of Jesus. No, this is someone new. But I feel like I *should* know. I squint, but the bright light muffles its features.

I close my eyes and when I open them, I am right next to her, staring up. Suddenly shorter, as if kneeling, but when I look down, I see that I stand to my full height. My clothes, once dark against the background, are white. They are the child's clothes. *I* am the child.

I glance around to see if we've traded places, but no one else is there.

She smiles at me. "See, you know what's in your heart."

"But I don't."

Her laugh is silent, but fills me as if it were a sonic boom. "Oh, my darling, yes you do! How do you think you're here if you don't?"

"The tumor?" It is more question than statement. I am so frustrated. I want to rip my hand away from hers, but it is too warm and comforting. She isn't speaking any truths to me. This whole time, she has only talked in riddles.

"Is that what you think this is?" She gestures to the white expanse.

"I have no idea, that's why I'm asking." She can see my heart, I know it, so how can she not see this? How can she not see how her words aren't helping?

126

"Why am I coming to you?" Her question is sincere and without mocking.

"To lead." I say the first thing that comes into my head.

"Then, you know what you must do."

The white flips into darkness so abruptly, it wakes me. Blackness surrounds me and I can't figure out where I am. There is no longer a dresser at the foot of my bed or a table to my right. A small moon-shaped light glows in the far corner, spilling across my desk.

My desk.

My desk in my room. I am home. Reality catches up, but I still feel the edges of her, tickling my outline with her light in the darkness. And I know she is right.

I have to follow my heart.

CHAPTER THIRTY-FOUR

T he cheap plastic of the chair sticks to my bare legs. I regret
wearing shorts to see the counselor, but it's so hot outside, I
can't bring myself to wear any more than the absolute minimum.

Five chairs sit in a circle around an oblong table. They are all
the same medium-tone wood which both dates them and tries to
look futuristic. It fails. The yellow vinyl seats don't help either
and announce each shifting position from my mom and stepdad. I
wonder if we can sit on the floor instead, or if this is the first test.
Can someone sit in these chairs long term? Or does the act itself
make them insane?

I wonder what category I will fall into.

The counselor rolls a plush leather-like office chair up, pushing
one of the lesser chairs out of the way. The nerve. Like she knows
how terrible the other furniture is and can't even pretend to be
okay with it, even for an hour.

Her warm smile tells me both that she knows I don't want to
be here, and that her chairs freaking suck. I nod back.

"So, Stevie, I know you're here today because the court has
asked you to," she starts.

"Ordered." I say.

"Stevie." My mom's voice is a low warning. The past twen-
ty-four hours haven't brought any thawing to her feelings, nor
does she try to act like it has.

"Well, I'm just being accurate." I try to hide my snide comment in an air of helpfulness. I'm pretty sure no one buys it, but
I don't care.

"Thank you," the counselor plays along, breaking some of the tension. "But be that as it may, I would still like you to keep an open mind. We're here to talk and see if we can figure some things out together. Maybe get some new perspectives, and most importantly, to listen to one another."

"Oh, so we're going to listen to me now?" I can't help it. I'm so angry, so pissed about this whole thing. The cancer, the doctors, my parents, hell, even Mr. Ackerman for not taking care of it all like he said he would.

And I'm too damn tired to try to act otherwise. In the back of my mind, I know I should play nice and answer the questions in a mature, adult way, to prove to her so she can tell the courts I know what I'm talking about, but I simply don't have it in me. She ignores my tone and doesn't take the bait.

"What I would like to do first is give each of you a platform to speak. We'll do this as a group, then I will talk with you alone Stevie, if that is all right with everyone." She addresses my mom. "If you aren't comfortable with that, you have full legal rights to stay while I speak with her, but I do suggest you allow part of this session to be one-on-one. It may help me get a better start if I can speak with Stevie alone where she doesn't have to worry about being judged or feel like she may hurt you with what she says."

"Like she could hurt me any more," my mom mutters.

This morning I gave myself a pep talk, an attempt to prepare myself for what this may be. I would stay strong, stare straight ahead, and not allow anything in this room to sway my convictions. While my meeting with Mary didn't give me the clarity I wished for, it was enough to know I need to stand firm. I won't let this shrink lady try to confuse me. And I will not let my mom hurt me.

But my mother's words penetrate the small links of my armor. They leave shards of words speckling my skin. Each breath digs them deeper into me. The pain is unexpected, which makes it even worse.

My stepdad stays silent. Through this whole experience, even my diagnosis, he's spoken little. It's possible he feels it isn't his place, that he's just a bystander to some other family's tragedy. He'd never been married before my mom, and while I know he loves her in a way my father never did, having children was never something he wanted. My mom was okay with not having any more kids, so it worked, but he inherited me when he made his vows. I never really thought what that must be like for him, especially now. But he's rallied around me in a way I wasn't expecting, even if he isn't going to fully say he is on my team, he tries to toe the line between us. He will try to calm my mother down, redirecting her anger or reminding her of the stress I'm under as well. It's a small thing, but a contribution I'm grateful for.

"I'm sure hurt has been felt on all sides," the counselor says to my mom, pulling me back to the present. "That's something we'll cover as well."

I turn my gaze down, the threat of tears has passed, and look for a nameplate somewhere. I didn't catch it when introductions were made.

The office is decent sized, but the table takes up most of it. Tucked into one corner is a small desk. Bookshelves and filing cabinets line each wall as if they make up the borders of the room and not the drywall and paint. Books are scattered over every inch. I don't see a single decorative item, just books. I strain to read the small sign on her desk.

Dr. Casey Lewis, LMHC.

"Dr. Lewis," I say. "Whatever I need to do to get you to sign off, I will do, but can we get started?"

The left corner of her mouth ticks up for a split-second before returning to its neutral position. "Of course. So, I've read your file, and let me start of by saying, Stevie, I am so terribly sorry this has happened to you. I imagine getting that kind of diagnosis wasn't easy."

This was a direction I wasn't expecting. "Umm, thanks?"

"I think it's important to acknowledge the obstacles we're facing, whether physical or metaphysical. Sometimes they blur the lines, but either way, we need to discuss them if we're ever going to make peace with them."

The tears build again, and I take a deep drink of water to quell them.

"I see you're getting emotional. Can you tell me why?"

130

I stare straight at her. It's easier to talk if I pretend no one else is in the room. Now I understand why she wants to meet with me one-on-one. I want to ask if we can do that now, but I guess that will break the rules.

"It feels like even though I'm the one going through this, even though I'm the one who needs to figure out how to live with this or if I *want* to live with this, I don't actually get a say. Or no one really wants me to have a say. At least the people who are supposed to care about me."

"But then you found the Church of the Eye, and they support you in what you want. That must be very hard to have strangers on your side when you feel your parents aren't."

I want to slap my hands on the table. Yes! Yes, that is EXACTLY it!

"Oh, please," my mother says, breaking the spell Mrs. Lewis is weaving, catching me in its threads.

"Mrs. Laurel, you'll have the opportunity to speak, but right now, I'd like to get Stevie's side of the story."

"So, I need to listen to lies? Just because she thinks they are truths doesn't make them so." My mom turns to face me and I can't help but return her gaze. "Stevie, these people are only supporting you because it helps their bottom line. Their agenda. You just happen to be the person they need."

It was the exact wrong thing to say.

I hear Mrs. Lewis's voice in the background, but I ignore it, the anger swallowing the sounds.

"What if I *am* special? Why is that so impossible for you to believe? You guys always talk about God and His plan and bring me to church, yet you can't use faith here? How do you think the Bible was written? By people who *experienced things*. By people like me. And people believed them and followed them and were saved by them because of the truth they spoke. A truth that you, hundreds of years later, still believe. Yet, you can't possibly believe your daughter may be experiencing this for real? No. It's staring you in the face and you just want to turn away. Worse. You want to take it away from me."

CHAPTER THIRTY-FIVE

························

There's lots of raised voices after I give my little speech. It feels satisfying to put into words the accusations of hypocrisy that have been floating around my head.

Luke asked me soon after I'd arrived about my family's religious practices. It didn't seem like his question was rooted in judgement, just a curiosity of how I was raised.

"We go to church every week," I said, thinking that answered the question.

He shook his head. "You're not a car because you hang out in a garage."

I laughed. It was a strange sensation, speaking with him. I had an urge to say things to please him and pull the radiant smile out of him and bask in its light. "I guess, but I mean, we go to church. We believe. I go on retreats and my mom volunteers when she can. It's more than sitting with a group of people."

"Do you save the planet by recycling one glass bottle?"

I'm not really sure what he's getting at. "No, I guess not."

"Okay, on the flip side, that bit does help. If you don't recycle the bottle you're adding to the problem, heck, maybe your one bottle will be the tipping point to the implosion of the Earth." He leaned toward me as if he's about to tell me a secret. "But, probably not. No, you have to commit. If you want to do something, really do something, if you want to save the planet, you have to recycle everything. You may even need to go out of your way, find a place that takes those curly lightbulbs. Go somewhere else that will take your grocery bags, or even get reusable ones. Do you see the difference?"

I nod. "Yeah, I mean, one is more a gesture where another is a lifestyle."

"Yes! Exactly. There are plenty of people who go to church, but what are they really doing with it?"

It wasn't an accusation, not really, but it made me feel inadequate. And more so—what I'm sure gets them more and more followers—I wanted to fix it. I thumbed through the Bibles in the meeting rooms. I discussed religion with the residents. Everyone was so happy, so eager to speak with me, to get close to the Girl Who Sees, but little did they know, I was searching just like them.

But returning home with new eyes, I see what Luke was talking about. How my mom and stepdad throw religion like a protective cloak around themselves, an excuse to feel better without really needing to do anything about it. And now that I'm back in the mix with the knowledge I have, I want them to *see*. See they can believe me and trust what I'm experiencing is true.

Trust that I can bring them the truth like Luke says I can.

But they won't even listen.

Mrs. Lewis suggests we switch to the one-on-one session, then she can meet with my mom and stepdad privately after. My mom gives a look to my stepdad and hesitates before getting out of the chair, like she is nervous if she leaves me out of her sight, I'll brainwash this woman into believing me.

Which, of course, is exactly what I plan on doing.

CHAPTER THIRTY-SIX

............(●✿●)............

Mrs. Lewis leaves for a couple minutes to speak with my mom and stepdad, so I take the opportunity to walk around her office. I'm surprised to find the bookshelves aren't just legal or psychology books, but general fiction as well. Some authors I am familiar with and others are new to me. I pull one out and thumb the black and gold cover.

"Poetry," she says, making me jump.

"Sorry." I rush to put it back and straighten the row like I found it.

"Don't be. You're welcome to borrow it if you wish. There are even some religious themes in that one. That's one reason I'm drawn to poetry." She stands next to me and pulls the book out again. "It's like people sometimes. There is a surface projection, words that if taken at face value mean one thing, but scratch the outer layer, investigate a little more, and a whole new meaning comes out. Just like us. We all have parts we let the world see, and other parts that stay hidden. Sometimes even from ourselves."

"Is that what you think this is? I am just hiding?"

"No. I think you're trying not to hide, actually, which I think is very brave."

"But you don't believe me." It's not really an accusation, more of a factual statement. She is paid to talk to me and to get me to trust her. She's pretty good at it from what I've gathered so far, but she's certainly not taking money to be my friend or on my team.

This is what I need to overcome. If only I had Luke's skills. I wonder if he can speak with her, make her understand.

"I think you believe them, which is a very powerful thing that can't be discounted. And I know that while your mother clearly loves you and is terrified, she isn't really helping you in this matter."

I huff. "You could say that again."

"But, I'm not letting you off that easy. You've got some homework."

"It's summer."

She covers her smile with her hand. "Yes, I know, but this one is simple. Not easy, but simple. Just try to understand where she is coming from. Try to put yourself in her shoes. Her daughter, her only child, getting a diagnosis like yours. Then, when she thinks all hope is lost, a doctor tells her it can be taken out. He can cure you. You can go on to lead a full, happy life. And you say no."

I take a deep breath. "So, does this mean that this isn't our only session?"

She shakes her head. "I'm afraid not. But that's not a bad thing, nor does it mean I think something is wrong with you. I need you to understand that. It just means I need a bit more time to get to know you and make a determination."

"Any ideas where you might lean?"

"Nope, but that's a good thing. It means that while I may not totally believe you right now, I don't *dis*believe you. Do you see the difference?"

I nod. I guess it's a starting point. I make a mental note to ask Luke about how to get her on my side the next time I see him, which reminds me...

"I want to have a visit with a member of the church. The court approved it, but my mom won't let me."

"Okay, that's something I can help with. Before we go, can you tell me what it is about this group? Why you feel you get something from them that you can't get from other people in your life? And don't just say 'well, because they believe me,' because you can find all sorts of people that will believe anything. It has to be more than that."

I say the first thing that pops in my head. "They don't make me feel foolish for believing it myself."

"That is a powerful thing." We stand for a few more minutes before she walks toward the door, handing me the book before letting me out. "Just bring it back next time. And read it, I think you'll like it."

"Thanks. And can I ask a favor of you?"

"I can't promise anything, but sure."

"Get better chairs."

Her laugh is deep and genuine.

CHAPTER THIRTY-SEVEN

When we get home from the appointment, the air in the house feels stale and filled with frustration. I think to the homework Dr. Lewis gave me and decide to make a small peace offering.

"Do you want something for lunch? I can make grilled cheese." I ask.

My mom smiles, the first one in days. "That would be great, thanks."

My stepdad pats his belly. "I wish, but I need to go to the office for a bit. I'll take a rain check though."

We don't speak as we eat, but we also don't yell, so that's progress. My mom collects the dishes to rinse them off.

"Did you cut your hair?" I ask her. Neutral enough of a question.

She reaches a hand up to touch it as if I've just reminded her it exists on her head. "Yeah. Color, too."

I nod. "Looks good."

She takes a small strand of mind and twirls it in her fingers. "You could use a cut yourself."

I shrug. We go back to silence. I take a rag and wipe the table off.

"Would you mind if I invite Jorge over tonight? I promise we won't stay up late, and we won't leave the house. I haven't seen him…" I hesitate, not wanting to draw attention to my absence even though it's all we can think about, "…in a while." There. Benign enough of a statement.

"That would be fine."

"Thanks."

Our conversation is stiff and formal, but progress all the same.

"Mrs. Lewis also mentioned that she would speak with the mediator about scheduling a visit," she says. "I am busy tomorrow, but I could drive you someplace local Saturday."

This is unexpected. "Thanks, Mom. Really, I appreciate it."

"Mmhmm. All right, I'm off to run some errands. Any requests for dinner tonight?"

"Ziti?"

"I think I can do that."

She runs her hand from my one shoulder to the other as she passes me, but doesn't bend down for a kiss.

Small steps.

When the doorbell rings, I leap to answer it. I'm dying not only for a much-needed distraction, but also to see Jorge. I feel so dif-ferent, I want to look at something familiar to ground myself and remember I'm still me.

He beams, gives me a quick kiss, and pushes past me, flowers clutched in his hands. I'm about to reach for them and thank him, when he takes a few steps forward and gives them to my mom.

Perfect, I think. Exactly the right move.

My mom asks him about college, then he chats with my stepdad about soccer and if he'll try out for the basketball team. While I want to get him alone to just hug him, I'm grateful he's taking some of the heat and tension off me. During dinner I say little, letting him fill the space with speech and laughter. For a moment, I can pretend that none of the past few weeks have hap-pened. No tumor, no running away, no courts. Just us, eating and laughing like old times.

But I know it's just an illusion.

After we eat, my mom suggests Jorge and I take our bowls of ice cream to the back porch and enjoy the unseasonably cool eve-ning. I flip the ceiling fans on to move the air and mosquitoes out of our vicinity and we sit side-by-side on plastic recliners.

The frogs that take over the retention pond behind our house bring a cacophony of noise to the night. Every few minutes ominous silence falls upon them in unison, some danger detected, then disregarded as their calls swell again.

"I forget how noisy they are," Jorge says, using his finger to wipe the remains of the ice cream out of the bottom of the bowl. I take the lady-like approach and press the ceramic to my face, licking the sides with my tongue.

"There must be more of them every year. I think that's what it is," I say.

"Maybe."

"So, did you come here to talk about frogs?" I say, an attempt at playful banter.

He leans forward and kisses me. It's the first bit of real affection I've had in days and I struggle to pull back from him, feeling the presence of the adults on the other side of the wall.

"How are you doing, really?" He moves to share my recliner, tipping the end forward slightly before I settle my weight back to counter his arrival.

"All the feels. Is that an acceptable response?"

He shakes his head. "Not for me. Spill."

I stretch my arms above my head before dropping them in my lap. He holds my hands with his.

I shrug. "It feels like the world has changed without me. Or, I don't know, maybe I've changed without the world."

"I haven't changed," he says.

"No, that's not what I mean." I struggle to find the right words. "When I got in that car, it's like I entered an alternate reality. Like the Stevie that left Atlanta was different than the one that arrived. And I'm still trying to put her back together, or see if I even want to put her back together."

"I did like her quite a bit."

"And now?" I chew on my inner lip.

"This Stevie is equal to the other Stevie." He leans forward and I think for a second he's going to kiss me again, but he stops, his nose poised millimeters from my own. "This one may be slightly hotter."

I laugh and push his shoulder. "I'm being serious."

"Oh, me too."

"Jorge."

"All right, all right. Look, you getting in that car on one level was dumb, you get that right?"

I nod.

"But I also understand you thought that was what you needed to do. I'm trying to support you, but you aren't necessarily making it easy."

My phone rings, interrupting our conversation. I look at the screen and silence it.

"Who was it?" Jorge asks.

I shrug. "Don't know the number, probably some media person. Somehow they got my cell number and call from time to time."

"You should consider talking to them."

"Yeah, right. My mom would *love* that."

"I'm serious," Jorge says. "You should do an interview. Stevie, people want to be on your side, *I* want to be on your side, but we don't understand. Help us."

I palm my phone as if I hope the universe will send the answer to me in the form of a phone call. It remains silent.

CHAPTER THIRTY-EIGHT

M aybe the counselor said something that resonated with my mom as well, perhaps her own homework assignment, because when I repeat Jorge's suggestion the next morning over breakfast, she doesn't immediately start losing her shit.

"Interesting. Who are you thinking of reaching out to?" she asks in a measured tone. I see the effort at hospitality she's making.

"Something small, local. I want people to understand what this group is and what it does. I've been reading a lot of articles online, and they're calling them all sorts of incorrect things."

"Like what?"

The images of the articles flash into my mind. "Calling them a cult. Saying they don't deserve religious tax exemptions because they aren't a 'real religion,'" I say this with air quotes. A faint memory of papers from the IRS passes through my mind. "I don't know, then some awful stuff. Like, for some reason people don't like that they give back. I mean, they grow all this food and give so much of it away, but they like, think it's for selfi sh reasons."

She nods. "Okay, but do you really think it's your responsibility to defend their reputation?"

"It's my reputation as well. When they call it a crazy fundamentalist cult, what does that say about me?"

She raises her eyebrows, as if I've made some point. I press forward, ignoring the look.

"It will be short," I assure her.

"You apparently know what's best for you, Stevie." It's backhanded, I know, but it's a concession, so I take it.

I search the missed call numbers in my phone until one matches a local news station. Nothing crazy, just to get the word out, like Jorge said.

When I call the number back, the guy named Mike on the other end sounds surprised even though he called me first. We speak briefly, and I agree to be interviewed by him for a five-minute segment. At first, he acts casual, pausing just enough between talking that I wonder if he's uninterested by the whole thing. He says it may be online content only, but he'll try to get the producers to work it into the five-o'clock news this evening.

"Like, tonight?" I ask. Jorge's idea is starting to sound like a bad one.

"Are you available in the next hour? We can come to you or meet someplace, whatever you are more comfortable with." The excitement in his voice is evident, the effort to remain aloof apparently too much, but I can tell he's trying to maintain his professional demeanor.

"Yeah, sure."

I give him my address before I can think too much about it, hang up, and promptly feel like I'm going to puke.

············(☉/☉)············

Forty-five minutes later, a camera light blinks red as the reporter asks me questions. We sit in the living room chairs my mom never lets me sit in for fear I'll destroy them somehow.

"So, what do you say to those who accuse this cult of kidnapping a young child and brainwashing her to further their cause?" Mike asks.

Jumping right in, I suppose. The man assures me the segment will be edited, so if I need a moment to collect any of my thoughts, he can work that out so it will look seamless. I am grateful as the blinking light pulls my focus away.

"Stevie, do you want to take a break?" He leans forward as he speaks.

"No, it's okay. I would say to those people, they need to open their minds. When religions first started thousands of years ago, people were killed for different beliefs. In some places, people still are." The reporter nods as if I'm saying the most interesting thing he's ever heard. It encourages me to press on. "But religions all start somewhere. This one actually started fifty years ago, so while newer in the great scheme of things, it is well-established in this area and moved to other parts of the East Coast." A bird calls outside the window, pulling my attention momentarily outside.

"Right. The founder, Jacob Gaines," he says.

My head swivels to face him, the pieces falling into place like a level of Candy Crush. *Gaines.* The same surname as Luke. I nod because I don't know what else to do.

"So, they discovered you based on a news story this station broke ten days ago, then came to Atlanta to find you?"

"Not exactly. I contacted them."

My mom sits in the far corner of the room pretending to be on her phone. Her hands hover over the surface as she listens to my answers.

"Because you're having religious visions?" Mike asks.

"Umm, yes, but, that's not really what I want to talk about," I rush to add. I need to pull the conversation back, to direct it to myself.

"All right," the reporter says, glancing at the camera woman. He leans back in the chair and puts his notebook down, like he's debating if coming here was a waste of time. Maybe it was.

"I want to let people know the Church of the Eye are a good group. They run a self-sustaining farm and work with green and organic materials. They are supportive of one another and try to live in a way that God would be proud. I think we can all do more of that."

"But they also brought an unaccompanied minor across state lines," he says. His eyebrows pinch together in skepticism.

"No, well, yes technically, but I asked them to do that. That's not the point. The point is—"

"That they do good. Okay," his words rush and he waves his hand in a dismissive manner. I must have made a face because he hurries to add, "We will edit this and clean it up, so don't worry if you stumble on the details."

I fight the urge to fidget with my ring. "I'm not stumbling."

"Can you tell me more about these visions? What kind of service they offer to the cult?"

"It's NOT a cult."

He doesn't seem to hear me, looking down at papers on his lap. "Can you tell me about the land they're residing on?"

"It's a farm, like I told you, they have crops and some livestock. I think they are looking to bring more. They want to bring more people in and allow them to work for their food, and provide for others. They are good people." Sweat forms on my hairline and I use a fingertip to quickly brush it away. The lights are so hot, I wish they would turn them off.

"But the land—"

"Look, I don't want to talk about the land. I've said what I wanted to say." It's childish, but I can't stop myself from crossing my arms. I stand to really drive home that it's over. He shakes his head at the camera person over my shoulder.

"Well, thank you, Stevie." He turns to face the camera. "This is Mike Tompson with News 6 reporting."

The red light turns off and he removes a piece of plastic from his ear as the camera woman unclips my microphone.

"That wasn't really what I was expecting," I say as they pack up.

He shrugs his shoulder like I should have known better. Of course they didn't really want to hear good things. They wanted an inside scoop on some crazy religious people.

He reaches out his hand, professional requirements trumping his frustration with me. "Thank you for your time and explaining a bit about the group you're a part of, but unfortunately that isn't what our viewers are really interested in these days."

I take it, hoping my hand feels clammy in his. "Not enough scandal."

He shakes his head. "Unfortunately, no."

Mike thanks us and leaves, the living room still arranged in the haphazard way he said would make it look lived-in, as if that wasn't what we did here.

My mom, to her credit, doesn't comment on the reporter trying to bait me during the interview. I am impressed by her restraint, because I totally would have if the scenario was reversed. Maybe Dr. Lewis is right. Maybe my mom *is* directed by love for me, in her own way.

I text Jorge, telling him it was a dud. He congratulates me for trying and says he's bummed it didn't work out better.

Me too, I respond back.

I'm in my room when my phone rings. I don't recognize the number and assume it's another reporter. I'm a little tired of this whole charade. They want answers, I give them, and they aren't the "right" ones.

I pick up to vent some of my frustrations when a vaguely familiar voice meets me on the other end.

"Stevie?" The question is a whisper and I picture someone hiding in a closet, phone pressed against their ear.

"Who is this?" I search my brain, but can't put a face to the voice.

"It's Abby. I can't talk long. I don't think I'm even supposed to be talking with you at all, but I saw your number on Mr. Ackerman's desk and swiped it."

"Abby!" It feels better to hear her than I thought it would.

"How *are* you? This whole thing sounds awful. I wish you could come back to us. I wish the stupid adults would treat you like one and let you make your own decisions."

"You and me both," I say, but then I'm at a loss for anything to add, the line silent for several heartbeats before she fills it.

"Well, we are all rooting for you. Mr. Ackerman and Luke have had a bunch of strange cars here. I think they're pulling every expert they can find to help you."

My mother's accusation plays in my head: *What makes you think they aren't doing this for themselves?* And I know how wrong she is. I remember the looks on the faces of the members. The hope and promise in their eyes. The assurances that we will figure this all out together. They are doing this for me. They want *me*.

"Are you coming to the meeting tomorrow?" I ask.

She lets out a deep, frustrated sigh. "Aunt Jackie won't let me, but she'll be there, Mr. Ackerman, Luke, and I think Sue, do you remember her? She does the pre-entertainment announcements in the evening?"

"I do. That's great, but I'm so bummed about you not being there."

"Me too. Oh, I almost forgot to say, in the last two days there have been exactly sixteen birds on top of the meeting house in the morning. Crazy, right?"

"I guess?"

She gives an exacerbated sigh. "*Birds*, sixteen of them. Like one for each year of your life."

"Right..."

"It's totally a sign. We're going to win. You're going to come back to us and live here for a long time."

"Agreed." I wonder if she can hear the smile in my voice.

"I gotta go—someone is coming. See you soon, Stevie."

"Yeah, see you." I look at my phone screen and the timer stops ticking. She's gone.

But to know she was there, they are all there, and not a figment of my imagination, means everything.

CHAPTER THIRTY-NINE

T he next morning my mom and stepdad take me to a community center about twenty minutes from our house to meet up with the group. When we arrive, a man in a suit with a clipboard stands out front to greet us. He's just as Mrs. Lewis described, medium skin, long hair pulled back into a ponytail, and thick-framed black glasses. He smiles at us, but there is no warmth behind it. His whole demeanor says he is here strictly for work.

He introduces himself to my parents—Mr. Patel—before shaking my hand.

"Stevie, I'll stay with you for the remainder of the visit and take notes which will be part of the court findings. They'll be available to your lawyers."

"The judge didn't mention that," I say, confused.

"It's standard." His words are brusque like he's said them a million times to a million families, and I bet he probably has.

"And do we stay for the visit?" my mom asks.

"That's entirely up to you. We have the space for an hour. You're welcome to stay for all or part, but it is requested that if you stay, you do not interact with the parties. You may observe from a distance that does not give you auditory information about the meeting, for the privacy of those involved."

"She is a minor," my stepdad says. "Don't we have a right to know what they're saying to her?"

Mr. Patel smiles his fake smile. "That's what I'm here for. I will record any relevant information and turn my notes over to the court." He turns to address me. "Ready?"

I nod and follow him through the glass doors to a small gymnasium. It smells of polished wood and soaked-in sweat, not entirely unpleasant, but certainly not something I'd want a candle made out of or anything.

Jackie rushes forward and envelops me in a hug. Mr. Patel shows my parents to two chairs at the far end of the room before he joins us again, scribbling a note on his clipboard. It makes me self-conscience, but I can't help but be excited to see Luke again. I quickly ignore the voyeur watching us.

I say hello to Mr. Ackerman and Sue and we sit in black folding chairs under a basketball hoop. It's a relief to know being back among them isn't awkward. My skin feels warm and strangely prickly, and I realize with panic I'm about to have an episode. I can't remember the last time I took a pill, which probably means it's been a while.

I look directly into Luke's eyes.

"Is it happening?" He leans forward, blocking Mr. Patel from my vision, and most likely me from his.

I nod. "I think it's starting."

Jackie reaches out and takes my hand. "We're right here with you."

"Keep talking," I say, fighting to stay lucid with the group.

Out of the corner of my eye, beyond where we're all sitting, Jesus stands. He's cloaked in cream robes, a Mona Lisa smile on His face. My breath whooshes out in one compression of my chest. It's different than with Mary. The world usually fades away a bit, the focus just on our interactions. Now, it's like I am present in both for the first time. The sensation is weird, like I'm half-way between a dream and waking up, and I worry if I stare directly at Him, He'll pull me straight from this world into His. Do I want Him to?

"Who's with us?" Luke asks. Sue moves to the edge of her seat, but he shakes his head in one brief move. He knows what I know. We can't bring attention to what is happening or someone will put an end to our visit.

"Jesus." I hope they understand I mean the actual son of God, and not that I am uttering a quasi-curse word.

"Stevie," Mr. Ackerman says. "Do we need to get someone for you, your parents, a doctor?"

I don't look at him, splitting my gaze from Luke's to the silent man to my left. I want them all to leave, except Luke.

"No."

"Stevie," Luke leans forward even more, holding both of my hands now. I squeeze back to ground myself in the present. I'm stuck between two worlds and if I let go of him, I'll be flung into the abyss. "Stevie, you need to ask Him what He wants."

I shut my eyes and concentrate on the words. When I reopen them, Jesus has taken several steps forward and stands directly behind Luke. I startle at his rapid movement, causing Luke to squeeze back harder.

"You have been so brave," Jesus says. His voice is like water, cooling liquid poured over me.

My voice rings clear in my head as if I'm speaking the words out loud, but I know I'm not. I swallow and try again.

"I don't feel very brave," I admit to Him.

"Stevie," Luke says, but I shake my head. Not now.

"Are you scared?" Jesus asks.

"Terrified," I say.

"But you are still here. You are still standing, still fighting, still seeking." He is all warmth and comfort, and I bask in His light.

"Please tell me why this is happening. Why me? I'm not sure if I can keep this up." I feel the weight of the last few days press me into the ground, as if the wooden floor will crack and the earth will swallow me whole.

"Oh, my sweet darling," Mary's voice cuts through, but I don't see her. I'm afraid to look around, worried the spell will be broken. I don't want them to leave me, not now, not yet.

"Your fear will guide you. Allow it," Jesus says.

"Allow it," Mary echoes.

My frustration builds as the warmth ebbs, releasing me inch by inch into the surrounding coldness. I try to hold on to it, the edges of it turn to a physical thing as I try to pull it toward me.

When full consciousness returns, I realize it wasn't the light I was tugging on, but the ends of Luke's sleeve. I tell them what

Jesus and Mary say and wait for them to be disappointed in how not Earth-shattering the conversation was, but Luke and Sue stare poignantly at one another.

Luke turns back to me, slowing pulling his arm out of my grasp. "We will win," he whispers to me. I want to believe him.

I see the eagerness of those sitting around me, they look practically poised to burst. But behind them, my mom and stepdad sit, perfectly still and gripping each other's hands. There's also anxiety and fear in their faces. They know they may lose me to the people huddled around me. It is out of their control as I chase whatever this is and refuse to give up. I won't let the doctors cut into me and take the one special thing I have away. It can't all be meaningless. I can't have this cancer just because.

With the timing of the visions, I know they can't be random. I know somehow this is important. I'm risking it all, my relationships and possibly even my health. I am taking a literal leap of faith and hoping what I find on the other side is firm ground. But it's for me. It's all for me and I wonder, what price is too high for selfishness?

CHAPTER FORTY

"You've become quite popular I see," Dr. Lewis says a few days later.

I shrug. "Yeah, I guess."

"Stevie, I saw you on Good Morning America."

"Yeah, well, I guess the local news was wrong, that I actually was a story. They interviewed me a few days ago, but decided not to air the footage. I guess some other markets got it, decided to run it, and The Today Show picked it up. Whatever."

It was cool to be on the national news and I was glad my story was getting out, but honestly I kept waiting for someone from YouTube to call. My mom on the other hand freaked out when she heard Savannah Guthrie was going to interview me. I decided to relent for her behalf. She was bummed it was just a teleconference but kept calling people and telling them about it anyway.

"It must make you feel partially vindicated though, right?" She sits in one of the uncomfortable chairs across from me. A peace offering?

"Yeah, it does. Now I get a bunch of emails from people thinking I'm crazy or the anti-Christ, which I fi nd particularly funny when I've never said that I'm competing for His position, just merely having conversations with the man and feeding some homeless."

"But people believe you."

"Yeah," I say, "they do."

Even Jorge seems to have come around, like he needed a trusted news source to say his girlfriend wasn't bat-shit for him to consider the idea. Even Stacey called me after the interview aired. Our conversation was brief and filled with long pauses, but it was nice to hear her voice.

"Hey," Stacey said.

"Hey back."

"So, you're like the second coming or something?"

I laughed. "No, not really."

"But you, like, talk to them? Like see them and talk to them?"

"Yup," I confirmed.

"Crazy."

"Crazy," I agreed.

She told me a bit about a job her mom made her get at a local laundry mat and how mind-numbingly boring it was. I joked that I'm glad I didn't end up having to get a summer job after all. It felt good to talk about something that wasn't "The Thing." Never much of a phone person, Stacey rambled for a few more minutes before saying bye with promises to get together soon. Promises I hope she keeps.

Dr. Lewis shifts in her chair and I'm brought back from my memory to her office. It has no pictures, at least not of people. I don't think I've ever been in an office with such little personality. I wonder what makes her choose to bring so many books, but no photographs.

The book.

"Oh, I forgot your book."

She waves her hand. "That's okay, next time. But make sure you remember, because it will be our last visit."

"Okay." I pull out my phone even though I know she has a policy against it and set myself a reminder before putting it back in my pocket. "Done."

"So, let's get to it. Have you been doing your homework?"

"You mean have I tried to be a little nicer to my mom?" I nod my answer. "I think she has been, too."

"That's wonderful! Do you think your relationship has been getting back on track then?"

The question makes me pause. Have we? "I'm, I'm..." I search for the words. "I don't know if we ever will."

She shakes her head. "No, I don't think that's true."

I chew on my cheek, it's raw at this point, but I do it anyway, rubbing the raised spot with my tongue. "I think I've broken it, broken us. Honestly, I really don't see how we can come back from what I did."

Dr. Lewis moves to the chair next to me and places her hands flat on the table.

"Stevie, I know it can seem like this moment is your whole life. That is the burden of the young. It all feels so big and so meaningful, it's impossible to think things can be any different. You still have decades of life to live. It can be so daunting you can't wrap your mind around it, but I assure you, if you don't want your relationship to be this way forever, it doesn't have to be. Your mom doesn't like this either."

I shrug. "You don't see the way she looks at me. Like I've ripped her heart out and swallowed it whole."

"That's parenthood." Her smile says she knows what she is talking about, but there are no pictures of children in her office.

"I'll keep trying, but like I said, I don't know what good it will do."

"I'm glad to hear you're trying. Don't stop."

"So, what now? I've done my homework, but I still need to come back next week."

"Well," she says, "there are still quite a few things we need to discuss. Some logistics."

"Like?"

She moves a few papers in front of me, forms with dozens of empty black lines.

"What's this?" I ask.

"Just some paperwork to fill out, basic questions to cover."

"Like what?" I ask.

"Where will you live?'

"The compound," I say without hesitation.

"And they will allow that? How about the school year?"

"There are kids that go to school there, public school."

"And your boyfriend, would you still like to see him?"

"Of course." Her questions are starting to irritate me.

"And your parents?"

"What about my parents?" I ask.

"Are you planning on seeing them? What will you do if they don't want to see you, or they are uncomfortable visiting you at the compound? Are you going to get a job? Go to college? Eventually have treatment?"

"I don't know. Yes, maybe. I don't know."

I stand, unable to contain my emotions while sitting. It's like I'm suddenly under attack.

"Well, you need to figure that out. You may be emancipated in less than two weeks. Not having a plan isn't an option."

My chest heaves and I grab the back of the piece-of-crap chair. I asked her to replace it and she just laughed at me. I grip it with my fingers, testing its weight.

"Please, don't take this out on the chair. I know it's not comfortable, but it will be so much paperwork to try to get a new one." One side of her mouth ticks up in a half-grin.

I let go. "I wasn't going to smash your precious chair."

"Stevie, look, I'm not trying to upset you." She sits ram-rod straight, unphased by my outburst. She probably sees them all the time, probably worse than this.

"That doesn't seem like the case."

She takes a deep breath in and lets it out slowly. It looks like it feels good, so I try it as well.

"If I'm going to sign off on this paperwork and agree that you are capable of making your own decisions in a responsible manner, I need to make sure that is actually true. I don't want to grant something I am later going to regret because I never challenged you to view what life as an emancipated minor actually looks like. I wouldn't be doing my job, and that is unacceptable to me."

She's right, I know, but it's still scary and overwhelming. Anger is easier. It feels better to be mad at her than see the reason in her questions.

I sigh and am surprised that tears prickle my eyes. I blink hard and look at the ceiling.

How do I get her, my parents, everyone to see I don't want all of it? I don't want my ties to be cut. I don't want to choose my mom, dad, stepdad, friends, Jorge, school, any of it. I just want control over this one small thing.

But I also know that's not an option.

"I can help you figure this out," she says, her voice bringing my gaze down back to her. "It's okay to ask for some help. That's what I'm here for. This isn't a one-way quiz or something."

I nod and sit back down. The anger starts to ebb, replaced by a wave of exhaustion. I'll write whatever she wants me to. I'll play along and get it all down. Whatever it takes to get her to sign off on her stuff for court. Everything else, well, I'll just have to figure out later.

I lean over and we get to work.

CHAPTER FORTY-ONE

·············(✿)·············

My mom doesn't meet with Dr. Lewis when I'm done, so we head right out after. I'm going to meet the group members at the community center today, but she has to work and grudgingly agrees to drop me off at Jorge's so he can take me a bit later. It's been a few days since our first visit and I'm not sure who all will be there, but am excited all the same.

"How was your talk?" My mom keeps her eyes straight on the road.

I wish we could just snap out of our funk. That I could crack a joke, she'd laugh, we'd each admit we were being dumb, and move on as if these last few weeks were just something we'll laugh about in the future.

But I know we're far from that.

"Good. I like her. I didn't think I would, but she's given me some things to think about."

"Oh, like what?" She glances at me. "Sorry, nevermind, you don't have to tell me. I know it's a private conversation."

She sounds genuine, and tears escape her eyes. She doesn't wipe them away, maybe hoping I won't notice if she doesn't draw attention to them. It crumbles an outer layer of my anger.

"Are you still going to want to see me, no matter what?" I ask. The question sounds as childish as I feel. It's like I'm trapped between two worlds, still young, still wanting my parent's approval for things, but also wanting to be independent and able to make my own decisions.

The car pulls over to the side of the road and my mom puts it in park. She unbuckles her seat belt and mine, her actions slow but purposeful, and leans over the center console to wrap me in a hug. Now I'm crying, too.

"Baby girl, I will love you no matter what, and I'll be a part of your life in whatever capacity you allow me to be. I know this is hard and confusing, but your dad, Reg, and I are trying to do what we think is best for you."

"That's what I'm trying to do, too," I say through sniffles.

"I know, and unfortunately those two don't align right now." She pulls back and looks me full in the face. "And this won't be the last time, God willing. We'll have disagreements, but that doesn't mean we don't still love each other and we don't still try. I know you're doing what you think is best, but I also need you to understand that I don't agree with you, and as your mother, it is my job to fight for what I think is best. Unfortunately, it means that fights you. It's not what I want, but I have to. Do you understand?"

I pull a deep breath in and let it out in measured intervals before nodding my head yes. Her lips form a sad smile, more of a straight line, before she puts the car back in drive.

"Put on your seatbelt, please," she says, and I obey.

After I get dropped off, Jorge and I have about an hour before we need to leave. His parents are both at work, and we laugh nervously at the unsupervised situation we've found ourselves in.

It feels like it's been years since we've been totally alone together, though I know that's not true. He kisses me deeply and I press into him, allowing a moment to forget about all the shit going on in my life and just enjoy the sweet taste of his mouth on mine.

He sits me on his bed, but I stop him when his hands reach the button of my jeans.

"Jorge," I say into his hair.

"I've missed you."

"So kiss me."

He complies, but soon his hands wander again and I break away from him.

"I'm not ready." Images of Mary and Jesus flash into my mind. I've never been a staunch wait-til-marriage kind of girl, but in this moment, with what I've been experiencing, it feels wrong.

"Okay." He sits behind me in bed, wrapping his arms around and kisses my neck. It sends pleasure tingles down my spine and I shiver.

Looking around his room, I'm struck by how different and bare it is. Most of the posters and pictures are off the walls. His bookshelf is half-empty. And I'm shocked to see a pile of boxes spread throughout the space.

"Jorge?" I break away and pick up one of the smaller boxes. It's filled with small trinkets, a baseball trophy, a miniature soccer ball, a side-by-side frame I got him with pictures of us in it. "Are you guys moving?"

"I am…" He stands next to me, taking the box and setting it back on the floor. My face must scream confusion because he rushes to explain. "Stevie, I'm going to college in just a couple months. You know what a terrible procrastinator I am, so my mom has been on me to start packing now."

"You're bringing all of this with you?" I'm not sure what all you need in college, but I doubt old year books and trophies are two of them. The picture though, he better bring the picture.

He shifts his weight and begins to swing his right leg back and forth, rubbing a straight line with his toe into the carpet. "I didn't want to add any more stress for you, Stevie. I'm sorry."

"About?"

"Well, my brother and sister already moved out, so it's just me and my parents. My mom said when I go to school, they're going to put the house on the market. They've always wanted to live in Virginia to be closer to my sister and nephews. I guess they were just waiting for me to be done with high school to do it."

"But, what will happen when school breaks? Where will you go for holidays and the summer?"

I see the answer in his face before he says it.

"I guess I'll go wherever they are."

The truth takes my breath away, and I'm crying fresh tears. Apparently, I didn't run out of them from the incident in the car.

"It'll be okay," he rushes to add. "I mean, I *am* going to college in Florida, so we'll see each other on weekends and maybe some nights if I don't have a lot of work to do. It'll just be over breaks that I might not see you. But other than that…" His words trail into nothing. "Look, I'm sorry, but I didn't want to upset you. I figured after the trial I would tell you."

"How do you feel about this?"

"Sad," he says flatly.

"Me, too."

He seems like the one person from my old life who believes me, who trusts me enough to stand by me as I navigate what this alternate future may hold. If he leaves, what will I have left to keep me rooted? I worry it will be the church on one side and my life before on the other with no medium in the middle bridging the gap anymore.

We embrace amongst the boxes that hold his life. I wonder if in ten days, I'll be doing the same thing.

CHAPTER FORTY-TWO

•••••••••◖◖◗◗••••••••••

My phone alarm goes off, giving a momentary break to the sadness.

"It's time to go." I wipe my nose on my sleeve.

"Do you want me to stay, or drop you off and come back?" he asks as we get into his car.

I think for a minute. Do I want him to meet these people that are helping me potentially uproot my life? Am I ready for my worlds to collide in this way?

"Yeah, sure, if you want to."

"I think I do," he says.

Mr. Patel greets us at the entrance again, wearing the same suit but a different tie. He seems unsure about Jorge coming with me, originally suggesting he stay to the side, but seems satisfied when I offer that he can record what Jorge says too, if that will help.

He clicks his pen three time. "All right then, that would be okay."

As we approach the gym, I'm confused by the noise emanating from it. I distinctly hear Abby's voice and get excited, but I wonder who else is here. Maybe more people decided to come and lend their support?

When we walk through the doors, I'm shocked to see about thirty people standing in small pockets, filling the gym floor. I recognize Abby, Jackie, some of the garden workers, and a few others, but most of these people are strangers. Jorge must feel my hesitation because he presses closer to me.

"A lot of people," he whispers. I flash him a concerned look, which causes worry to crease his brow. He's about to ask something else when Luke pushes through.

He opens his arms wide to embrace me before introducing himself to Jorge. I'm so flummoxed by all the people, my manners have completely left me. Abby rushes up, and seeing her helps me regain some of my composure.

"Abby, this is Jorge." I gesture next to me. She bypasses his outstretched hand and hugs him.

"I'm so glad you were able to come, too. This is such an exciting time! You must be thrilled to be a part of it!" she says.

Jorge looks at me, eyes narrowed in confusion. I shrug back.

"What are these people doing here?" I whisper, not wanting Mr. Patel to know something strange is going on. I'm not sure why I think he will have a problem with all these strangers, but something in me says it won't be super helpful to point it out.

Luke beams. "Isn't it wonderful? They are interested in joining the church. And *you*," he leans close to me, "you are the one who brought them. Come meet them."

Electricity courses through me as Luke grabs my hand and pulls me away from Jorge and toward the group.

A pit forms in my stomach.

I was ready to see some familiar faces and maybe talk about the case a bit. But this? Getting paraded in front of a bunch of strangers? Not really what I was signing up for today.

I look back to Jorge, for what? Help? But he's too far for me to reach and he's not looking at me. His eyes are wide as he takes in the scene around me. Abby is chatting with him and I see Jackie introduce herself, but I can't make out the conversation, though it doesn't look like he's responding.

As I step to the crowd with Luke, a woman comes up to me and takes both of my hands in hers.

"My son is sick. I have been praying, but he isn't getting any better," she says, an urgency to her words. "Can you ask Mary what I should do?" Tears swim in her eyes as I try to snatch my hands back, but her grip only intensifies.

"I, I don't know…" I stammer.

A man comes up, towering over both of us. "My mother passed. I want to tell her I'm sorry. Can you see her? Can you talk to her for me?"

"No, I… it doesn't work that way." It doesn't seem like anyone is really listening to me. More people press in, they reach forward and touch my arm, my hair, one woman takes my face in her hands.

And throughout it all, Luke just stands there. He doesn't push these people off of me or try to explain that it's not like I have a pathway to the underworld. He smiles, shakes hands, and remarks that *yes, it is wonderful, isn't it? This amazing gift that has been given to me. And how* his *group is working with me to harness it. That together, we will bring peace and salvation.*

The crush of people overwhelms me. Heat builds and I panic that I'm going to have another vision.

Not now. I say over and over in my head.

The visions are still so unpredictable, I don't want to pass out or have to fight to focus through all of this. But soon I realize the heat is just the press of bodies on me. Sweat beads on my forehead, and I struggle to free my arms to wipe it away. I catch a glimpse of Jorge through the crowd and wonder if the bewildered expression on his face mirrors mine.

After about twenty minutes, Luke finally steps in and asks the people to give me some room. I'm not sure what prompted his sudden rescue, but it came not a moment too soon. Exhaustion, both mental and physical, cause me to shuffle my feet and hunch my shoulders. I long to sit down, stretch my back, and crack my neck. Luke brings me a chair and I collapse in it as the group mingles but keeps their distance. Relief flows through me.

"What was that?" I ask, a bit of edge in my voice.

I catch Jorge's eye and he takes a step toward us, but I shake my head. I don't want to draw attention to my anger and have Mr. Patel, who is currently staring at his phone, come over too.

Luke's face turns bewildered for a moment before sliding back into a smile. He quickly glances to the far corner. Evidently, he's keeping tabs on Mr. Patel, too.

"What do you mean?" he asks.

"This." I fight the urge to throw my arms wide. "What is this? An ambush? Who are these people?"

"Stevie," Luke says, all seriousness in his tone as he keeps a smile plastered to his face. "You can't help people, *I* can't help people, if we don't have people to help. We need new members."

"I wasn't aware parading was part of the job," I say. My hurt and anger mix to a toxic combo in my chest.

He turns and looks at me, the smile dropping. "Our goal is getting the word of God out. That's been our goal since day one. Teaching people about God and helping them. You can help us further that. God has contacted you, for what purpose if not to help? Not to help people? If that's not something you're interested in doing..." he lets his voice trail.

I feel put on the spot, stupid for not seeing the big picture, not cluing in before. He's right, of course. What's the point if I can't use this for good?

I nod.

Luke turns and addresses the group, his hand on the back of my chair. I can't help but wish it was resting on my shoulder instead. Guilt makes my cheeks go hot in embarrassment. Five seconds ago, I wanted to throttle him and now I want physical contact.

What is wrong with me?

"Brothers and sisters," he says, bringing my attention to him. Mr. Patel stops looking at his phone. "I'm so pleased you chose to join us today and met the remarkable Stevie. She is truly a blessing from above." Now he does touch my shoulder. I try to ignore the flip in my stomach. "We're on the brink of great things together, and we're so excited you're here to be a part of that as well!"

The room breaks into clapping. Again, I can't help but feel like I'm a half-step behind.

CHAPTER FORTY-THREE

M y car door isn't even closed before Jorge starts in on me. "What the hell was that?" he asks.

I shrug, not sure how to answer him. Not sure what the answer *is*.

"Seriously, Stevie. That was like the Spanish Inquisition there. All those people. Were all those people from the compound place?"

"Calm down," I say, stalling for time.

"Calm down?" He looks at me, jaw clenching and unclenching.

"I don't know why you're so angry."

He throws his hands up, smacking them against the roof. "Really? You really can't possibly understand why I might be angry? Stop playing like you're an idiot in all of this, Stevie. I'm really getting sick of the game."

"Hey! I'm not playing anything."

"Oh, please. You act like you're the only one going through this and that it's a personal affront to you if someone doesn't completely understand, but you don't even try to let them. Let me. You say you want me to believe you, but you can't even trust me enough to let me know *what* I'm supposed to believe?"

"I…" What? I have no words.

"This isn't going to work if you keep secrets from me. I can't be on your side if I don't know what I am signing up for. What *was* that in there? Abby was telling me all this stuff like you might go around and speak to different chapters up and down the coast?"

The comment blindsides me yet again, but I make sure it doesn't show on my face. It's clear to me now that I don't have all the answers and feel a bit foolish, but I damn well won't admit that to anyone.

"Okay, okay, look, I'm sorry. I don't really know what all that was back there. I've never seen most of those people. I guess Luke said they had a bunch more people interested in joining the church, so he brought them to meet me."

"So that was what, them parading around their new toy? Hoping to have people fall in love with you and join them?"

"I'm not a toy," I say.

"You certainly looked pretty bright and shiny."

I bristle at his implication. "Luke was just introducing me to new people. I talked to lots of people when I was staying with them. I don't see the difference."

"Anyone who could see your face while you were being bombarded would know that is bullshit. You looked like a deer in headlights. Worse, like you'd already been run over and another car was barreling toward you. Then it seemed like you and that Luke guy were having a pretty heated discussion. Stevie, stop lying to me. You know damn well that was screwed up."

I lower my gaze and feel about an inch tall.

"I'm not trying to pick a fight with you, I swear." His voice softens as he reaches for my hand. I let him take it. "It just looks like they're using you, and I don't want you to get hurt."

I snatch my hand back and stare right into him. "How are they using me? Because they have some people who maybe want to change their life for the better and meeting me may help them do that? That I might have something they want to hear? You're just as bad as my mom, thinking that I can't possibly be this person that others look to for comfort."

"How much do you know about this group?" He ignores the bating words. "I'm sure I did the same Google searches as you, and aside from a few new articles that mention you, there is little about them out there. And what is being written isn't particularly nice. I did find something about financial troubles for a 'COTE LLC' with Mr. Ackerman's name on it. Right, isn't he that lawyer guy? I thought I saw his name on the papers your mom got."

Shock dissipates my anger. "What? Do you think it's the group?"

"I don't know what else C-O-T-E could stand for. Stevie, I want you to be careful. I think you're really valuable to them. But not in the way you think."

·············(☉✍☉)·············

Jorge's words play in my thoughts any time I let my mind wander. Even two days later in Atlanta. I lay on the cool white table in my yoga pants and tank and struggle to push the nagging feelings out of my mind. I've slept terribly the last two nights, toggling between thinking Jorge was right, that I was being used to further Luke's goal, and thinking he was wrong, and I really was the prophet they were looking for, and the group was more concerned with what I could do for the world than for them.

I beg for Mary, Jesus, anyone to come to me and guide me, but my dreams are fitful and useless.

A shiver runs through me, stopping my mind from spiraling again. I wish I'd worn the extra thick socks I'd packed. The prep room is cold, but since I need my arm free, I had to take my zip-up off.

I should be used to MRIs by now and the contrast medicine they have to pump in my veins, but this time the needle appears to be larger than necessary and hurts about twice as much as I thought it would.

"Sorry," the nurse says as she tapes it in place. "I'm going to start the drip now. I'll be back in ten to wheel you over. You need anything?"

"No, I think I'm good," I say, proud that I kept the nervous shake from my voice. I close my eyes and take measured breaths through my nose. While I'm prepared for it, the warmth of the contrast IV as it works its way through my veins dulls my senses so I don't immediately realize something is going on. But then I hear a shift in clothing to my right.

I turn my head and meet the gaze of a man. He is in dark red robes, which seems out of place since everyone here appears to wear blue scrubs. His face is shadowed by the low light and glows

166

softly blue from the machine next to me, making it difficult to decipher his features.

"Can I help you?" I ask, the IV making me groggy. It's difficult to speak and reminds me of when I was trapped between the present and my vision.

Exactly like that.

He smiles. "You are."

Oh my God.

Literally.

"It's you. I didn't know if *you'd* ever come to me." My tongue feels too large. I look at the clock, hoping the nurse is true to her word and doesn't come back for a few more minutes.

"I come to you all the time. Can't you feel it? Can't you feel us around you always? Since when do you need eyes to believe?" His voice sounds like an echo bouncing off my bones. It reverberates around my insides until it settles into a soft buzz. The room darkens even more, His robes and voice the only things left that are real.

"Believing is so hard," I say.

"It is, but imagine how much harder not believing would be."

I try to picture a world without Them in it. Emptiness is all I can come up with.

"I'm not sure what to do."

"You don't always need to be," He says.

"Then how do I know what to do?" My frustration builds. In each conversation with Mary I've been unable to get real answers. I was hoping He would at least be able to give me some.

"Trust."

"I am worried I'm being used. That there are people around me trying to exploit me. I'm not sure how to tell who is righteous or not."

"If you always speak truth, make sure you follow the light inside yourself, and everything else will fall into place. There will be people in your life who will help or hurt your purpose. But you mustn't let them. Stay on your true course. Don't let them sway you."

I'm about to ask Him what side of the coin Luke is on when the door opens, breaking my attention. The warm sensation is still there, but it's different, muffled now. I know without looking He is gone as the darkness in the room ebbs back into the blue light.

"How you feeling?" she asks.

I open my mouth to speak, but have no clue how to answer her.

CHAPTER FORTY-FOUR

Back with my mom in the exam room after the scan, I can still feel the echo of my conversation with God. It feels so good when I get the visions, when they visit me, but my emotions get so jumbled because it's also so frustrating. What is the point of being a prophet if I have nothing to say? Nothing to show for it? It's not like I'm really helping anyone, much less myself. They tell me this has meaning and to stay the course and be ready to help, but I'm missing the how.

I am risking my health. A small risk. One that isn't too pressing at this exact moment, but what happens when it is? When I reach the point where I have to cut the tumor out of my brain? Will that light a fi re under Mary's butt to make something, anything, actually happen? I'm worried now that I'll reach the point of no return without answers and nothing to show for it, dying without helping anyone.

I turn to my mom, wondering if she can sense the desperate internal turmoil going on inside of me, but from my vantage point up on the exam table, I see she's just scrolling through her phone.

There's a soft knock at the door before it opens. Dr. Oppenheimer is followed by another doctor. My heart seizes. I wonder if this means something terrible.

He introduces the woman and she tells me she was hired by Mr. Ackerman.

"My offi ce is also in this hospital," Dr. Jamis says. "I thought it would be easier for me to observe this appointment instead of having a separate one. I hope that's all right with both of you?"

My mom and I nod. I'm glad I won't be stuck in this place all day. I'm still so lost in thought and a bit rattled. I want to get out of here as soon as I can. We aren't leaving til tomorrow, but this urge to *leave* makes my right eyelid start to twitch.

Both doctors stand huddled over a screen in Dr. Oppenheimer's hands. They speak in low voices as if they haven't come to a consensus yet. On what? Who is going to give me the bad news? A pressure builds in my chest as my heart begins to race.

"I'm worried," I say, trying to break the building tension, "that you're all here to tell me I'm dying or something."

Dr. Oppenheimer is the only one who laughs at my lame joke. "Not today."

He hands Dr. Lewis the tablet and steps forward to press his fingers on either side of my neck. He nods to himself before asking for his tablet back and pulling up some images on it. They look like duplicates of each other.

"We're looking here at your original scans on the left and the scan from today on the right."

I peer over.

"They look the same."

Dr. Oppenheimer smiles broadly. "Exactly. This is really good, Stevie. It shows there hasn't been growth since your last scan."

I feel empowered by this. "So, there's little risk at this point, right? Little need for removal?"

The doctor shakes his head. "I saw your story on the news. I take it you're still having visions. Do you find the medicine limits their frequency?"

I shake my head and bite my lip before answering him. "I haven't exactly been great about taking them."

My mom is about to say something, but stops herself.

"I wasn't kidding when I said the seizures can create complications for you completely separate from the tumor. Stevie, it's dangerous to not take them."

"Well, that's the thing I wanted to ask you about. The last two times I've had the visions, I haven't had a seizure."

"How can you be sure?" Dr. Jamis asks.

"I'm awake during them, lucid, conscience, whatever you want to call it. They used to happen like dreams. I would wake up on the floor or something, but not anymore. The room is still there. I am still fully aware, and I can still talk."

"Interesting," Dr. Oppenheimer says.

"Have you seen that before?"

Dr. Jamis shakes her head.

"No," Dr. Oppenheimer says, "but if I've learned anything in medicine, it's that new symptoms can present themselves all the time. But, if you're reluctant to take the medicine because you *liked* that the visions accompanied the seizures, I hope this encourages you to take them as they no longer seem to be related."

That seems fair.

"When are you heading home?" he asks.

"Tomorrow," my mom says.

He fishes in his pocket and pulls out a bright green flyer and hands it to her, but addresses me. "Stevie, this is information for a local support group that meets Tuesday nights at this hospital. It's for people with or recovering from brain tumors, some the same type as yours. I really suggest you go. This is something not a lot of people can understand, but they can.

"I think you can benefit a lot from attending. You don't have to talk, but just listening may help. I also wrote the location of a local chapter in your area. They meet on Saturday mornings. Maybe if you get something from this meeting, you can check out that one as well."

My mom's face looks hopeful.

I nod in agreement. "Maybe I'll check it out."

"I'll send a copy of these to Dr. Jamis, who will provide her findings to your respective lawyers. If you don't have any questions, we're done here. I'll need to see you back in four weeks to check on your progress, but I think if we still see the same level of stagnant growth, we can extend the scans to six months."

"That sounds good," I say.

They turn to leave, but Dr. Oppenheimer hesitates.

"I'm your doctor, Stevie," he says. "But even if you don't wish for that to be the case anymore, I hope no matter what the verdict is in your trial, you will decide to seek treatment."

I nod, clutching the paper as if it will give me the answers I can't seem to find anywhere else.

CHAPTER FORTY-FIVE

I call my dad after the appointment, telling him the good news that the tumor hasn't grown at all. I see my mom also on the phone and assume she's talking to my stepdad.

I wonder how she's delivering the news.

My dad seems excited, but I can hear the exhaustion behind his relieved words. No growth is good, but for the side he's fighting for, it certainly doesn't help his case.

When I hang up, my mom is wrapping up with Reg. She takes a breath so deep, it visibly pulls her shoulders up and down. She nods, though I know he can't see her, and says bye. When she looks over at me, she gives me a small smile before we turn to leave.

"What do you think about the support group meeting?" she asks as we walk, handing the neon paper over to me. I skim it over.

"I don't know."

"I can drop you off and we can get dinner after. It starts at four thirty and I think lasts about an hour and a half," she says, not hearing or ignoring my hesitation.

"Umm, okay." I'm not really too keen on going to it, but I know it won't hurt and will make my mom happy.

I realize today's update must be a strange mix of emotions for her. She's probably stoked that the tumor isn't growing—no imminent death today—but at the same time, just like I read in my dad's tone, it's certainly not going to automatically sway the judge to rule in their favor.

When we return to the hospital a little after four, she goes to the cafeteria to get coffee and "catch up on work" as I walk to the desk and ask where I'm supposed to go. The man points me to the end of the hall.

Glass doors open to a courtyard with chairs set in a small garden. It's warm out, but sun shades and mist fans make it bearable. It's not at all what I expected.

Okay, so I'm young, I think that's been established, so there are quite a few things that I assume are the way things are, but only because of movies and TV. I expect this support meeting to be the in the basement of the hospital, an ancient coffee maker on a table with brown rings littering it and white mugs, some of which are stained by lipstick.

I couldn't have been more wrong.

A Keurig—seriously—sits on a small bistro table. Bright colored mugs surround a k-cup stand. I pick one with a donut on it and wait the sixty seconds for the sweet-smelling coffee to steam out.

I'm not usually a coffee drinker when it's a million degrees out, but it gives me something to do with my hands, helps me feel like I am properly playing the part.

Six people filter out of three other doors to the courtyard. Two have hospital gowns on and shaved heads, one pulling an IV stand behind him. The other four are in street clothes like me, full heads of hair. Or wigs? A man in khakis and a plaid button-up calls the meeting to order.

"For those who don't know, I am Dr. Ike. I work as a support staff member at this hospital and run these meetings. Please feel free at any time to get yourself something to drink. Some of you have been here before, but I'm pleased to see a few new faces." He smiles at me, the woman with the IV, and the guy sitting next to me. "We usually start these meetings by introducing ourselves. You're welcome to say what you're here for, be as specific as you like, then we'll open the floor for any issues anyone wants to speak about. Why don't you start, Tonya?"

The woman sitting next to him waves her hand. "Hi, I'm Tonya. I'm two years post-op from grade two ependymoma. Had my six-month scan last week, and," she pauses, as if waiting for a drum roll, "I am still cancer free."

The circle claps, and I join in a beat late.

"Tonya, that is so wonderful to hear," Dr. Ike says. "Next?"

"Theo," the man next to Tonya says.

Everything about him is large. His hands look like they'd swallow mine up, and if I tried to encircle his biceps with both of my hands, I'd fail. I noticed that he only clapped half-heartedly during our celebration, and I wonder what small mass of cells could bring this giant guy down.

Theo shifts in his seat. "Pilocytic ast, ast…"

"Pilocytic astrocytoma," Dr. Ike jumps in.

"Yeah, thanks. I guess I should get better at pronouncing it." He stares at the ground.

"You will," Tonya says. I wonder if this is meant as encouragement or ominous.

"I got diagnosed last week, and I go in for surgery Friday," Theo continues.

"Good that they're taking care of it quickly," the woman with the IV says.

"I was having seizures at work, and my doctor said it can start affecting my memory soon." He leans forward and places his head in his giant hands as his shoulders start to shake. I am not prepared for this. Tonya gets up and gives him a quick hug. "Thanks," he says. "It's all very new to me. But I've got four kids, so you know, I gotta do whatever to stay around for them."

The circle nods.

The woman with the IV says she has glioblastoma multiforme. The mood shifts in the circle, but I'm not really sure why.

"That is tough," Dr. Ike says.

"It is, but that doesn't mean I'm not going to fight. I beat it once before. I'll just beat it again."

Uncomfortable heat builds through me, and I fight the urge to run and throw my chair through the glass walls, to escape this place as quickly as I can. The warmth builds as my stress increases. These people are *dying*. Here I am, wrapped up in my problems, and they are DYING.

I look over and see Mary sitting in the corner on a wall of stones in front of a fountain. She is silent, and I don't dare talk to her—especially since all I want to say is "why aren't you helping these people?! These are the people who are sick, who need you!"

A small part of me realizes the warmth was probably from her, and I'm about to get lost in my thoughts of how I'm seeing her along with everyone else, when it's my turn. I hesitate.

"Oh, honey, we already know who you are," Tonya says.

"You do?"

"Right?" Tonya looks at the group, who nods.

"Okay, yeah, I'm Stevie. I have grade two oligodendrogliomas. Whew, that's a mouthful. I guess you do get the hang of saying it." I smile at Theo. He doesn't return the gesture.

"That's a good one to have," the woman with the IV—I can't remember her name—says. "High success rate."

I'm not sure how to respond, so I shrug and give a half-nod. I'm glad none of them press me further, especially if they've heard of me. Mary sits quietly.

Once everyone speaks, Dr. Ike asks if anyone has anything they'd like to discuss.

I turn and stare at Mary. "Do any of you get visions?" I hear myself ask, my eyes locked on her. I don't remember giving my voice permission to talk.

They shake their heads.

"Do..." one of the men trails. "Do they follow you around?"

I shake my head, ignoring the figure sitting off to the side.

"But I did get the euphoric feelings," Tonya says, pulling the conversation back.

"And when you had your tumor removed, did they go away?" I ask.

"Yup."

"How did that make you feel?" Dr. Ike steals my question from me.

Tonya shrugs. "Honestly, empty. It made me regret my choice, but then I think about my husband and three dogs and my future, and it was worth it."

Her answer, while truthful, doesn't really help.

There are conversations about treatment, about talking with a spouse, how to tell kids, but I have trouble following, my attention torn between Mary and my own thoughts.

I keep getting hung up on Tonya's answer. How can you regret something, yet be happy you did it? The juxtaposition doesn't make sense to me.

At the end of the meeting, we all clap, like we've accomplished something, but I don't think we did. I look around, to see if Mary approves of this showing of excitement, but she is gone. I do a quick scan of the courtyard, but she is nowhere to be found. My body again feels like a normal temperature, and I wipe the sweat that had collected on my forehead. The unceremonious way she came and left makes our encounter seem unfulfilled.

As I'm about to leave, seeing my mom standing in the middle of the hall, Tonya stops me.

"No one can make your decision for you..." she pauses. "...I guess maybe they can in your situation. But anyway." She waves her hand as if that motion can remove my problems. "There are plusses and minuses for everything, just make sure your positives outweigh your negatives."

"Thanks."

"And keep coming to meetings."

I smile at her, for the first time feeling a bit of kinship since all this started.

CHAPTER FORTY-SIX

········•••◦⊙◦•••········

'm a bit disappointed when Mr. Ackerman says we're going to meet in an office space he rents near downtown to go over last-minute stuff about the case instead of the community center with the group. I was really hoping to see Abby one last time before the trial. Especially to set the record straight in my head after the disastrous last meeting and subsequent fight with Jorge.

I want to see Luke, have him apologize and say this was all a misunderstanding. That no, I am needed, just me. The rest of it, the *show*, is just that, an honest attempt to get more followers. Something to make me feel like what I am doing is right and I'm not being used. Not that I agree with Jorge, but the seed he planted has found a small patch of fertile soil to start taking root.

Mr. Akerman's office is close enough to my house, so I ask my mom if I can walk. She hesitates, but agrees.

I know we're all counting down the days until I can drive. Well, I guess hoping that I will be able to drive. That's another thing I'll have to figure out. I haven't gotten my learner's permit yet even though I'm old enough. I haven't pressed the issue since I'm pretty sure my doctors would advise against it, and I doubt any licensed driver would be willing to be a passenger in my car.

As I leave my house, the summer heat seems bearable when I first set out, but by the time I walk the half-mile to his office in a converted single-story house, I'm a literal hot mess.

My hair, which I decided to straighten for some reason instead of just throwing it up in my normal ponytail, clings to my forehead and neck.

"Screw it," I say out loud and tie it up.

I readily accept the water the secretary at the front offers me and wait for him. I'm a bit early, and he's apparently meeting with another client. For some strange reason, I assumed that he worked exclusively with the group, but I guess not. This is where he meets his "outside clients," the secretary informs me.

Am I one of those?

Two minutes after our appointment is supposed to begin, a woman and two young children walk down the narrow hallway followed by Mr. Ackerman. He nods to me but follows the group to the front door, speaking to them in a low whisper. The woman nods, though seems like she is about to cry, and leaves, gripping the kids' hands.

"Stevie!" His smile is bright when he turns around, like whatever sad events just transpired has been instantly washed from his memory.

"Hey, Mr. Ackerman."

"How are you feeling?" He gestures for me to follow him.

"Like I might throw up."

His eyes narrow and he leans slightly forward. "Stevie—"

I put up my hand. "No, not like tumor related. Just nerves."

He relaxes back in his chair. "Okay, nerves are totally normal."

The office is larger than his one at the compound and considerably neater.

"There's no pictures here," I say, walking the perimeter of the room. "Aren't you supposed to have your diplomas hanging up, too? At least Dr. Lewis has that."

He laughs. "This is a space I rent two days a week. It's part of a co-op with other lawyers. We all share the staff assistant up front and the space. I don't have enough need for a full-time operation outside of the compound, but I do need somewhere I can conduct outside business. This lets me do that, but since we all share it, no one keeps any personal items here."

"Oh, cool."

"It's a bit late to ask, but I can show you my diploma if it's important to you."

I shake my head. "No, that's all right."

"Why don't you take a seat and we can go over your case."

He pulls out a large stack of papers from a rolling briefcase. My file is no longer a single green envelope. It runs the gambit of sizes and colors, papers everywhere.

"We can go over a few of the reports, then discuss your testimony."

"Mine? I thought I don't have to talk. Isn't that like an amend-ment, right?"

"If this were a criminal trial, yes. But you aren't being accused of anything. You are making a case, which means you are actually going to have to be a part of making it." He lifts one corner of his mouth up in a half-smile, a show of sympathy I think.

"So, we've got the final report from the counselor," he says, voice bright and trying to lighten the mood. He pulls out one of the stacks of papers connected with the largest staple I've ever seen. My heart tightens.

I met with Dr. Lewis yesterday afternoon after we got back from Atlanta to go over my plan for the future, which to her credit, she didn't laugh at. It involved a lot of crying and second guessing, but after our meeting, I did feel like I had more of a plan.

Hopefully, she agreed.

"Great news," he says, flipping to the last page. "She did approve you for mature minor status."

I let out a gush of air, relaxing into the chair. "Seriously?"

"Why do you seem so surprised?"

"This whole thing is surprising, truthfully. I keep expecting someone to come in and say it's all been a joke. The tumor, this legal battle, the Church of the Eye, all of it."

"Why?" He looks concerned.

"Because, this is stuff that happens to other people."

"No, Stevie. It's what is happening to you." He leans forward, the most serious face I've seen him wear. "Stevie, this is a huge deal. And we are one giant step closer. Dr. Lewis included your post-trial plan, if it goes in our favor. I find it well thought out and reasonable, but do you think you can actually execute it? Do you think you can move into the compound? Switch to their homes-chool program? See your parents on the weekends? You're asking a lot of yourself, but also everyone else. You need to be sure."

The doubt surrounding me since my diagnosis has been crushing, least of all from myself. It seems that everyone thinks they know what's best for me, and as easy as it sounds to allow them to make all the decisions for me, I can't.

"I am terrified," I say. "I'm not going to lie or sugar coat that. I don't know if everything will work out exactly like I hope it will. It might be a huge mistake, one that I will struggle recovering from."

He raises an eyebrow. "This isn't encouraging," he says.

I hold up my hand. "Please, let me finish. It might be a mistake, but I don't think so. I know people think I'm crazy with these visions. There are probably even members of the church that doubt me, maybe even you." His face doesn't indicate if I'm right or not. "But *I* know it's true. And so, I have to do this. I have to go forward and trust that what is supposed to happen is because God is behind these visions. I need to trust that even if I have no idea what I'm doing, He does."

Mr. Ackerman nods. "All right then. Let's get started."

CHAPTER FORTY-SEVEN

·············(C✦ᴅ)·············

W hile I'm walking home, I pull out my phone to call Jorge. It rings once and goes straight to voicemail. The tell-tale sign of being ignored. I tell myself he's probably just busy. He didn't return my call from yesterday either. He's probably working, though I can't remember if he was supposed to be on yesterday or today. I try not to read too much into it, which of course sets my mind into a tailspin.

Stacey picks up on the third ring. I can picture her looking at my name on her phone, pausing a moment before answering.

"Hey!" Her voice is too bright, too excited, a weak attempt at covering her hesitation. I wonder if she was the right one to call and unload my drama on. But I'm not sure who else there is. If this whole experience has taught me anything, it's that I don't have as many real friends as I thought I did.

I take a deep breath and jump right in.

"So, the trial is about to start," I say.

"You're going to go through with it?" she asks.

The question takes me aback. I didn't know she thought changing my mind was a possibility.

"Yes, I mean, there's no other way…"

"Oh, of course. I know," her words rush out. "I'm sorry. So, what's up? Is that lame to ask? I mean, I *know* what's up, but I'm guessing there's a reason you called?"

"I met with my lawyer for the last time today."

"Is that a strange sentence to say, *my lawyer*?"

"Oh my God, the strangest," I confess.

"Anyway, sorry, so your met with your lawyer."

I fill her in on the last few days. Meeting with the counselor, and the news today that she signed off on my paperwork, agreeing that I'm of a mature and sound mind.

"And she figured that out by talking with you?" Stacey asks.

"And this form I had to fill out. That's what I was going over with Mr. Ackerman as well."

"Form?"

I hear a crinkling noise and then the sound of her eating chips or something similarly crunchy. My stomach growls in jealousy. I quicken my pace, just minutes from my house now.

"Yeah," I say. "They had me fill out this questionnaire-type thing. Like, what are my plans if this goes through. Where I'll live, where I'll go to school, stuff like that."

The crunching stops, sudden silence on the other end.

"Stacey? You still there?" I pull the phone down, but see the line is still connected.

A shriek explodes out of the phone.

"What *school*? What the hell are you talking about?" she yells. Her voice is still loud, but bearable enough that I can press my ear back to the speaker.

I didn't really expect her outburst. "Stacey."

"You aren't going to graduate with me?" her voice is quiet now, worse than the yelling.

"I don't know. I was thinking I'd go to school there, but I guess, I mean, nothing is set in stone."

"First, I thought I was going to lose my best friend to cancer. I watched you have some fit and get taken away in an ambulance and thought you were going to die. Then you said, while the cancer was removable, you were going to keep it in, and God spoke to you and for some reason, He wants you to stay sick. I didn't understand, but I love you and wanted to support you. But this? So, now no matter what, I'm going to lose you." Her voice is thick with sadness and I find they choke my speech as well.

"Stacey…"

"Look, Stevie. I gotta go. I don't know what all this is. What exactly you're doing. But please reconsider. Just…just don't leave us."

This time when the phone goes quiet, I know it's because she's gone.

CHAPTER FORTY-EIGHT

M y sleep is fitful and I wake up more tired than before I
went to bed. I kept hoping Mary would come to me in my
dreams, but they are void of appearances from any of Them.

I originally felt better after my meeting with Mr. Ackerman.
Having his affirmation for my plan and knowing what to expect
during the trial took some of my anxiety away. Not only will I be
speaking, but so will Dr. Lewis, Dr. Oppenheimer, and Dr. Jamis,
as well as my parents. That part I'm not totally ready to hear.
But that calm was quickly wiped out and now I'm freaking out
because of my phone call with Stacey.

I play her outburst over and over. I guess I never pictured in
all of this, even potentially leaving school, as me also leaving her.
She's right. I can't imagine graduating without her either.

To take my mind off it, and with Tonya's voice in the back of
my head encouraging me to keep attending meetings, I ask my
stepdad if he will drive me to the one Dr. Oppenheimer wrote on
the back of the paper he gave me. My mom is out running errands
and the motivation to go hit me after she left.

He happily agrees, I think glad to have something not only to
contribute to the cause, but also knowing that it will please my mom.

When he drops me off, I decline his invitation to stay, which
he looks relieved about.

For as welcoming and full of light as my first meeting was,
this one—held in the basement of a local church—is exactly how
I thought these things would be. Right down to the sad coffee pot
and questionable mugs.

Row of chairs fill up quickly. I pick up a handout, just to have something to do while I'm waiting for the meeting to start, and notice this is for all cancers, not just brain.

The same uncomfortable feeling creeps in as the room becomes crowded with bodies and voices. Most are older than me, about my parents age, but there are a few kids my age and one a lot younger, clinging to her mother. The mom seems like she doesn't notice, half walking, half dragging the little girl behind her as she chats with a few others.

A woman in jeans and a polo stands at the front of the room and brings the meeting to order.

"Hello, I'm Alix, and I'm so happy to see you all today! It's a true blessing to have you all with us to share in your experience, your troubles, and to gain strength from one another. Since we are a larger group, for those of you who have not been here before, we allow an open forum for speaking, we do not go around the room. This helps keep us on time." A heckle in the back makes her laugh. "Okay, *somewhat* on time, and it also allows things to be comfortable if you're not ready to share."

This I can get behind.

"But first, and this is very difficult for me to say, but I received word that Aubrey Jo passed away yesterday morning."

A shockwave passes over the room. Some people cry out, some cover their mouths with their hands and shake their heads in disbelief, while others spring up to embrace one another.

"Aubrey Jo was a member of this group for nearly nine months as she battled leukemia. I think she touched every person in this room who was lucky enough to meet her. And while she will be missed, we'll keep her spirit alive, like we keep the spirit alive of all members that leave us too soon. I ask you all to bow your heads in prayer as we have a minute of silent reflection for Aubrey Jo."

I look down at my untied shoelaces, a numb feeling through my body. I'm not stupid. I know people die all the time, and that people die all the time of cancer. It's not like I know anything about this girl other than her name, but I feel affected all the same. There are people in this room who may not live very long, myself included. And sure, a bus could hit me at any second, but before a few weeks ago, there was a pretty slim chance I wasn't going to make it til at least eighty.

"Thank you," Alix says, breaking the silence. "Now, who wants to share?"

The meeting runs the gambit of emotions. Some people tell stories of their treatment in such a humorous way, I even find myself clutching my sides with laughter. A few times I wipe tears from my eyes, hoping I get to them quick enough that no one notices. One person is the parent of someone who passed, and while it seems this is the wrong meeting for them, no one tells them to leave or stop speaking.

The hour meeting, as predicted by the heckler in the back, runs a half hour over before Alix finally calls an end to it. There's a senior yoga class arriving, so we need to move the chairs to the sides of the room and start heading out. I'm about to walk through the open doors when an older man calls my name.

I turn around, expecting to see someone familiar, but I don't recognize him. He introduces himself as Bill and holds out a trembling hand.

"They keep saying that will stop, but it's been about six months, so I think I'll just have to live with it."

"Sorry to hear that." I shake it and ask him if we know each other.

"Not really," he looks from my eyes to the floor for a beat before gazing back up again. "I saw your story on the news, but before you think I'm some crazy person, I'm really glad you came here today because I kept thinking about reaching out to you."

"Okay…" I scan the room and see Alix talking in a small group. I try to catch her eye just in case, but she's too deep in conversation to look up.

"I'm about six months post-op from surgery," Bill says. "I had oligodendrogliomas too, but mine was anaplastic grade three," he pauses, probably realizes I'm not up to date on all the lingo. "Means it was, or I guess is, malignant."

"Oh." My initial alert at his cornering is relaxing bit by bit.

"I just wanted to let you know if you had any questions about the surgery, I'd be happy to answer them."

I've never met anyone with my exact cancer before. The thought of getting to hear more about his treatment is too enticing.

"Do you mind walking with me?" I ask. "I'm sure my stepdad's been here waiting for a while."

"Sure."

We walk up the stairs together, and I signal to my stepdad that I'll be there in just a minute when I see him at the end of the hall. I have a million questions to ask this guy, and also have no idea where to start. Maybe with the most basic.

"Did you have visions?"

He nods. My chest tightens.

"Of what?" I ask.

"Nothing as special as you. I would see dead relatives. Which, don't get me wrong, was great. Some I wasn't as much of a fan of in real life, but got along really well with as ghosts."

"Do you see them anymore?" I'm dying to know.

He shakes his head. "No. But you know what was great? My entire surgery, while I was under, I was with them. Damndest thing, because they said the actual removal happened relatively quickly. It was stopping the blood and sewing me up that took the longest. But I swear, for the entire ten hours I was with them. When I woke up…" He clapped his hands together. "…gone. Haven't seen them since."

"That's so sad."

"Sometimes. But heck, I'm all about living. I have plenty of time to be with the dead when I'm one of them." He barks a laugh. "Not quite ready for that though."

"You seem like you're doing really well."

"Doc says I'm making great progress. It's been the last month or so where I feel like my speech is finally back to normal, so that was frustrating, and my coordination isn't one hundred percent yet, so I still can't drive, but I'm here."

We stand in silence for a few seconds. The myriad of questions I had for him moments ago evaporated in my thoughts. All I can think about is how nonchalant he is. The visions were there and then they were gone. Simple as that.

"Thank you for speaking with me," I say, "but I really gotta go. Take care, Bill."

"You too, Stevie. And hey," he calls to me and I turn around, "don't forget to say your goodbyes during the surgery. I forgot to. My only regret. I woke up and never got to say thanks."

The thought of losing my visions without getting to see them all one last time, to thank them, to tell them all the unsaid things between us, is one more reminder that I'm not sure if I'll ever be able to let them go.

Not yet at least.

CHAPTER FORTY-NINE

·············(C/O)·············

My mom is so glad I went to the meeting, she doesn't hesitate to say yes when I ask if I can go out with Jorge tonight.

"What are you guys planning on doing?" she asks in a low tone, as if she's just asked me for some big secret she can't reveal to anyone.

"Umm...dinner? Very scandalous."

"Who's doing something scandalous?" my stepdad asks, walking into the kitchen and grabbing a soda.

"Stevie is going out on a date tonight."

"Oooooh, a *date*," he says.

"You guys are jerks."

They laugh and I join in, despite myself.

It's like a magical spell, transporting us back to The Before. I wish we could live here, standing in the kitchen without a care in the world.

But just like that, the spell is broken. My stepdad's phone rings and my mom goes into the laundry room to fold clothes. I'm not sure how we'll look at the end of this. If causal meetings around the kitchen island are in our future, but I sure as hell hope so.

·············(C/O)·············

I'm disappointed when Jorge picks me up and says he wants to go somewhere to talk. My stomach growls loudly, but he doesn't notice I guess.

"Can we maybe get some dinner first?" I'm worried my stomach may eat itself then turn on my other internal organs if I don't get some food.

We pull into a Burger King, which wasn't exactly what I was thinking, but for the benefit of my spleen and appendix, I order something.

We drive to an abandoned lot at the far end of the little complex we're in and park. I dig into the bag, shoveling fries into my mouth as I fumble with the paper wrapping on my burger.

I notice Jorge is still. A terror fills me. Is he going to break up with me? Sitting in his car with my mouth full of fries? I freeze.

"I need you to tell me what it's like," he says. "What it's *really* like."

I swallow hard. "Like?"

"You've told me about the visions, but that can't be the whole story, the whole reason why you don't want to get this tumor removed. Is it this group you're in with? How they make you feel? How the visions make you feel?"

I take a sad look at my burger before answering him.

"A little bit of all of it."

"I need more than that," he says.

I quickly shovel a few more fries in my mouth, swallow, then answer him.

"I almost can't even describe how *good* I feel when the visions happen. You know how sometimes on a cold day, your mom will take a fuzzy blanket right out of the dryer and wrap you in it? Holding you in the warmth?"

He shuts his eyes, remembering the feeling. "Mmhmm."

"It's like that times a thousand. The warmth penetrates into my insides, making me feel totally safe, like I don't have to worry about a single thing because it is all being taken care of. And then they speak to me, and while it doesn't all make sense, in the moment, there's a truth that give me instant peace."

"What do they say?" he asks.

I fumble. Other than a few people at the church, I haven't told anyone the details. It's hard to put them in the proper words, to make the simplistic not seem meaningless.

"They tell me they believe in me," I say, carefully picking my words, trying to put them in an order to make him understand. "But it's not just what they say. It's this whole notion that I'm here for something really important. That they're coming to me, me specifically, for a reason. It's this pure calm feeling like I know I can do anything."

"Sound really intense."

I nod and take a huge bite of burger. I'm starving. He'll get over me talking with my mouth open. "It is, but it doesn't stay for very long. Once they go, once I am back in reality, I can kinda remember what it feels like, but then each time it happens, I'm like, 'this is so much better than I can even hope to remember it being.'"

"And how is the group going to use this? What, try to send you in a trance to get answers for them? Are you being given like the eleventh commandment or something?"

"Har har. No, they said I'm just supposed to tell them what I see. It's up to them to translate it. Their founder had a premonition that a girl who spoke to God would help bring them to salvation."

He takes a drink of soda before continuing. "And you're going to be that for them? Are you prepared for that? The meeting at the rec hall was overwhelming enough for you. How are you supposed to talk to possibly hundreds of people? Have them pick your visions apart, especially when you can't *make* them happen?"

"I know it won't be easy," I say. "And I know I won't have all the answers, and as cheesy as this sounds, I just really have to have faith that God will show me the way."

"And in the meantime, you get euphoric feelings each time you get a visit?"

"Yup," I said.

"How can I possibly compete with that?"

"What?"

"Vi, seriously, I'm never going to be able to make you feel that way. I was planning on talking you out of it tonight, asking you to drop this whole lawsuit and just get the treatment, offer to do more outreach with you at youth group until I have to leave, but then what? You'll know what you gave up, and I'll know I asked you to do it."

"So, don't. Don't ask," I say, my voice flat.

"And what, we keep going on pretending that this isn't a big deal? That you can sever legal ties with your parents, go live on a...a...whatever you want to call it, and I go off to college and see you during breaks? Is that really a viable future you see?"

"Jorge..." my voice trails.

"Seriously, Vi. You think you're trying to do this noble thing or whatever. But really, you're just being selfish with the lives and emotions of everyone around you who actually gives a damn, and choosing people who probably couldn't care less about you, the real you."

His shoulders rise and fall with his quickened breath, his hand gripping the steering wheel so hard I wonder if it will break under the tension.

I'm suddenly no longer hungry. Anger and hurt, confusion and fear fill the space in my stomach.

CHAPTER FIFTY

················○○○················

My eyes feel half-swollen shut when I wake up the next morning. I check in the mirror and am glad to see they don't look as bad as they feel. Hopefully my mom and stepdad won't notice I was up crying most of the night.

After Jorge's speech, we sat in the car in silence for about ten minutes before he drove me home. My goodbye was a small, sad smile, and he drove off. I waited until I was safely in my room to bawl my eyes out.

When I get into the kitchen in the morning, my mom asks if I'll join her at church and I agree. It's been a while since I've been to a service there and I'm hoping if nothing else, Stacey will be there. Jorge's family usually goes to the later service, so I'm not too worried I'll run into him.

I haven't spoken to her since she nearly bit my head off about school. We've texted a little, but really, I just want to sit and talk with her. I want to make sure we're still okay and fi ll her in on all that went down with Jorge last night. I need her opinion on what the hell is going on.

And maybe what to do about it.

My mom and I sit in our "normal" pew and I grab a program someone inadvertently left behind from the last Mass. I flip through it as the choir sings softly in the background. I notice there's a call to prayers for me in the back of the program. My skin feels hot and I flip it over quickly, hoping my mom didn't catch me. I'm sure she is the one who requested it there, but I really don't want to talk about it. There are too many connotations.

What kind of prayers for my recovery? Prayers for what I have been seeing? Or simply prayers I will lose the court case and get the tumor removed?

Father Hugh walks up to the pulpit, the choir finishing their last note as he arrives. His sermon today is about acceptance of God's will. Fitting.

He says faith and trust are tightly entwined. We must put trust in God that He, in return, will take care of us. And He trusts that our faith will stay strong even when we may not understand the path we're on, or what His will may be.

It's like he's reading my brain and knows what I need to hear. I keep waiting for another vision—it should be here of all places, right?—but no one ever comes.

We say our prayers, our welcomes to those around us, sing, and listen to a few Bible readings. The hour goes quickly and soon my mom and I are heading to the social hall. Stacey stands in the entryway and I have to fight back a shout of relief.

She embraces me tightly, and I am keenly aware that people are staring at us. Well, probably me. People have kinda been staring since I arrived, like I'm someone different than the kid they've known since I was born.

Stacey has a strange expression on her face, like she can't figure out what to say to me.

I decide to rip off the Band-aid.

"I'm really sorry," I say, tears welling in my eyes.

She reaches out a hand and squeezes my arm. "Stevie."

I wave her interruption off. "No, I am. I haven't been thinking about how you're feeling and ignoring you."

"I don't blame you."

"A lot has been happening, and I forget who knows what and it's so exhausting to talk about. I've just slacked. I'm a really shitty friend."

"No, you're not. It's just complicated. I haven't been that great either."

"That's not true."

"I know, but I thought it would make you feel less shitty by me saying it."

I laugh despite myself and she hugs me. We both wipe tears from our eyes as we pull apart.

"Let's get some cookies and go outside," she says, then leans in and lowers her voice. "I think there are too many eyes and ears on us here."

"Sounds like a plan."

I make eye contact with my mom and motion to the courtyard. She nods and holds up two hands to indicate she'll be ready to go in ten minutes.

We head outside, Stacey holding the door, and me clutching about a dozen cookies. As if knowing I'd be attending today, they'd put out the lemon sandwich ones, my favorite. We settle on the brick half-wall surrounding the courtyard that holds the bell tower. I look up at the series of bells, each progressively larger. I wonder how big the one at the top is. It doesn't look that impressive from down here, but I bet I can't even put my arms around it.

"All right, spill," Stacey says.

"About?"

"Oh my God, you're the worst. The trial. The cult. Everything, anything."

"It's not a cult," I say, defensively.

"Ugh, you know what I mean."

"Yeah, I do. It's not a cult. They are a religious group just like us."

She takes a cookie. "I'm sorry. You know I act stupid when I'm nervous. You know me well enough to know that, right?"

"You're the worst."

"I totally am!"

I eat one of the cookies because I'm afraid she's going to eat all of them otherwise.

"I'm sorry, too," I say. "I'm really sensitive about it. I keep getting crap about it." I sigh. "Let's start over."

"Deal. So, how's stuff going, really? Your brain still ticking away?"

I laugh. "That's supposed to be an improvement?"

"If you love me, you also have to love my faults." She flashes a huge smile. I laugh.

"I think Jorge broke up with me," I say it in a rush, like ripping off a Band-aide. And I'm really proud of myself for not crying, not even a little.

She almost falls over she hugs me so quickly. "What? Oh my God, I'm so sorry. Why? What happened?"

I shrug. "I think he couldn't handle what's happening. He was blaming it on other things, but really, I think it was that."

I decided to leave out the whole "you're selfish and terrible" part of his speech. I wasn't quite ready for anyone else to hear that, or worse, to agree with him especially since it feels like Stacey and I have just come to a tentative truce.

"Oh babe, I'm so sorry. Honestly, me and Malik haven't seen much of him lately. All the stuff going on with his family and college I guess made him a bit of a recluse. They don't seem to come to service anymore, even the later one. We've tried to get him to go out a few times, even with just Malik, but he doesn't seem interested anymore. Maybe just give him some time? Seems like this moving stuff is really messing with him."

Anger flares in me. "Oh, and what, having a brain tumor is like, not a big deal? I need to be accommodating to *him*?" I know I shouldn't raise my voice, that she isn't the one I'm angry with, not really, but I find myself yelling anyway. The few people also standing outside turn to look at us. Stacey sticks her tongue out at them.

She places a hand on my shoulder. I don't shrug it off. "Look, I'm sorry. You're right. I'm just trying to tell you that he's going through a lot as well. I'm not trying to make an excuse for him. He acted like an ass, and you *should* be mad at him. But I'm trying to let you know what a mess he is. Maybe don't totally count him out yet."

I look up again, blinking hard against the tears. I can't help but feel like I'm making a mess out of just about everything in my life right now. I thought talking with Stacey would make me feel better, but somehow, I feel even crappier.

Her parents come out a few minutes later to tell her they're about to leave. She gets up to hug me and I grip back tightly, needing something to hold on to. She squeezes me hard then kisses my cheek before going back inside.

I promise myself as she leaves that I will be a better friend. I'll check in more, see how she's doing. We keep only talking about me and I forget to ask her anything back.

I'm in a fog as my mom and I drive home. I still can't seem to get Jorge out of my mind. It takes my mom saying my name a few times before I realize she's speaking to me.

"Wait, sorry, what?" I ask her.

We pull into the driveway and she cuts the engine.

"What's going on with you? You haven't been yourself since this morning. Are you nervous about—"

"I think Jorge is going to break up with me." I cut her off and bury my head in my hands. "God, and I thought about having *sex* with him!" Fresh sobs stop me from speaking.

"Were you?" she asks.

I shrug. "I don't know. Maybe?"

She laughs a little, and I can't help but be even more hurt. I'm guessing she can see the sadness on my face because she briefly places her hand on my knee.

"Honey, I'm sorry to hear that. Did you guys get into a fight last night during your date?"

"Some date," I huff, wiping my eyes. "I don't know if fight is the right word, but he made it pretty clear he's not interested in sticking around to see where all this goes."

"I know this isn't the easiest to hear, but if that's true, maybe it's best you know that now, right? What does Stacey think?"

I shake my head. "That he's got a lot on his plate and maybe I need to cut him some slack. Uhh!" I stare up at the roof of the car. "Like I need one more thing right now."

"God gives us the challenges we can handle, right?"

"I think He thinks too highly of me."

We both laugh a little.

"I'm really sorry, baby. Maybe you've got it wrong. Maybe he's just a little freaked out and needs some time to think. Why don't you ask Stacey about it? But later. I think for now, you should relax tonight. We have a big day tomorrow, a big week coming up. The last thing you need is more stress, right?"

"Yeah, I guess," I say. It's the irst time she's brought up the trial, and I don't want to draw too much attention to it so she'll keep speaking.

"Your dad and Karen land in a bit. Why don't you figure out a place for us all to go out to dinner tonight?"

"That sounds good. Any requests?"

"Nope. Whatever you want that can take a reservation. We don't want to be out too late. Your dad and Karen are staying in a hotel downtown, so maybe something between here and there."

I get myself together, and we go inside. I immediately start searching for the perfect restaurant. I remember a steak place close by and use their website to make a reservation.

The last spot asks what occasion we're celebrating.

The beginning of the end.

I type it in.

CHAPTER FIFTY-ONE

···········•••◦(●╱◉)◦•••···········

"**M**orning," Mr. Ackerman says. I walk up to him and Luke as they stand in front of the courthouse.

My parents and stepparents walk past us with their lawyer. They keep their heads up as if we are strangers and not like I rode with them here.

"How was the morning?" Luke asks.

"Awkward. I guess it was fine. But we didn't talk much."

"Would you like me to petition for you to stay somewhere else? A hotel? I can see if your parents would agree to the compound, but that may not go over well..." Mr. Ackerman's voice trails.

I think about staying someplace else for the next few days. It may be nice to get away, but would that make things worse?

"No, I think I'll stay. I've been working at making peace with them. I'd rather not mess that up."

Luke puts his hand on my shoulder. "A very mature decision."

I can't help but feel proud, like I've accomplished something huge. Part of me realizes I'd do anything to chase his approval. Even just his presence brings a relief. The thought of being back on the compound, of actually getting to *live* there, fills my mind's eye and gives me a strange rush.

"So, we'll go in the same order we spoke about Friday," Mr. Ackerman said. "First will be Dr. Oppenheimer, then Dr. Lewis, the social worker assigned your case." He looks down at his sheet to remind himself. "Mr. Patel. Then your parents, Dr. Jamis, Luke—"

"You're testifying?" I cut Mr. Ackerman off and turn to Luke. He gives me a half-smile that makes me just about die.

"Oh, yes, I'm sorry," Mr. Ackerman says. "I forgot after we discussed the matter on Friday, we decided since Luke's name will be on the petition to be your healthcare surrogate, he should also speak. Shouldn't be anything too long. They'll ask him what level of care he's willing to provide should your condition become more serious, and if he'll get you treatment at that time. Also a bit about where you'll be living and how you'll be cared for. Originally, I was going to have Jackie do it since—"

"I thought I was going to be out of town this week," Luke said, finishing Mr. Ackerman's sentence. "But then I realized how important this is. How important *you* are, and I was able to rearrange my plans."

I glance at Mr. Ackerman, who's expression surprises me. Exacerbated? Annoyed? I guess at being interrupted, but could there be something more to it?

"This will probably take the better part of a week," Mr. Ackerman says, ushering us through the security line. "The judge will want to be thorough and give both sides plenty of time to speak, but don't be concerned if it takes longer than that, or shorter. It really just depends on how much information the judge feels he needs to make a decision."

We take the stomach-dropping elevator to the tenth floor, enter the courtroom, and start the proceedings that will dictate my fate.

CHAPTER FIFTY-TWO

·············(⊙/⊙)·············

Dr. Oppenheimer looks handsome in his suit, like he just walked off a movie set where he saved the day. It's strange seeing him without his white coat on, like he's missing an appendage. It's not like I know him well or anything, but it makes me wonder if I saw him on the street, would I even recognize him.

Sitting in the courtroom, the small lunch I ate from the diner across the street from the courtroom feels like a buffet for how uncomfortably my stomach gurgles. The judge was a little late starting this morning and after Mr. Ackerman and Ms. Kwong hand him a bunch of different papers, the judge decided to break for lunch before having anyone testify.

The door opens behind us and I reflexively turn around. Stacey and Malik slip in and take a seat in the back. She lifts a tentative hand to me, and I give her a small wave back. Relief helps take some of the nausea away. Even with my promises to be better, I haven't talked to Stacey since our conversation after church and part of me worried she wouldn't want any of my baggage just like Jorge. Her presence feels like a life preserver. I crane back, hoping that maybe Jorge came with them and realized that I just might be worth it, but the door remains shut.

My parent's lawyer, Mrs. Kwong, starts speaking, drawing my attention back to the front. She asks Dr. Oppenheimer basic questions, his education, how long he's been practicing, his experience with tumors like mine.

"Each tumor is unique," he answers.

"Yes, I would imagine," she says. "But as to the type, how many have you seen?"

"I've had several patients with oligodendrogliomas, however, it's quite rare to have it in a patient so young. Stevie is my first under the age of thirty-five."

"So, does that make her situation more or less dire?"

I lean forward, curious about his answer.

"Each case really is unique, so I wouldn't say it makes it more or less, but certainly her age and relative health makes her a good candidate for recovery."

"And what is her rate of recovery?"

"Her five-year rate is almost ninety-five percent, which is in line with this type of tumor, but I feel her recovery time may be decreased."

"Thank you." The attorney sits down, shuffles some papers, and nods to the judge.

"Mr. Ackerman?" the judge addresses him.

Mr. Ackerman gets up and approaches the doctor.

"Doctor, you've talked about her rate of success and her pro-posed speedy recovery." He says this last bit while making air quotes. "But what you haven't properly explained to the court is the urgency of her need for treatment."

"Urgency?" Dr. Oppenheimer asks.

"What I'm asking, doctor, is that from my understanding, there is little immediate risk to Ms. Albie at this time. Is that a correct assumption?"

"These types of tumors are slow-growing, if that's what you're asking, yes."

"So, if they're slow growing, do you have an estimate on how much time she'll have until it becomes medically necessary to remove the tumor? Until her success rate will start dropping and it will become urgent to take it out?"

Dr. Oppenheimer shifts in his seat. "There is no real way of knowing."

"How would you try to know? Let's say for some reason you're unable to perform a surgery on a patient, how would you know how long they have until whatever it is, let's call it an under-lying health risk, is outweighed by the need for removing the foreign body?"

"Again, that is not something I can hypothesize, but that's why we do scans on a routine basis. That way, we can keep an eye on any growth and develop a plan."

"Has this been a treatment plan for any of your patients?"

Mrs. Kwong stands, but Mr. Ackerman raises a hand.

"I will rephrase. Without using any names or identifying features, can you tell the court if you have ever had to delay treatment for a patient, and if the routine scans have been an available alternative."

"Yes, I had a patient once who had high blood pressure and was overweight. Treatment was delayed until the patient's weight could get to a healthy range to eliminate additional surgical risk."

"And how long, in that case, did that process take?"

Dr. Oppenheimer takes a deep breath. I can tell he doesn't really want to answer the question—he's gone down a rabbit hole he's trying to work himself out of.

"Doctor," the judge addresses him, "please answer the question."

"Two years."

The room goes quiet.

"And did you follow the protocol of regular scans to keep an eye on your patient's tumor?" Mr. Ackerman asks.

"Yes."

"And what was the patient's 'five-year success rate'?"

"It's been seven years and the patient is still alive without reoccurrence. That trend is expected to continue for the foreseeable future."

Mr. Ackerman nods. "And, if at the end of these proceedings, the judge determines that Ms. Albie can make her own decisions regarding her medical treatment, and she decides to forgo treatment at this time, is this the same method of observance you would suggest in this case?"

Dr. Oppenheimer momentarily chews on the bottom corner of his lip. "Yes, it is."

"Thank you. That is all." Mr. Ackerman sits, and I fight the urge to high five him. I feel like we've just won the case when I know it's far from over.

Mrs. Kwong stands up. "Doctor, while this treatment plan worked for one of you patients, does that guarantee it will work for another?"

"No, of course not. That was a very special circumstance. There were risks far greater for this patient than the sole risk the tumor posed. In Ms. Albie's case, that is not the situation. The tumor is the largest risk to her life currently."

"And in your medical opinion, what would be the best course of treatment?"

"Removal," he says without hesitation. "Suggesting anything else would be unethical on my part."

"Thank you, doctor." And she sits.

The excitement I feel deflates. I look to the judge and wish I could peak in her head and see if that last bit affected her. Have I gotten closer or further away from getting what I want?

CHAPTER FIFTY-THREE

························

Late that night I sit in my room scrolling mindlessly through Instagram. I even make it to the end of my feed and start searching for random hashtags when I can't resist the urge any longer. I close the app and open my starred contacts. My finger hesitates over Jorge's number.

Part of me desperately wants to hear his voice, and another part of me never wants to talk to him again. I am so hurt, but also so lonely, desperate for some positive human contact. They conflict in me until I am a soup of emotion.

I turn it off, then back on again. Twice more before I finally say, "screw it," to no one in particular, and call him.

He answers on the sixth ring. Either he wasn't by his phone, or he was debating on answering.

He doesn't sound out of breath, but I don't really want to admit it might be the latter.

"Hey," he says after a beat.

"You weren't there today." I didn't mean to call him out right away, but the words tumble out on their own accord.

Silence meets me. It was a mistake to call him. I can feel it through the line. My skin breaks out into a nervous sweat. I wonder if I can just hang up. I doubt he would ever call me back. My, how far apart we've gotten.

"I didn't know if you'd want to see me," he finally says.

"Why wouldn't I want to see you? I'm in the middle of an incredibly stressful and scary point in my life, and you didn't think I'd want to see you?"

He sighs. "I'm sorry, really I am. But I couldn't get away anyway."

"Why not?" I take the bait, it chipping away at my hurt.

"Had to go to a signing today…" he trails, "…my parents sold the house."

"Really?" I keep interest in my voice. Trying to be normal.

"Yeah, strange."

"Totally strange. When do you guys move out?"

"That's the really crazy part. This couple that bought the house wants to move in by the end of the month. Did some super fast all-cash closing."

"End of the month?" I am shocked. "That's only two and a half weeks away."

He laughs. "Crazy, right?"

"Totally insane. But you don't start school for almost two months. Where are you guys gonna go?"

He sighs again. "Gonna have to move twice, I guess. I tried to talk them into letting me rent an apartment close to school. I mean, I'm going to be there, living on my own soon enough, but my mom kinda freaked at the suggestion. Said I was still a child and children live with their parents. They're the ones that decided to sell my house out from under me, not like I asked them to do it."

My mind is swirling. A little more than two weeks and he won't be living ten minutes away. I bet he wasn't even going to tell me. Anger flares, and I struggle to keep my voice even. "Were you planning on saying goodbye?"

"Crap, Stevie." His voice sounds like it's already a thousand miles away. "It's not like we're on great terms, right? You haven't called me in days, and now you do, out of the blue, and are pissed?"

"I wasn't sure how we left things, and I kept thinking you'd call me. When you didn't, I thought maybe you didn't want to hear from me anymore. I didn't know what to do, but, but..." my voice breaks as tears fill my eyes. I try to get a deep breath to steady myself, but it just seems to make it worse. I'm sobbing now, embarrassed and angry at myself, and consider hanging up again.

"Stevie." His voice is all sympathy.

"I'm sorry." I finally get myself back together. "I'm sorry for calling."

"Don't be. I know things are all messed up right now, but I'm also not sure if I'm ready to have you out of my life. I'm sorry I didn't come today. I'm just really confused." He takes a loud breath. "I know it's childish, but I wish things could go back to normal, before, you know...."

"...a tumor invaded my brain, brought religious visions, and made me sue my parents?"

He laughs. "Yeah."

"Yeah, me too."

It's only half true. Sure, I wish that things between us were back to normal, but do I really want to wish my visions away?

We talk for a few more minutes before my yawn brings the conversation to an end.

"All right, well I'll let you get some sleep. I bet you need it. Plus, I gotta finish packing," he says.

"Crazy."

"I know."

We hang up, and I wonder, as I drift into a fitful sleep, if I will ever talk to him again.

CHAPTER FIFTY-FOUR

·············•••••◦(ℰ⁄◦❀◦)◦••••·············

I can feel the bags under my eyes the next morning as I'm sitting in the courtroom. I can't remember the last time I had a good night's sleep. Between the stress of the trial and the quasi-fight with Jorge, I stayed awake well into the night. I had to peel myself out of bed this morning, all memories of my bright-eyed five a.m. wake ups a thing of the distant past.

I cradle a cup of weak coffee as Dr. Lewis takes the stand. Mrs. Kwong asks about her qualifications, which even I have to admit, I'm impressed by. It helps wake me up a bit. She should have way more plaques on her walls.

Hearing everything she's done makes me wonder if I could even be half as successful in college. Heck, at this point, I wonder if I'll even finish high school. The way the doctor talked yesterday, if I have to get the surgery, it can put me really behind while my brain recovers and I learn how to do simple tasks again. Shit, and that is if the surgery goes well. I don't even want to think about what would happen if they screw something up. Maybe higher education will be the last thing on my list.

I think back to that guy Bill from the support meeting and how he struggled with tremors after his surgery, how resigned he was that he wasn't going to improve. That could be my new normal. I shiver in my seat.

Dr. Lewis flips through some of her notes when Ms. Kwong continues to ask questions. Once they get past her qualifications and more on to her assessment, it becomes strange, hearing someone talk about me in such a way. Sure, Dr. Oppenheimer was talking about me, but more about my tumor, not me as a person, not really. It was more clinical, for lack of a better word.

But this is about *me*, my mental state, how my upbringing was—it's like someone reading my diary out loud to the world. I expected her to go into some detail, but some of the things she said, I even forgot that we talked about.

"And these visions," the lawyer continues. "In your clinical opinion, she is still of sound mind even though she is seeing things?"

"Well, it's certainly not schizophrenia, or something similar, where the visions can be explained, in a way. Based on my research, I believe these visions could be a result of the tumor's size and location. Stevie has no prior history of such visions."

"But that doesn't mean they haven't just come on though, right? I've heard some mental disorders don't show themselves until the mid-teens," the lawyer interrupts.

"True." Dr. Lewis nods her head, making my stomach clench. "But I do not feel that's the case here. She has no other symptoms people with such mental disorders tend to have. She is hyper-aware the visions are happening, and they're isolated to a particular theme, in this case, religious in nature. The visions aren't telling her to hurt herself or others."

"Isn't refusing treatment a way of hurting herself, though?"

Dr. Lewis pauses over this question. I do as well. "Not in the way my patients with schizophrenia do, and she's not trying to directly hurt herself. She feels that at this time, the treatment is not worth the cost of what she has to give up. Though I do believe she's an intelligent woman, and if the time comes where treatment is the best option for her, she will do it."

"Thank you," Ms. Kwong says and sits.

I wish I was able to represent myself. I want to get up and ask Dr. Lewis a million questions. Prove that I am not crazy, have her say over and over again she thinks I am of sound mind and body, but I can't. I feel helpless all over again.

Mr. Ackerman starts simple, asking her to reiterate some of the things she said previously, clarify a thing or two, but no real information. I want to scream at him, give him a piece of paper with my questions and force him to ask her.

"Now, you said in your report, and I am paraphrasing here, that you think Ms. Albie is of sound mind and body and should be free to make her own medical decisions."

"Yes, that was my finding."

"Can you go into how you're able to make that determination? What factors go into approval or denial of such a finding?"

Dr. Lewis nods. "Of course."

I relax a little.

"I obviously met with Stevie on a number of occasions, as well as her mother and stepfather. That helps me get a picture of what the home dynamic is."

"And what was your determination in that?" Mr. Ackerman asks.

"She comes from a stable and loving home. Her parents' divorce seemed to have a minimal detrimental effect on her. It appears that her mother and father have worked hard to maintain an amicable relationship, which is at a high benefit for any child. She knows right from wrong, and can clearly demonstrate empathy. She has empathy for her parents and friends and the strain this is putting on their relationships."

"Yet she's interested in pursuing this anyway?"

"Yes," she says.

"And you believe this is a decision she's made in a logical and mature manner?"

"I do. I know it must be difficult for us to hear these things about visions and treatment, but Stevie has thought long and hard about this. She has come up with a post-decision plan I feel will be very successful, and if those in her life can continue to support her as they have, I see no reason why she can't explore this part of her life to its fullest before entering the next chapter which will include treatment."

"Thank you, doctor. Is there anything else you would like to add for the court?"

Dr. Lewis takes a deep breath, ratcheting up my heart rate again. "I am not a mother, so I cannot begin to imagine what her parents are going through, but I must say that Stevie is an intelligent young woman. She does not appear to be taking this matter flippantly or without weighing the consequences. While I understand this is no easy decision and have advocated them to work this out on their own, I do hope that if this gets to the point where court intervention is needed, her wishes will be treated like the adult decision it is."

"Thank you, doctor." Mr. Ackerman says. "No further questions."

Mr. Patel gets on the stand next. He talks about the visits I had with the group. Whether he noticed something strange in the last one or not, he doesn't say. His testimony is pretty boring and I zone out.

Luke elbows me gently in the side and I about jump out of my skin. I look around and see everyone standing and hurry to do the same. The judge says we will break for the day, starting in the morning with my parents.

I am relieved the day is over, but already have dread building for what is sure to be a tough day tomorrow. I wish we could skip all of this and get to the end. I need to know what my fate is.

The waiting.

The waiting is almost the worst part of all of it.

Besides the dying. And my parents fighting me. And Jorge's kind of break up. And me not really being sure where I fit into any of it anymore.

Besides all that.

CHAPTER FIFTY-FIVE

········•◦◦(ℓ✦◎)◦◦•········

My mom takes the stand, sits up tall, and laces her fingers together. I inhale a deep breath and hold it for a count of fifteen, long enough that the edges of my vision get black dots, but not long enough to keep the nausea at bay. My head is throbbing, sure, but I'm more worried about what's about to happen than what is actually occurring in me. It's a bit hard to tell from how far away I am, but I swear it looks like the polish on her right pointer finger is half-peeled off.

I can't remember a single time in my life when her nails weren't perfectly painted. It's made us late for dinner, flights, school plays, but no matter what, if she takes off one layer, another one immediately replaces it. Maybe one time she will paint my nails. Maybe we'll lead a life in the future that will have space for that.

My dad went before her, but wasn't on the stand for very long. It was basic stuff, how mature I am, what role I play in our family. Strange really. It wasn't until this moment that I realized how he has such a separate life from us. I know that sounds ridiculous. I know he is remarried and lives pretty far away, but the times we spend face-to-face with one another is usually short and filled with activity. My stepmom is perfectly nice and we get along, but I don't think we've had a single solo conversation.

When he got off the stand I couldn't tell if his testimony did anything to sway the judge one way or the other.

My mom is then introduced to the court, states who she is, and the questions begin.

How she felt during my diagnosis. What the treatment means to her. How she will assist in my recovery if I'm ruled to have my brain sliced. Of course, they didn't ask it quite that way, but that's pretty much what they meant.

"Do you know if your daughter has ever had an alcoholic drink?" Ms. Kwong asks.

I'm just as shocked as my mom. Mr. Ackerman objects, but the judge allows it.

"I don't think so. As far as I know, no," she says.

"But you can't say for certain, under oath, that she's never had a drink?"

"Objection," Mr. Ackerman calls out. The judge agrees and I'm glad she doesn't have to answer it.

"Do you know if your daughter is sexually active?"

If the tumor doesn't kill me, this literally might.

Mr. Ackerman stands. "Your Honor."

"Ms. Kwong, I am not sure how this line of questioning pertains to the discussion at hand."

"Your Honor," she says. "We're trying to establish that Ms. Albie is capable of making adult decisions. I'm trying to determine if there are other adult decisions she is already making to help establish her level of maturity."

The judge allows it. I sink in my chair hoping I can disappear into the hard wood.

To her credit, despite it all, my mom defends me. She doesn't allow Ms. Kwong to use my age against me. A few times when the attorney attempts to belittle me, suggesting that maybe I sneak out after curfew or have taken money from her, my mom comes to my defense. She certainly doesn't have to, hell, it makes her case look stronger not to. Sure, play me up as the fitful youth, unable to make responsible decisions. That's what they want the judge to believe. But she can't do it. She can't let this woman say bad things about me. It helps bring me back up to a fully seated position and makes me smile a little.

I'm also grateful, somehow, shoplifting isn't mentioned.

Now it's Mr. Ackerman's turn.

Instinctively, I want to pull on his sleeve, tell him to forget about it, to not cross examine her. I should stand up for her the way she stood up for me, but I'm a coward, and let him go. Shame warms my cheeks.

My mom shifts nervously and rubs a spot on her left hand, a sign showing how uncomfortable she feels. When she first talked to me about sex and periods, I was surprised she didn't wear a hole straight through her hand by the end of the ten minute conversation.

"Good afternoon, Mrs. Laurel."

"Good afternoon." My mom drops her hand.

"I have a few questions for you." Mr. Ackerman goes up to the podium and shuffles a few papers. "Do you believe in God?"

There is an immediate objection from the opposing counsel, but the judge overrules her when she can't come up with a reason.

No, this is all wrong. He shouldn't be doing this. I try to catch his eye, even turn to Luke, begging with my thoughts to have him put an end to this. I don't need her to say something for me to win. The doctor took care of that, I'm pretty sure. And I don't think anything she says will undo that. Sure, her attorney didn't make me look great, but the judge is an intelligent person. I'm sure he can see through what she was getting at.

"I will ask you again. Do you believe in God?"

"Yes," she says.

Mr. Ackerman nods. "And you take your daughter to church every Sunday?"

"Most Sundays, I would say, unless we have a family event."

"Of course." He walks closer to her. "When you first heard your daughter speak about her visions, what did you think?"

"I was scared," she says, her voice small.

I'm taken aback. Scared?

"Can you explain why?"

She takes a deep breath. "I was worried what it meant. If it meant the tumor was growing bigger, or affecting her brain in some way that would be irreversible."

"I see. Did you ever think these visions could really be sent from God, along with the tumor, to fulfill a prophecy?"

"No."

Her answer is so quick and concise. No hesitation. No thought needed. It hurts me that she would dismiss the idea so readily.

"So, even though you consider yourself a religious woman, a woman who takes her daughter to a house of worship every Sunday she is able, you can't then believe when your daughter says she sees visions of God?"

My mom shakes her head.

"Please speak up for the court," the judge asks.

"No. She's seeing these things because she's sick." She starts to cry and I feel nothing. My anger competing with my sadness until all emotion is wiped from me, canceling it all out.

"Are you a follower of the same religion as your parents?" Mr. Ackerman asks.

She raises her eyebrows for a moment before remembering she needs to speak. "No, they were Methodist. I was raised Methodist, but converted to Catholicism before I got married. The first time," she quickly adds.

"And how did your parents feel about this conversion?" Mr. Ackerman asks.

"They weren't happy about it. Their religion meant a great deal to them. It didn't to me until I got older."

"Yet, you still did not return to the church of your youth? Even after your first marriage ended."

"No," she says.

Mr. Ackerman rubs his chin like this is the most compelling thing he's ever heard. I'm completely lost about the point he's trying to make. Reading my mom's expression, I think she is, too.

"So your parents, while they may not have been very happy with your decision, did they support it? Still talk to you? Still love you?"

I can see the realization hit her the moment it hit me.

"Yes, but that was a different situation."

"But isn't your daughter looking to pursue a different form of Christianity? I'm not sure I see the difference between what you did and what she's doing. Only maybe, your parents were more understanding."

"Objection. Relevance." I almost yell it as well, but the other attorney gets to it first.

"Mr. Ackerman," the judge warns.

"Apologies, Your Honor." He turns back to face my mom. She is flushed with anger and I think a bit of embarrassment. "Are you supportive of your daughter's wish to be part of a different religion than what she was raised in?"

"That's not what we're talking about here. We're talking about her health. I don't care if she never goes to church again. I just want her to live."

Mr. Ackerman shakes his head. "That isn't what I asked you. Are you supportive of her being a part of a different religion?"

She chews her inner lip, thinking of her words carefully. "Not this one."

There. That's it. So, it's not just about my tumor. She doesn't want me being a part of the Church of the Eye. Even if I remove it, I'll lose them. I'm not sure if that's something I can live with.

"Thank you. No more questions."

Mrs. Kwong refrains from asking more questions.

When my mom returns to her seat, my dad tries to pat her arm, but she brushes him away. Angry at what—herself, Mr. Ackerman, me?—I'm not sure.

CHAPTER FIFTY-SIX

‧‧‧‧‧‧‧‧‧‧‧‧◦◦◦◦◦‧‧‧‧‧‧‧‧‧‧‧‧

D
r. Jamis testifies in the morning. She pretty much says the same thing Dr. Oppenheimer did yesterday, but in such a way that it makes my decision seem more reasonable. There's a bit of back and forth between the two lawyers, but it ends on a high note when she reiterates there is no immediate threat with the interest in my case. No doctor, her or Dr. Oppenheimer, would risk not recommending removal the second it really became necessary.

This makes me feel a bit better, too, as the question of when we reach that line seemed a bit up in the air to me.

Now, it' Luke's turn to get on the stand.

Mr. Ackerman introduces Luke to the court and has him spell his name, the normal routine, before asking him a bit of the group's history. This I'm also interested in as the internet has some holes in the story.

"After the death of our leader, my grandfather, I was nominated to take over and guide our followers." So, he was voted in. Funny, I thought he inherited it, like a king-ship or something.

"But all along, have your teachings stayed consistent? Or have some changed?"

"Oh no, we're still following the original doctrine as told to my grandfather. Well, that is, until now."

I sit up a little straighter, unaware that their teachings had changed.

"And what is different now?" Mr. Ackerman asks.

"Well, Stevie, of course."

I am stunned. There has been no discussion with me about any updates to their teachings.

"And what about her has influenced how your organization moves forward?"

"Because we are in The Now."

"Can you please explain what that means?"

He shifts in his chair and laces his fingers together before continuing. "According to our original doctrine, we were living in The Before. This is to say, the time between our transition to the other side. We were preparing ourselves and our souls that whole time, trying to live the life we felt God wished us to, until he deemed us ready to accept the next step."

"The Now?" Mr. Ackerman interrupts.

"Yes. This time would occur once the person came to show us the way through, to bridge the gap between The Before and The After."

"And who do you feel is that person?"

"Stevie." His voice is so sure, so full of conviction. He doesn't look at me, but I can feel his words and presence directed straight at me.

"And how is this person supposed to be able to do that?"

"The doctrine says that a person with the ability to communicate directly with God will seek us out. We must help this individual in any way we can, and because of that, we will be rewarded by walking the path of salvation with them. We believe that Stevie's ability to speak with God, Mary, and Jesus fulfills this prophecy, and she'll teach us what we need to know to reach The After, our next life."

I shift in my seat. I've heard him say this before, but it still seems so outlandish that I'm going to be the one to "save" them. I can't think too much about "the after" of this case and how I'll transition from being a normal teenager to a prophet. Essentially, how the rest of my life will shape up.

Mr. Ackerman shifts some papers before continuing. "And you believe her teaching you is the sole way, even at the possible medical risk she may be undertaking to do such a task?"

The way Mr. Ackerman asks his questions, I almost believe he's on my parents' side. Isn't he a believer? I'm sure he's not just a paid lackey by Luke. I doubt someone would spend the hours he does, hell, even have an office on the same property as the church if he doesn't in some way follow the same teaching.

But here he is, grilling Luke as if *he's* the one on trial, as if he alone is preventing me from gaining medical care.

"We believe God has brought her to show us the way, and He will show her the way to healing. When her work is done and the direct connection is no longer needed, He will either call us all home, or she'll get treatment and be able to live a full life in His light until He reunites with her once more."

"Thank you."

Luke's words swirl around me. I've never heard him lay it out so simply before and I'm desperate to ask him a million questions. I know exactly what he means. My parent's lawyer gets up, and I'm nervous for the onslaught I know he's about to get.

"Good morning, Mr. Gaines." Her tone is light and pleasant.

"Good morning." He sits back slightly in his chair, appearing to relax a bit by her friendly demeanor.

He shouldn't have.

"So, your group, the Church of the Eye, would you consider yourselves a cult?"

"Objection!" Mr. Ackerman stands in a flash.

The judge holds up his hand.

"Your Honor," Mr. Ackerman continues, either not noticing or ignoring the hand gesture. "Mr. Gaines's group is not on trial here. Ms. Kwong's tone and suggestion are highly unprofessional and unappreciated."

"Mr. Ackerman," the judge raises his voice. My hands tremble with anger at the other lawyer's brashness. "While it's true that he's not on trial, nor his group, it is also true that this court needs to know about the people who are seeking to become guardians of this child."

His use of the word "child" stings. It's as if I'm not sitting right here.

"I will allow this line of questioning," he continues, "but be warned Ms. Kwong, make sure you stick to information that is relevant to the case, and not a witch hunt on the schematics of religion."

Chapter Fifty-six

"Of course, Your Honor. I will rephrase my question though. Mr. Gaines—"

"Luke," he interrupts. "You can call me Luke."

She smiles and tilts her head down slightly. "Luke. Is your group recognized by the Christian church or any other religious organizations as an approved sect?"

"We are a sect of Christianity, yes."

"That's not what I asked. Have you been *recognized* as such?"

"No, but only because they have rigid views on what Christianity should be. New branches are always resisted at first, but—"

"Thank you, that answered my question." She cuts him off. "And you would like the court to believe that a sixteen-year-old is the second coming of Jesus?"

Luke shakes his head. "No, that's not what our teachings say. We believe she will show us the path to righteousness, to prepare us for The After."

"Right. The After." She talks as if Luke is about seven years old. I understand it's just an act, something she plays up to make her questioning sound more compelling and his answers seem less so, but it's still infuriating.

"And after she has shown you the way, so to speak, what then?" Ms. Kwong asks.

Okay, this one I'm interested in hearing, despite myself.

"Then?"

"She will show you 'the path,' which, my apologies if I don't fully understand, is this a physical path or a metaphorical one?"

"We believe it will be a mental state that may also bring us to a physical location," Luke says.

"All right, so once this has been achieved, then will God take your group away to heaven? Will Stevie get to go with you? Or will you not need her anymore? What happens to her once she is no longer of any use to you?"

"It doesn't work like that."

"So, how does it work?" she asks. I'd kinda like to know, too.

"She will educate us on the way, and when her role in that is complete—which I don't believe will happen any time soon—if it's not time to depart to The After yet, we'll live in harmony with the peace she has brought until the end of our days on Earth."

"And how will you know?"

Luke sits up straighter. "I will just know," he says.

"And does God bring you to The After, or do you?"

"I don't like your implication," he says.

"Ms. Kwong…" the judge says, his voice trailing.

"There have been cults in the past—"

"We are not a cult!" Luke cuts her off.

She raises her hand. "There have been groups in the past who felt God has called them home, and those members have to die to make good on that."

"Objection," Mr. Ackerman says.

"Please ask a question, Ms. Kwong," the judge says.

"We need to make sure that Stevie will be safe with you." She turns and opens her arms to the room implying she's speaking for everyone. "I would like to know if Stevie goes with you, puts you on 'the path,' and delivers you to 'the after,' will she then be required to end her life?"

My breath gets catches between my throat and my lungs, and my body goes rigidly still. Luke's face turns red with anger.

"You people always want to do that," he says.

"Sir, I am just asking you a question."

"*You* are allowed to have your religious doctrines. They get to be the standard and no one can challenge them, but to think anything differently…"

"I am not arguing religion here, Mr. Gaines," she says, not calling him Luke anymore. "I'm trying to establish what exactly your teachings are and see if Stevie will be hurt because of them."

"I would never hurt her or any of our members," Luke says, his chest visibly rising and falling. "God is the only one who can call us home, and the only one who can decide if and when we're supposed to cross over to what lies beyond this life."

Ms. Kwong nods and paces in front of the witness stand, forcing Luke to move his head back and forth to follow her.

"And what happens if along this journey your group's need for her guidance clashes with her need for treatment?"

222

"We believe God will show us the way in all things. If treatment becomes necessary, we'll trust in Him to either provide a method, or remove what ails her."

"You think you can just wait for a cure and trust God will provide it?" she asks incredulously.

"No, I'm not a believer in faith healing." Remarkably, he has regathered his composure. I would have jumped up at least a half dozen times and lost it on this lady by now. Hell, I'm tempted to do it for him.

"So how will He provide then?"

"That's faith, Ms. Kwong. We must trust He will give the answers, in whatever form they are."

"Even if that form includes removing the tumor that may be the direct communicator to God?"

"Yes," he answers without hesitation. "If that line of connection is removed, for whatever reason, we trust that another one will open in its place. We do not believe He would place Stevie's life in jeopardy."

"And you think that, when the time comes, if she's sick and unable to make her own medical decisions, even if it may be at the detriment to your mission, you'll agree to medical intervention if she's unable to?"

This question does create a pause. One that makes my breath catch again. He leans forward and locks eyes with her.

"I will do any and all things to protect her. So, yes."

I let out a long breath, but it doesn't quite make me feel better. With the group's mission fully laid out, I'm left feeling like I'm on a speeding train and can't get off.

Sure, he *says* he will, but after all that stuff about me being the one person that can truly save them, the only one who can tell them exactly what needs to be done, can I really believe he'd let all that go just to save me?

CHAPTER FIFTY-SEVEN

··············(❦❦❦)··············

The week weighs on my shoulders, pushing me a few inches further into the ground than gravity alone. I haven't had any visions since the trial's started, and while I've been better about taking my meds since I've been home, I wonder if stress and lack of sleep are a bigger contributing factor. My bones creek, like they will snap under the stress. My head is *killing* me. I quietly took an extra ibuprofen during our earlier break, but it has barely taken the edge off.

I hope no one notices when I rub my temples with the pads of my fingers as we descend from the tenth floor. Luke looks at me. Of course he notices. He always notices everything.

He glances at Mr. Ackerman then back at me, one eyebrow raised. I shake my head and force a smile, dropping my hand. The removal of the pressure causes the throbbing in my head to intensify and I have to shut my eyes against it.

"Stevie," I hear Luke's voice say through the darkness.

"Mmmm, fine. Just a long day." I force my eyes open. The harsh light isn't doing me any favors, but I fight against reacting.

Mr. Ackerman turns as the metal doors slide open. I focus on the round circle pattern pressed into the metal of the elevator to steady my nausea.

"It will be over soon," Mr. Ackerman says.

A sentence that can apply to a million things.

In our normal routine, my parents will be standing near a tree speaking with their lawyer. Mr. Ackerman will stop us away from earshot, go over final instructions, and walk me to them, like I'm a baton they're passing around.

224

Today I feel as beat up as getting hit by one.

He touches my arm to stop me, his eyebrows almost crowding together in concern.

"Stevie, is everything all right? Are you feeling okay? Do you want me to call Dr. Jamis to take a look at you?"

I shake my head, huge mistake. A sound escapes my lips before I'm able to stop it. I try to cover it in a throat clearing, but I don't think I'm fooling either of them.

"Stevie," Luke looks straight into me. Not at me, not through me, no, *into* me. Like he can see my soul and speaks directly to it.

"If you're having second thoughts," Mr. Ackerman says.

I open my mouth, but Mr. Ackerman holds up his hand, stopping me.

"You can be having second thoughts," he says, "but you need to communicate with us. There are," Mr. Ackerman pauses, searching for the right words, "resources being used in this matter that can be used elsewhere if you don't want to proceed."

"I want to proceed. Unless, you don't want me to?" I ask, turning to Luke.

His smile could light the solar system. Forget the sun, I want to bask in him.

"Stevie, we believe in you, *I* believe in you. I want nothing more than for you to lead us, but I also know firsthand what the burden of leadership can be. It's asking a lot," he says.

Anything, I realize. I'll do anything for him.

"We don't want you to do anything you don't want to do," Mr. Ackerman says as if reading my mind.

"What about the prophecy?" I ask.

From his expression, Mr. Ackerman looks keenly interested in Luke's answer as well. I still can't tell what the lawyer thinks about all this. At times, he seems like a true believer—I doubt he would be spending all this time, energy, and probably money on me if he wasn't—but I've also never heard him speak one way or the other about the matter. Maybe he's a "quiet believer," as my mother calls them.

"I believe God has sent you to help us, and I'm usually good at seeing the signs God lays out for me." Luke says this in a way that is more factual than boastful. "But I also believe in free will. And I think God knows and trusts us to have it. If you decide you don't want to pursue this anymore, He will find a way for us."

My breath deflates me as his words put themselves together in my throbbing head. The surprise of his implication—that I may not be as important, critical as once thought—does something unexpected to me. It's like the shock has thrown my headache away and replaced it with a deep hurt.

He must see this.

"You misunderstand, Stevie." He puts his hand back on my shoulder, leaving it there this time. The warmth of it feels wonderful. "I don't want God to find another way, unless you do."

"No, I don't."

"Well, I'm glad we got that settled," Mr. Ackerman says and the proceeding of the passing-of-the-Stevie commences.

CHAPTER FIFTY-EIGHT

···········•••••◉(ℰ✒◉)◉••••···········

When we get home, I go up to my room and take stock of my surroundings. If the verdict goes my way, I'm not clear on what the next steps will be. While the plan is for me to go live at the compound, no one has really set up a time frame for that. Should I be packing a bag, just in case? My whole room, like Jorge had to?

I haven't spoken to Jorge since the awkward phone fight that turned into him telling me he was moving soon. We didn't end on bad terms exactly, but I was still hurt about his no-show at court. He hasn't even texted me to see how the trial is going. Even if he hasn't technically broken up with me, how can I let him back into my life after such a shunning?

It pains me to think I can't.

Stacey has texted me a few times. I thanked her for showing up to court, saying it really meant a lot. She's slow to respond to my messages. I can tell she has no idea what to say or how to act, but that's okay, I guess I don't either.

A ping sounds on my phone and I pick it up, a part of me hoping it might be Jorge, but it turns out to just be an email. I open it mindlessly, needing some distraction, and see it's an invite to support programs at the Episcopal church. I wonder how the heck they got my email address. I don't remember signing up to be on any lists, but who even knows these days. My phone's probably been hearing my struggles and sought this out on its own.

I'm a bit burnt out on the whole "sharing my feelings" thing the meetings do, but read through the different offerings to further procrastinate having to deal with my current predicament. I'm surprised to find there's a group meeting tonight. It isn't about any certain form of cancer or death, but looks to be a group that meets to talk about faith. For some reason, the hairs on my arms stand up. I reread the listing, and I'm not sure what triggered this response, but there's something about it being focused on faith that seems like it's calling directly to me.

Maybe the email wasn't a coincidence.

I go downstairs and find my mom and Reg talking over coffee in the kitchen.

"Hey, mom?" I start.

She doesn't answer me at first, and I have to try again. She must have thought she was imagining things since we haven't really spoken since the trial started. The morning car rides to court have been super fun and our dinners at home are silent. I clean my plate and go up to my room till morning where we repeat the charade over again.

"Huh? What sweetie?" she asks.

"Um." I hold up my phone, as if that's all the explanation I need. "I got an email about a support meeting tonight. It starts at six thirty. Could you take me?"

My mom's face looks stricken. "I, well I…" she stutters.

"Absolutely," my stepdad answers without hesitation.

My mom walks up to him and squeezes his arm before heading upstairs. Neither says anything, and I wonder if there's just a point in a relationship where you know what the other person is thinking. It's sorta strange.

When we leave around six, my mom hugs both of us tightly. It's such an odd gesture, like we're about to head out for a long trip and not just a few hours. I haven't seen her since our quick conversation earlier this afternoon, and I get the feeling she's about to ask if she can come, but then after another wordless conversation with my stepdad, she lets us leave.

"She has dinner reservations with Cammie," my stepdad says when we pull out onto our road.

"Oh," I say. "Why didn't she just say so?"

"She doesn't want you to think she's picking something over you." He shrugs. "She hasn't seen Cammie in a long time. I told her she needed to go," he says.

I nod. It's again a reminder that I'm not the only one going through this even though I'm technically the only one with a tumor.

"You know, I can go in with you," Reg says.

I'm about to say no when there is a hint of desperation in his eyes. The last few weeks have been hard for him, too. While we have no blood that ties us, I understand how connected we are anyway. Maybe it's because my parents still have such a great relationship, and I'm so in touch with my dad, that I've never really felt the need to rely on Reg like maybe some other divorce kids do. It's probably left him feeling a bit out of place. I always thought it was great. He could be there for my mom and wouldn't have to worry about parenting me since I already have that covered, but I never stopped to think how that may be pushing him out, how that may make him feel.

"Yeah, sure, thanks," I say. What could it hurt?

We sit in traffic for several more minutes, and I can't help but check my watch every few seconds. The meeting is dangerously close to starting and I hate being late. The thought of opening a creaking door in the middle of someone talking and everyone turning to stare at me.

Just picturing it makes a shiver run through me.

"You know," I say, checking the map on my phone, "it's right up here." I gesture to an open parking spot to our right along the street. "We could just walk?"

"Yeah, sure," he says and pulls the car into the spot. "Wonder what's going on."

As if on cue, the sound of sirens and the flash of lights seem to explode all around us. We get out of the car and start walking up the sidewalk, right in the direction of all the commotion.

People sitting in their cars crane their necks to see what's going on. One woman even gets out to get a better look.

A small crowd is gathered on the sidewalk in front of where we're supposed to be going. The façade of the church glows intermittently red and blue as the emergency lights flash, now silent except for their clicking as they rotate. My stepdad moves slightly in front of me like he is trying to protect me from something.

I see that he is.

Broken glass and ripped pieces of plastic from two cars are scattered on the street. I push around my stepdad, unable to look away as police, fire rescue, and EMTs move around the scene. I am shocked to see Lewis, the EMT from when I first needed that ambulance ride that started me down this path.

For some stupid reason I move forward, hoping to catch his eye, but my stepdad pulls me away.

"Stevie, let them do their work," he warns. "Maybe we should go?"

I shake my head. Frantically I look around, begging Mary or Jesus or God to show themselves. People need help now.

The sound of ripping metal pulls my attention back to the scene. The fire department has a giant mechanical lever attached to the smaller of the two cars and is using it like a can opener to rip the roof off.

The scene comes into greater clarity for me. The smaller car is half-stuffed under a larger and taller pickup truck. The two crushed into what looks like a third vehicle, all three the same black color, making them blend together. The image of wildebeests crossing crocodile-infested waters enters my mind. Moving together to confuse, hoping in the pack they will all make it out alive.

But they never do.

A man is moved to the sidewalk near us and Lewis kneels over him. It's hard to tell how hurt the man is in the fading light, but he appears to be talking. I remember Lewis asking me questions, my mind racing with confusion as to what was going on. I bet this man is going through the same thing.

For the briefest of moments, Lewis looks up and locks eyes with me. I can feel his gaze in the recesses of my soul.

He looks away without a hint of recognition.

"Maybe we should go," I echo my stepdad's words.

We take a step back and bump into someone, a face I recognize from the last support meeting. As I look around the sidewalk, I realize there are a couple more people I saw that time as well.

Everyone must have congregated here as they were arriving. Now we're unable to walk away from the tragedy unfolding even if there's nothing we can do to help.

The pastor's off to the side, his lips moving in what I guess is a prayer for the victims.

Where are you? I demand to the void where Mary should be.

There are other people I don't recognize, quietly crying and holding one another. A young man, probably early twenties, with no legs sits in a wheelchair. A woman around the same age clutches his hand, but he seems not to notice, the scowl on his face creating deep lines on his forehead as he stares intently at the car crash.

Panic fills me, tightening my chest until I have to fight against the painful breaths. Ice stabs my lungs with each pull of air. My head starts to pound.

Looking around, my problems seem silly and insignificant. It was a mistake to come here and bring Reg. I'm not dying, not really. I'm not being ripped out of a car. I haven't had tragedy hit me. Okay, so I have a brain tumor and will probably never speak to my boyfriend again, who six months ago I was wondering if I'd marry. But I haven't lost anything, not really. My life has taken a one-eighty turn, but not in any terrible way. Nothing has really *happened* to me.

Shit, what's happening to me *I'm* creating. This is all *my* doing. I could have had this tumor out weeks ago, been well on my way to the miraculous recovery everyone was sure I was going to have. I'd be out with Jorge right now, getting a bite to eat, maybe speaking a bit slow, but he'd be patient.

And then I remember, no—he'd be gone.

He'd be on the other end of the country, so far away he might as well be on the moon. My tumor had nothing to do with that. His parents would have sold their house and demanded he move with them. He'd still be gone.

But the rest of it, the rest of it is all me.

Why is this happening if I can't help anyone, not really?

Mary, Mary, Mary! I yell over and over in my mind. What's this connection worth if she doesn't come when I need her? When someone else needs her?

There's a distant scream and it takes me a moment to realize it's not my yelling but coming from the accident. It sounds like the yelping and cries I've heard from injured animals. The primal need to put pain into noise. Automatically I feel tears burn the backs of my eyes.

What is the point if you aren't going to help them?

I came here hoping to get some answers, hoping to hear other people's versions of what faith means to them to give some validity to my own. And yet, all I see is how fragile life is. How parts or all of a person can be taken away so quickly.

The woman cries out again, and it's all too much. There's just too much suffering here and I need to get away.

I turn to my stepdad to apologize when I see he has tears running down his face. I about lose my breath at the shock of it. I've never seen him cry before, not in the years I've known him, not even over the death of his father, but here, standing on this sidewalk, the droplets flow as quickly as he can remove them. I pretend not to notice. Something tells me he wishes to be alone in this, and if there's anything I can understand, it's that.

The pain in my head builds and I'm about to sink to the ground under the weight of it all when I notice Mary sitting on the church steps. I almost cry out in relief and fight the urge to run to her and fling myself into her arms.

I'll be strapped to one of the gurneys and carted away for sure if I do that.

The sirens remain, but the men and women racing around the scene shout and holler at one another. The roof of the car is now open and a group ladened with bags and boards struggles to remove the driver.

I try not to think about the fact that the woman has gone silent.

"Let us pray," the pastor calls.

The group on the sidewalk, some maybe not even here for the meeting, press in closer to him. Mary gazes at the pastor as well and I can't help but wonder if she realizes I'm even here.

The typical warmth that accompanies my visions hasn't reached me. The woman they pull out of the car is bathed in red I hope is just the ambulance lights. Maybe I don't feel her presence because she's not here for me. My selfishness is thrown into stark relief again.

To think I'd be the only one she'd visit. To think her presence in the world is for my sole benefit and those I could possibly help.

Jorge's words about my selfishness play over in my head.

When the prayer is over and people lift their gazes, Mary wipes her eyes then catches me looking at her. She smiles broadly, like she's surprised to see me here.

I'm both sad and relieved I haven't been singled out, but a small voice in the back of my mind says "maybe you aren't that special after all. You called for her, and she did not come for you…"

I scan the street, but don't see anyone else looking in her direction. The ambulance door shuts with Lewis' full focus on the injured man, just like he was with me.

My stepdad grabs my hand and I jump slightly at the touch but don't pull away. I glance up at him, but he's staring at the ambulances pulling away. He squeezes and I squeeze back before he releases my hand.

The cars now lie vacant in the street, open and gaping, crying their own miseries to the heavens.

The pastor announces he will be canceling the meeting for tonight, but gestures to the small gated garden to the side of the church. "There is coffee and juice for anyone who wishes to have some."

My stepdad looks at me and I nod. The thought of having burning liquid pouring down my throat, to have any sensation that isn't the current pounding in my head and ache in my heart feels like a desperate need.

I scan the street for Mary, but she is gone. I wonder when she left. Maybe when the ambulances pulled away? The notion she was here for the victims seems even more solidified.

As I look around, I lock eyes with the pastor who makes his way over to me.

"Stevie, right?" he asks and I nod. "I recognize you from the news. I hope it's all right I'm approaching you like this. I certainly don't want to make you feel uncomfortable, especially if you need time to process what you saw tonight. This terrible tragedy," he says as he gestures to the road.

I think about it for a moment before answering him. "No, it's fine. I hope everyone will be all right."

"All we can do is pray, and we have done that."

It seems a little too simplistic for me, but I nod. We stand in silence looking out to the road. Officers take pictures of the crash and another helps divert traffic so the waiting cars can get through. I'm about to make some excuse to walk away when he speaks.

"You know, if there is anything on your mind..." He opens his arms and for a moment I'm worried he's going to surround me with them, but realize it's just a gesture when he lowers them again. "I hear us pastors are pretty good listeners."

It's a lame joke, but I give him a consolation laugh and then shrug.

"I've been following your story. I know it can't be easy, but convictions never are," he says.

"Is that what you think this is, a conviction?" I've never heard someone give it that name before.

"Isn't all faith? You believe something and fight for that belief."

"What if you're fighting for the wrong thing?" I ask, my voice a mere whisper.

He lifts one side of his lips up. "Are you worried you're getting the message wrong?"

"I don't know. Maybe? Or that I'm making the message up."

That gets a real laugh out of him. "Can you imagine Paul the first time God spoke with him? He must have thought he was going insane. Or Adam. Or Moses. How about Mary?"

I stiffen at her name. "What about Mary?" Had he seen her, sitting feet away?

"Imagine, you're a young woman and have been told you're carrying the son of God. Do you think you'd believe instantly?"

I shake my head.

"Of course not! I doubt she did, either. I know I wouldn't."

"That's a relief."

"Stevie, no one has all the answers, but that doesn't mean we don't stop searching, stop learning, or stop to listen. Do you think the people involved in this crash tonight, their families, aren't questioning the point? Possibly questioning God?"

"But my tumor..." my voice trails.

"Exists. You can see it on a scan. It's a real thing."

"But the visions?" Everything feels like a jumble. My emotions, my words, his words. I want to leave. I want to bury my head under my blanket and clutch Al and pretend I have some other life. Pretend this is happening to someone else.

"What makes you think they can't be just as real?"

"Because it's confusing." I admit, taking deep breaths to steady the panic building in me.

He nods. "I bet it is. You're dealing with two very real things. A threat against your life, but also a threat against your belief these visions are real and provided by God."

"Do you think they are?" I ask, needing further validity from him, needing an answer.

"Oh, I can't *tell* you what to believe. But I can say, I have seen miracles in many forms. There's no reason for me to believe this can't be one of them."

"But if I get the tumor removed, I'm afraid they will leave along with it."

I see my stepdad walking toward us with two cups in his hands, and the need to have the pastor put my mind at ease turns desperate.

"Do you believe God will find a way?" the pastor asks. His voice is firm and serious.

"I guess."

"Then you shouldn't be relying on a tumor or risk your life over it. That's what faith *is*. You need to believe if He wants to speak to you, He will."

Chapter Fifty-Nine

·············•••◦(ℰ✐☉)◦•••·············

After the fifth fast food place we pass, my stepdad asks if I'm
hungry. I say no.

"Hard to think about eating, huh?"

I nod.

"I saw you speaking with the pastor. Did you find anything he
said helpful?" There is hope on the edges of his voice that burrows
straight into the depths of my heart.

"I think so."

When we get home, my mom is putting away dishes and
straightening up. I go to her and kiss her cheek and let her hand
rest just a beat longer on my back before heading to bed.

I lay in my room with the lights off and stare into the darkness, the pastor's words weaving through my head. They mix with
Jorge's voice. Then Dr. Oppenheimer's. Mr. Ackerman's. Luke's.
My parents. The voices rise and fall, compete with each other for
my attention.

Then God's voice breaks through, as clear and sharp as it was
that day in the hospital, making the words form a single echo.

Faith. Faith. *Faith*.

I am pulled into a swirling sleep filled with light and voices,
chanting me on through my dreams.

·············•••◦(ℰ✐☉)◦•••·············

My head is clear when I awaken. I push my fingers along my hair
line and am met with no resistance of pain.

I am cured.

I know it's impossible, but it seems so real. I feel different, like there's no way that I'm sick anymore. Should I suggest another scan? To see if it's for real, if the voices carried away the damaged cells in the night, leaving behind fresh, clean ones? A brain free of disease?

I look at my watch. There's no time. I'm needed at the courthouse. This is it. I will take the stand, speak what truth is left in me, and lay myself upon the mercy of the judge. I say a prayer of thanks as I get ready and ask for strength. When it comes down to it, that's really all I need right now.

It feels strange leaving my room, wondering if I'll return to it as a resident or a packer. I have a sliver of sympathy for Jorge, but remind myself at least he knew when he left his room, he'd never be coming back.

I'm not sure which way is worse—having hope, or realizing there's no point in wishing.

Mr. Ackerman picks me up today and I'm surprised to see that Luke is not with him. I'm told he is arriving separate along with some of the residents, Abby included. The excitement at seeing her helps ebb some of my nerves.

That is, until we get to the tenth floor.

My parents and stepparents look terrible. I know people say after like one bad night of sleep, "Oh, you look awful!" But this vision before me doesn't hold a candle to that. It's like their insides have been scooped out and they've been forced to go through the day without them. They look ready to collapse at the smallest touch. Or word. Or ruling, I suppose.

I have to turn away, sure I'll ruin my mascara if I look at them for one more second. I think back to my stepfather last night and the silent tears he shed, how I kept his secret. And he, in turn, kept mine. Both of us allowing the other to suffer without comment, even though we both knew, no words needed, what it was about.

This.

This day.

Mr. Ackerman said unlike a normal jury trial, the judge will probably make a ruling after I speak. He may take a small break, but has most likely been going over his notes each night. A long deliberation won't be necessary. In a few more hours, he'll know, and so will we.

I wonder if words can kill a person, the pen mightier than the sword and all that. Taking one look at the four people standing at the end of the hall, if it hasn't happened before, it's sure to now.

The pit in my stomach reaches such a level, I'm certain it will swallow all my internal organs like a black hole.

Mr. Ackerman holds the door open for me and we enter the courtroom, my parents close behind. The panicked feeling rises in me, competing with the nausea from my nervous stomach for the top emotion. I'm not sure now what makes me feel like throwing up more—the pain in my gut or in my heart. Maybe it's both. It feels as if I'm already destroyed.

I see Abby and embrace her. Luke smiles at me and squeezes my arm. Sue, Jackie, and a half dozen other Church members are with him, all wearing the matching pants and tops I associate with outreach.

"It's easier for people to find us," Abby had told me.

I'm glad they did.

They sit together, leaving me alone at the table with Mr. Ackerman.

I wish I'd texted Stacey last night and asked her and Malik to come. For some reason, I have an extra desire to be surrounded by those I love today.

The judge enters and after some announcements, we begin. I swallow the weight in the back of my throat as hard as I can, but it still hovers too close to the edge. I wonder if I should bring a trash can up to the stand with me. I bet that would draw further attention to the fact I feel like I'm going to puke. No, best to just get up there and get it over with.

I raise my right hand and swear to the woman sitting to the left of the judge that I will tell the truth. There's no Bible, but I don't need it. I know what this means, and lying really isn't going to help anyone.

Mr. Ackerman stands up at the podium and addresses me. "Good morning, can you please state your name and spell your last name for the court."

"Stevie Albie, A-l-b-i-e." I keep my voice slow and measured, just like he taught me, telling myself over and over not to rush. The court reporter needs to record everything and the clearer I am, the easier their job will be.

"Thank you, Ms. Albie. We've heard testimony the last several days from various doctors, community church leaders, as well as your parents. You've been present for all this testimony, correct?"

"Yes." It's a strange question to ask. Of course I have been. He's sat next to me the whole time. The judge has acknowledged me each day.

"So you've been able to hear what all these people have had to say about you and your condition?"

"Um, yeah. Yes." I catch myself, adding the last part in a clear voice.

"Do you have anything to add in your defense? Anything about being awarded medical emancipation?"

Okay, I know we went over my testimony, but the words feel sluggish in my brain. I wasn't really sure how to answer this one, the words stuck in the back of my mind.

"Defense?" I ask, mainly to buy myself some time.

"Okay, maybe that was too broad a question." Uh, you think? He shuffles through some papers before continuing.

"Your doctor in Atlanta, Dr. Oppenheimer, went over a bit about your initial diagnosis. When he first discussed that with you, did you feel like you fully understood what he was saying? The gravity of your condition?"

I nod, then quickly add when I see the look on Mr. Ackerman's face, "Yes. I didn't fully know what an oligodendrogliomas was, and I had to do a bit of research when I got home, but when he first said it, it sounded like it was really bad."

"But you didn't feel like it was that bad when you looked into it more?"

"I knew it was a brain tumor, and it would eventually create enough trouble for me that removal would be necessary, but from what I read, it seemed like they were slow-growing enough that the immediate threat wasn't, um, as intense as Dr. Oppenheimer made it seem," I say.

"What did you decide to do?" He takes a step closer to me with a sad smile on his face.

"It was dumb, I know, but I panicked." I take a deep breath. I know it's going to have to be addressed, so might as well be now. "Along with the tumor, I've been having these religious experiences. I worried that removing the tumor would remove the visions, so I reached out to someone from the Church of the Eye, and they sent people to get me from my hotel."

"And this was done with one hundred percent approval from you?"

"Yes, fully. They'd reached out to me before, once they saw my news story, but something just drew me to them. Like I knew they could help."

"And this was before you met Luke or any of the other members officially?" he asks.

I nod. "Yes."

"Can you tell us what your visions are and in what capacity they occur?"

I take a deep breath and look over at my parents. They are holding hands. This shocks me a little. While they are possibly the poster children for co-parenting, they certainly aren't intimate at all with each other. Even from where I sit, I can tell their knuckles are white from clasping on to each other so tightly. It picks at my resolve.

"I'm not sure *why* they occur," I say. "I don't usually see it coming, they kinda creep up on me."

"Okay, and when they 'creep up on you,'" he says with air quotes around my words, "what do you see? Can you describe the experience a bit for us?"

"It's warm. And I see Mary usually, but sometimes Jesus. And one time I saw God." I look from Mr. Ackerman to my parents to the judge. I'm doing a terrible job at explaining this, and I realize how crazy I sound. Maybe the bad experience from saying this to Jorge has my mind all jumbled. Plus, my God, my head is suddenly killing me. I rub my fingers along my hairline, but the pressure is making it worse this time.

Despair and panic rise again. *I thought I was cured.*

"Let's back up a little," Mr. Ackerman says, also realizing how much I'm sucking at this. "Tell us about how the first experience you had was."

I appreciate that he calls them "experiences" and not visions. Definitely takes some of the crazy out. I take a deep breath to steady myself. "I was at home, in my room, and thought I was dreaming when this peacefulness washed over me. A woman was standing there and I knew without question that she was Mary, mother of Jesus."

"You're sure someone hadn't broken into your house? That it wasn't a *real* woman standing there?"

Actually, the thought had never crossed my mind until this moment. Even when it happened, I had no fear. This wasn't a scary intruder. This was someone come to help me. "No, not for a second. It's weird, I recognized her."

"From the pictures at your church?" Mr. Ackerman asks.

"You know how sometimes in a dream you're some place and even though it doesn't look like the place, you know it?" Silence meets me. I rush to clarify. "Sometimes I will have a dream that I forget my class schedule for school, and I am running all around the building worried that I'll be late because I don't know where to go, and even though it doesn't look anything like my real school, something in me knows it *is* my school. Like that."

"And you have had somewhat similar visits in the months since then?"

"Yes, like I said, it isn't always Mary, but I have had experiences since that one. But they're all similar in the sense that I know who's visiting me, even if they don't look like I'd necessarily expect them to."

"And what do you think is causing these experiences?" he asks.

"The tumor, maybe. Even I have to admit the coincidence of when they started happening. But maybe it's just the tumor that let me see what was already there. Or maybe they would have happened anyway and the tumor was a happy accident." Something dawns on me in this moment. "Maybe..." My voice trails as I try to work my thought out. "...maybe the tumor was there, and they were sent to me so it would be found. I'd been having headaches for a while, but didn't really think much of them. Maybe they came to save me."

"But you still don't want to have it removed?"

"The doctors said it isn't growing very fast and my immediate threat is low. But for whatever reason, the experiences keep happening, and I'm afraid that removing the tumor will take them away."

"But why is it so important to keep these visions?" he asks.

I take a deep breath. I've been thinking this question over for days on how to properly answer it. To put all my feelings and emotions in just a few sentences.

I look over at Abby and she smiles at me. When I glance at my parents it's like they've shrank three sizes since I started talking.

I think back to Mr. Ackerman's question about the cause of the visions and the new-found possibility that Mary has come to help me. Just me. Maybe this wasn't part of some big scheme. Maybe I wasn't meant to save an entire community, religion, the worlds, or whatever. Could this all have just been for me?

"You know what you need to do." Her words echo in my head.

Is helping myself what I need to do?

I look up and she is standing there, smiling serenely, and nodding.

Can you hear my thoughts?

She nods again.

The warmth spreads through me as the pain in my head hits a crest and falls, only to build up again. The nausea comes in similar waves and I'm relieved to see there's a small trash can by my feet. I scooch it toward me, hoping no one will notice.

I'm trying to do the right thing, but I'm so confused.

She is in front of me now, between my seat and Mr. Ackerman. He is still talking, unable to see her. She doesn't speak, but reaches out her hand. I can see my parents over her head. Tears are streaming down my mother's cheeks as my dad rubs her back with his other hand. Behind them, my stepparents are also holding hands. It is this, the outpouring of comfort they are giving each other that cracks the rest of my resolve.

I can't do this. How am I going to leave here, go live in another house, in another city, away from them? How am I going to figure out how to split holidays now three ways? Do I really want to not see them? Is this feeling, while wonderful in its brief moments, really worth the trouble and pain that surrounds me as soon as it leaves?

For even as Mary's warmth and love helps ease the pain in my head, it always lingers under the surface, an alligator waiting for me to let my guard down so it can snatch me up and pull me under.

I can't escape it forever. Nor can she keep the predators at bay.

Faith, I repeat to myself.

Faith, she echoes in my head.

I stand, shaking on my feet. "I'm sorry," I say to all of them.

"Can I get you some water? Are you feeling okay?" Mr. Ackerman says as he approaches me.

Mary moves out of his way, and I turn and repeat my apology to her.

"There is nothing to be sorry about," she says. Her voice is sweet and honest. I blink my eyes hard against the pain that's building as she slips away from me.

I open my eyes wide and see her walking backward. I want to tell her to wait, to scream, to tell her it was a mistake. But is it?

"Ms. Albie?" Mr. Ackerman is at my side now, the bailiff behind him. My parents hover above their seats, unsure what they're supposed to do. I see Luke stand. The judge is staring at me as well, and the heat of everyone's eyes remain focused on me.

I look at the judge. "I'm so sorry. I'm sorry I wasted everyone's time and energy." My words begin to slur as the wave of pain rises again. It constricts my breathing, and I attempt to start over again. A thin voice in the back of my head reminds me to speak slowly and clearly. I move to take a step off the stand when my legs buckle under me. The last thing I remember before my head slams on the wooden railing is my mother's look of pure fear before everything goes to black.

CHAPTER SIXTY

••••••••••◉(❦⁄✪)◉••••••••••

My head aches, but in a new way, like it's deep inside, through to my core. It's dark, and my eyes struggle to adjust. I can just make out a figure sitting in a chair next to my bed. No, not my bed. A bed. The sheets are different, white, crisp, but scratchy. Not like my sheets.

I raise my hand to my head and am met with something soft, but when I press against it, it hurts. I can't help but mess with it. Gauze, I think, some type of cotton batting or covering, but covering what?

Gingerly, as if I may be made of spun sugar, my finger explores the wrapping on my head. Something bumpy, right where the pain is concentrated, is right under my fingertips. I want to pick at it, but the pain at any increased pressure prevents me from investigating more.

I sit up and the figure from the chair stirs. I hear my mother's voice before I can see it's actually her.

"Oh, baby." She presses a button and tells no one in particular that I'm awake.

Who cares if I'm awake?

"Baby, I'm so sorry."

I try to ask her what for, but it comes out as a gurgle. For some reason my mouth won't say what my brain wants it to. I ball my fists in frustration, but loosen them when her hands touch mine.

"Shh, don't try to talk. The doctors are coming. They'll explain, but they said it may take a little while for you to get your voice back. You had a tube at first and..." her voice trails for a moment. "...and it may take a bit for you to talk like you used to."

244

Okay, now I really have no idea what she's going on about. The words are perfectly fine in my head. I understand everything she's saying, so what is she actually talking about? I open my mouth to ask her, but the words don't form properly. I want to scream in frustration, but I'm unable to do that as well.

"Oh baby, I'm so sorry, but we had to. They said we had to take it out."

The doors open, flooding my eyes with light before the darkness pulls me back under again.

••••••••••(❦)••••••••••

Mary stands in all her warmth and glory above me. She takes my hand and speaks to me softly.

"They couldn't understand me," I tell her. I'm relieved my voice is working again and want to ask her what was wrong with it before.

"Do you understand yourself?" she asks.

"Yes."

"Then that's what matters, that's what you have to hold on to. Don't let anyone tell you what your truth is. You have to find it for yourself and when you do, protect it."

"Aren't you my truth?" I ask her.

Her smile is everything. Bright, true, good. "If you would like me to be, then yes."

I look around, but none of the objects surrounding me are clear. Where am I? Still in the hospital? Or are we back in the court room? I try to reach out my hand to ground myself, but no matter how much my brain tells my arm to move, it doesn't.

I wonder how long I've been here with her and how much longer I'll be able to stay. I want to ask her to go with me, wherever that may be, but a part of me knows she can't. Knows with the same understanding that she always provides. I can't see it, and really, I have no idea where it comes from, but I know that it comes from her and I can trust it. That I *should* trust it.

I want to ask her a million more questions, but I hear my name being called behind me, and I turn, I must follow it. I must answer.

················•••◖◉╱◉◗•••················

The room is filled with light the next time I open my eyes. For a moment, it disorients me, and I expect to see Mary standing there again. In her place, my mother is at the window, my stepdad now the one seated in the chair. When my eyes lock on his, he calls her over and they both approach my bed.

Her soft weight shifts mine to the left slightly and I want to move over, to let her have more space, but I'm unable. I try to lift my pointer finger, the effort exhausting me.

"You need to take it easy," she says. "The doctors said you can't rush anything. Brain surgery is a mysterious thing to recover from, but you're doing an excellent job. They really do think you'll make a full recovery. They said this time next year you won't even be able to tell they cut into you."

She gives a small laugh, caught somewhere between that and a cry, and turns away from me. My stepdad rubs her shoulder before coming back by my side.

"Stevie, we're here for you. We aren't going to leave the whole time you're here, and when we go to the rehab place, and finally back home, we'll be there for you, too. You don't have to worry. Us, your dad, your stepmom, your friends, all of us. We're all going to help you get through this. You aren't alone."

I try to nod and tell him thank you even though I have no freaking clue what he's talking about. Rehab? They will stand with me? Against what? They're going to let me refuse the surgery? They will stand with me as I see where God had decided to take me?

I open my mouth, but find no words pour out. My vision gets fuzzy and I'm pulled back under.

················•••◖◉╱◉◗•••················

This time when God comes to me, He is no longer in the beautiful robes as before, but in a navy blue top and pants. He reminds me of the nurse that came to take me for my MRI.

"How are you feeling today?" He asks.

"Confused." I think the words, my throat still too raw to speak.

"About what?" He stands at the foot of my bed and I see I'm still in the hospital. He must be coming to me in real time and I'm relieved He knows how to find me here. I wonder who told him, Mary? Or does He know this like He knows all things?

"They keep saying something about my surgery?"

He turns to me and His face looks different than before, but I blink and it returns to normal. I shake my head slightly to clear it.

"You were very sick," He says. "They were very worried."

Panic rises in the back of my raw throat. I can feel the place where the tube resided, dry and tight, barely letting enough air in to breathe properly. "How worried?" I ask.

"Stevie, you have to understand they love you and think they're doing what's best for you. You have to find a place in your heart to forgive them. Forgiveness is the greatest gift you can give someone. Forgiveness gives peace to an ailing heart and allows it to open to accept My presence. Forgiveness, Stevie, you must remember."

"I will remember."

"They thought what they did was best."

"For whom?"

The light ebbs again, getting brighter and darker until I can't tell where I am, the in-between, the now? The place where both exist?

I blink hard and when I open them, He is gone.

Chapter Sixty-One

················⟨●⟩⟨●⟩●················

When time finally catches up with me, I'm told ten days have passed since I stood in the courtroom and announced I had something to say. My mom tells me I collapsed right after that, knocking a whole glass of water right on the court reporter, and banging my head on the wooden railing as I fell. The ambulance rushed me to the hospital and a scan revealed the tumor had grown, not a lot, but in a misshapen way, perfectly pressing into my frontal lobe. Dr. Oppenheimer and Dr. Jamis were luckily still in town and were called immediately to assist the local surgeons in the removal of my tumor.

They took it out. It's gone.

"It all happened so fast," my dad says. "But the judge rejected your request for emancipation, feeling not only the immediate medical need dictated it, but also that you were about to announce you no longer wanted to pursue the medical emancipation. Your mother and I agreed, and the decision was made."

I nod, still unable to speak properly. I think that was what I was going to say, too, but the memory is fuzzy.

They try giving me a pen and paper to write on, but I find holding the pen so impossible, they quickly give up when they notice tears in my eyes. Time, I'm told. I just need time and it will all come back to me.

I'll be moved to a rehab facility where they'll work extensively to get my motor and language skills back up to snuff. Unfortunately, it means I'll miss my senior year of high school, well at least most of it, but the school already agreed I could take summer classes next year and hopefully graduate in the winter

instead of having to wait until next spring. Colleges would understand, hell, this will be a good essay on overcoming adversity.

Stacey says that last part in feigned jealousy as she sits on the
edge of my bed.

"Ugh, you are totally going to get into Harvard because of this.
Even though I've worked my ass off my whole life and have a
four-point-oh, I'm going to have to slum it in some state school
while your God tumor gets you into the Ivy Leagues."

I breathe a one-beat laugh, about all I can muster, and shrug
my shoulders. The effort requiring a two-hour nap after she leaves.

·········••••◖(✪⌒✪)◗••••·········

A vaguely familiar man in blue scrubs is at the foot of my bed the
next time I wake up. He smiles at me and something about him
speaks comfort and healing.

"I know you?" I slur out. The speech therapist has been coming
twice a day and while I hate her visits, I notice I can talk a bit more
clearly. The work is hard and I don't feel like doing it, but I don't
have a choice in the matter.

"Stevie, I'm Doctor Iver. We've spoken a few times, but I don't
know if you remember. I was here when you were coming out
of your surgery and I'm on the team tasked with your transition."

"Ition?" my words slur. Hey, I'm a work in progress.

He nods. "Yup, Dr. Oppenheimer and Dr. Jamis had to return
to Atlanta, but they left me as your primary doctor in their absence.
Don't worry." He holds up a hand at some face I'm not aware I'm
making. Apparently even though I can't speak it well, my
sarcasm has found ways of revealing itself. "I was part of
your surgical team, so I know what we have been up against. Do
you remember anyone going over your surgery with you?"

I think back. Other than my mother telling me about it, I don't
remember any doctor or nurse mentioning it.

"That's okay. You'll experience brain lags for the next few
days. Some things may take months to really 'stick.' I'll go over
it and if in a few days you need a refresher, that's okay, too. I can

talk about the brain and surgery all day, so it's no skin off my back to go over it again. Yours is a fascinating case.

"Your tumor was slow-growing at first, really up to a few days ago, and then we aren't sure what caused it, but a growth spurt of sorts occurred which caused it to increase in size by 1 millimeter. Now, that may not sound like a lot, but there isn't a whole bunch of room in your scull for any increased mass, so just that little bit can cause problems. You had a seizure when you were on the stand and were rushed to the hospital. We gave you medicine, but were unable to get your seizures under control. That's when, with court approval, it was decided the tumor would be removed.

"You came through the surgery remarkably well. It helps that you're young and healthy and it was centralized in one location, so we think we got all of it. You'll need to come back for scans every three months for the first year, then we can go to six months after that, but your prognosis is good. You have maintained your ninety-five percent rate of reoccurrence, which means there is a very low five year rate it will come back. Do you understand?"

I nod, wondering how many times I've nodded to this same speech over the last few days. I clear my throat, still sore, but starting to heal from the tubes. "Home?"

He shakes his head and gives me a half-smile, half-frown.

"You're a bit away from that. Let's try to get our first goals first. You'll have your first chemo treatment here. Then we're hoping to discharge you to the rehab center in the next few days. After that, they'll reevaluate you and your progress and will know a better idea of when you'll be going home."

He sits on the foot of my bed. I want to move my leg out of his way, but the effort is too much, so I let it rest right near him. He doesn't appear bothered by it, but it's all I can concentrate on. His blue scrubs, a blue that looks so familiar but I don't know why, are a stark contrast next to the pale sheets.

"You're doing remarkably well," he says again. "But you still have gone through a major surgery. That can't be downplayed or rushed. You'll heal when you'll heal. It will take as much time as it takes, but we'll do everything to make you comfortable while making progress. Sound good?"

Chapter Sixty-one

I nod. "Good."

As the doctor leaves, my parents come into the room. They smile at the doctor and my mom sits next to my bed. My stepdad stands by the window, looking out as if he thinks the view riveting, but I know it's just the parking lot. I've had words perched on the edge of my tongue for days now, my speech difficulties making it impossible to push them out of my mouth.

I concentrate hard and press my tongue to the roof of my mouth to help form the word while I purse my lips.

"Slorry," I attempt.

Tears instantly well and fall down my mother's face. "Oh baby, no, we are sorry, oh we are so sorry."

She leans forward to embrace me around all the cords and wires. A second set of arms engulf me, letting me know my stepdad has pulled his attention from the window to us. I'm pretty sure we're all crying, but it's such a wet mess, it's hard to tell whose tears are splashing who.

There's so much more I want to say to them, but for right now, sorry-with-an-l will have to do.

CHAPTER SIXTY-TWO

························

"**T**oday is the day!" Nurse Rubens announces as she comes into my room.

With effort and concentration, I pull both sides of my mouth up into what I hope is an even smile.

She nods at me, her own lips curving in appreciation. "Better," she says. "Your parents are just wrapping up with the doctor now, then the transport staff will come in, then you'll be off."

My dad and Karen returned to Knoxville the day before, him promising to return in two weeks, but correcting the nurse about my parental situation is too much right now. I stick with a simple "Thank. You."

I say each word as a complete sentence, needing to get this right and show how appreciative I am of everything.

She waves her hand and is about to say something else when shouts erupt from the hall.

It's a strange sensation to have part of my body work perfect while others lag behind. I can understand, see, and hear everything, but my speech and motor skills are still a bit off. I understand for the first time why little kids have meltdowns over stupid things.

Not being understood or having the world rush around you while you're slowly trying to find your way is incredibly frustrating.

Before I can ask her what's happening, she leaves my room. I let out a frustrated growl in the back of my throat.

That sound I have no trouble making.

As the shouts get louder, I recognize one of the voices. My skin grows cold, and the heart monitor beeps faster. *What is he doing here?*

Luke appears in the doorway holding a small bouquet of flowers. From their variety and lack of cellophane, I guess they're from the gardens at the compound. A small, recessed part of my heart pinches with longing.

But that's over now. I'm not sure if that was ever destined to be my life, but it sure as hell isn't now.

My mom and stepdad stand right behind him as he enters my room. For a hilarious second, I wonder if she's going to pounce on Luke's back and attack him.

"It's fine," I slur.

"Stevie," my stepdad says.

I shake my head, movement easier than words. Plus, I want to save my energy for this conversation.

"We're going to grab a cup of coffee. I think the transport team will be here in ten," he says. "Leave the door open," he addresses Luke, who nods.

"Press your call button if you need something," my mom says as my stepdad pulls her away.

Luke places the flowers near the window, the petals facing out toward the sun. I catch a flock of birds swooping past outside as he does it and suppress a smile.

We stare at each other a few moments as I prepare the words in my head. Do I want to salvage whatever connects us, or sever it completely?

"I didn't plan," I say, needing a break halfway through my sentence, "to end like this." The effort makes my jaw and mouth ache, but I know I need to get these words out.

"I can believe that."

I laugh, an easier reaction than speech.

"What?" he asks.

"You always...believe me."

It was meant as a joke, an icebreaker, but I can see the real hurt my words inflict on him.

"Of course I believed everything you said. Because I have faith God brought you into our lives for a reason, and I have to trust Him and you, but honestly Stevie, I don't know where we go from here."

There's so much more I want to say. To defend myself and my visions. To defend Mary and what she was to me. I want to make a case for why I still matter, why I can still have a place even if I don't have a direct connection anymore. At least not one that is visible. The words sit poised between my brain and my mouth.

"I tried," I say.

He takes a deep inhale. "I know you did."

I shrug. "I guess," I pause, trying to form the right words. "I'm just a girl now."

"I guess so."

It feels like he punched me in the gut. I was hoping for so much more. For him to tell me, *Oh no, Stevie, you are still important. It was you that mattered. You were the one we sought.*

My mom and stepdad return, two people I don't recognize in scrubs behind them. I'm guessing they're the folks from the rehab team, but I'm too exhausted from the exchange with Luke to ask.

I'm worried I've said all I'm able to.

Luke nods to no one in particular. My mom looks between us, hoping for some kind of cue for how the conversation went, how she should proceed accordingly. My stepdad just looks like he wants to punch Luke or drag him out of the room. A small part of me wants him to.

I realize, to an embarrassing level of clarity, this salvation was never my responsibility. As much as I wished it wasn't true, as much as I tried to be older and more mature than I was, Luke should have been the one looking out for me.

I want to call out and ask him to explain himself and tell me his truth, once and for all. Now that there are no stakes. No one to impress. No God directly watching over us.

Was he using me?

"Why," I force out.

He turns and looks at me. They all do. Five sets of eyes glued on me. One by one, they drop their gaze, all except him.

He has words at his disposal, able to throw them around like confetti as if they're worthless, while I treasure each one I can form.

But he turns away, saying nothing, and leaves.

CHAPTER SIXTY-THREE

One Year Later

The sun burns the back of my neck. I put my fingertips to it and feel the heat radiating there. I look around for a kiosk that sells lotion. I'm pretty sure I forgot to put any on before I left the house, which means I probably didn't. My memory is still a little foggy from the chemo and sometimes I lose track of things I feel like I should remember.

My hair is finally growing back, but it's barely to my ears and offers little protection with how thin it still is. While I'm getting the lotion, I'll probably pick up some aspirin, too, since I feel a headache coming. Probably didn't drink enough water yesterday.

Stacey and Malik skip down the faux street ahead of me. She turns, cheek pink with the sun and heat, laughing at something Malik said.

"What do you want to do next?" she calls back to me.

I'm walking slowly, well, slower than normal I guess. But great progress! According to my physical therapist.

Nine months ago, if you'd have asked me if I'd be walking this quickly again, I'd have told you no. Nine months before that, if you had asked me if I'd be walking this slowly, I'd have told you no.

What a difference perspective gives.

I have to formulate my words in my head before I say them, just like the PT told me to. "I don't care."

I barely slur at all anymore when I talk. Another feat of accomplishment. I'm considering making bumper stickers for my parents.

My kid walked ten steps unassisted today!

My kid ordered lunch and the nurses could understand her!

Small, but I think worthy of print.

Today is the first time my mom and stepdad have allowed me to go any place without them for the day. I'm heading to my dad's in two weeks, so they're probably realizing they need to relax a little. I haven't been to Knoxville since before my diagnosis, and I'm looking forward to the change of scenery and to see my dad for longer than a weekend visit here and there.

When Stacey called me yesterday, tentatively asking if I'd like to join her and Malik at the park, I said yes instantly. My mom and stepdad don't understand why I'd want to go a theme park, especially since I can't ride much, but I insisted. I need some normalcy.

I ache to feel the rush of air and G-forces when I hear the shouts of those riding the roller coasters, but then I think back to how much I'm accomplishing already and vow to myself that this time next year, I'll be riding them.

We'd pretty much done everything I could go on in the parks. The easy kiddie rides like E.T. and the Dr. Seuss stuff, and rode the train from one park to the other and back twice. I appreciate them wanting to include me, but even I was getting bored.

"Why don't you guys go on one of the roller coasters?"

"We can do something together. I think there's that animal show that starts in a little bit," Stacey says.

I shake my head. "No, it's like over an hour. We can do that, but why don't you guys go on a ride? I'll get a snack, and by the time you're done, it'll be time for the show, sound good?"

She hesitates, but I can see on Malik's face he desperately wants to go on something that wasn't made for babies.

"Seriously," I say. "I really appreciate you guys staying with me, but I want you to have fun, too."

"We *are* having fun!" she insists. I stare at her until she shrugs. "We go on the rides all the time. Today is about hanging out."

"Go."

Malik pulls her hand toward the alley which leads to the red tracks. I walk to a kiosk across from it and get a soda and churro. The lotion and pills can wait for now. The hot cinnamon sticks to my fingers and burns the inside of my mouth, but is delicious.

It feels strange being back here again without Jorge. He keeps in touch with Malik who passes along bits of information when I ask. He says Jorge's enjoying school, and while Malik talks about vague promises Jorge says about coming to town, that he wants to see me and apologize in person, he typically goes to his parents' new place up north on breaks instead of visiting. He doesn't text me even though Stacey said Malik told her he was going to. I know it bothers Malik, he doesn't want to hurt me and is annoyed at his friend, but Malik doesn't talk about it too much to me. I think he doesn't want to upset me.

People do that a lot around me, try to protect me from things. My mom would get rid of the paper as soon as she was done with it in the morning, ignoring the fact I could just go online to get any information. But the news hadn't covered anything about the group in a long time.

They did a couple follow-up stories after the trial was over and when I got my tumor removed, but other than that, they faded back into obscurity.

I still hear from Abby. Her hair is back to purple, but she says it's a lot darker from the blue, but she's hoping to get it brighter soon. Our conversations are short, so I'm pretty sure no one there knows we communicate. With how the rest of them cut me off, I can imagine it's frowned upon that she hasn't shunned me.

I think part of her hopes something will be worked out and I'll be able to come back, but with the removal of the tumor, the visions have stopped, so there really isn't any use for me there anymore. Plus, I know they're upset I "wasted" all their resources on the trial.

Apparently, the group was in dire money troubles and were banking on me to help pull them out of it. Luke thought with the addition of me and my visions, donations and support would flood in. He'd taken a second mortgage on the property to help pay for getting me out of Georgia then for the medical second opinions.

Some increased donations did come, but as soon as the trial was over and it was clear I wasn't going to save anyone, they dried up.

The last I saw on an internet search, they were starting to file proceedings for chapter eleven bankruptcy.

About a week after Luke visited me in the hospital, we got served by a woman who yelled out my mom's name as we walked a slow lap around the outside of the rehab facility. She handed my mom a paper telling us the Church of the Eye was suing us for my legal fees. My mom immediately called Ms. Kwong. Their phone call was brief, but I could tell by the way my mom paced back and forth and chewed on her thumb nail, the lawyer didn't put her at ease. Luckily, a few days later we got word the judge threw out the case before it really went anywhere, but the church's message was clear. Stay away. We no longer want or need you.

I try not to be hurt by it, but I am. But I'm not sure by whom. Them, or God?

I was so sure I was chosen and I was going to help these people and myself find salvation. But in the end, the doctors cut that little mass out of my brain and *Him* along with it.

I held firmly to the hope that the visions would return, just once, but no luck. I think back to Bill from the support group, telling me to say bye. I feel cheated I didn't. I know my parents and doctors had my best interest in mind, but not knowing it was going to happen, I had no idea those last visits were it.

I can barely remember what it felt like anymore. I'll get a little too close to the stove or lean on the dryer while it's running, trying to recreate the feeling of warmth, but it's never quite right.

There's this missing piece in me that I know their presence would fill, but I'm unable to describe it well enough to find anything else that could take their place. It's like trying to itch a scratch but it keeps moving right when you think you've gotten it.

It was strange going back to my old church at first, being surrounded by statues when I used to have the real thing, but enough time has passed that people don't really stare at me anymore. I haven't had someone throw themselves at me and ask me to cure them in about six months.

Literally throw themselves at me. It was super awkward.

But I know that while I don't have the visions anymore, it doesn't make the fact they happened any less real or make God and Mary and Jesus any less a part of my life. I have to be on my own journey now to figure out what their presence means.

I have to have faith.

My scans since have all been clear. I went every six weeks at first, then three months once those were clear for the first couple. If my next scan, scheduled for two days from now, is also good, I get to switch to every six months.

I can't wait. The scans are such a drag.

A scream pulls my attention back and I look up. The car goes up the track in front of me, dropping its residents beyond my vision, their cries carrying through the square. I take off my flip flops and let my toes squish on the faux grass beneath them.

Next year.

I shut my eyes against the warm sun, allowing it to radiate through me.

Suntan lotion. I need to remember suntan lotion.

The heat intensifies and I reluctantly get up to move into the shade. Sitting on the fake sidewalk in the shadow of an awning, I wait for cooling relief, but it doesn't come. I'm even sitting out-side the open doors of an air-conditioned store, but I still feel a hot tingle.

A familiar tingle.

I search the crowds and they part just enough to see her.

Mary stands, a smile on her face and arms open wide enough to encase the entire world, welcoming me home.

The End

Acknowledgements

······••••◦(◖◗)◦••••••·······

No book sees the light of day by itself, and this one is no exception.

To my early reader and later Stevie champion, I can't thank Arielle Haughee enough for her words of encouragement (and lots of suggestions) to help make this book the best it can be. I couldn't have done it without you.

Erin Homs, your thoughts and feedback on one of my earliest drafts were instrumental in getting this story off the ground. Thank you so much.

Jennie Kendrick, you found the slow spots and holes and pushed and plugged them. *Mass* is better because of you.

Diogo Lando at Red Raven Book Design, you persevered through endless tweaks and adjustments. Thank you for putting up with me and providing such an amazing cover.

Valerie Willis at Battle Goddess Productions. You are a force. Thanks for lending some of that to my work.

Marriah Herro, for giving me insight on diagnosis and treatment. Sharing your experience was invaluable to me.

To my family and friends, for asking me about my work and being my cheerleaders—thank you.

To my husband, for putting up with my zoning out in the middle of a conversation because I just figured out how to fix a part of my story and I have to write it down this second before I forget...even if you don't have the obsession, you understand and give me the time and space I need to create.

And as always, to the Three Little Bears, for making me laugh and bringing me joy.

There are no easy parts in life, but the search to figure out what one's truth is can be a particularly difficult road, one that winds and changes sometimes day to day. Surround yourself with those who bring more light than darkness, and it's that much simpler. All those in my life do that, and I am grateful for each and every one of you.

About the Author

K ristin Durfee grew up outside of Philadelphia where an initial struggle with reading blossomed into a love of the written word. She is the author of the young adult fantasy series Four Corners, as well as short stories appearing in several thriller, speculative, and contemporary anthologies for adults. She currently lives in Central Florida, and when not enjoying the sun with her husband, son, and two quirky dogs, you can usually find her on a run, horse-back ride, or wandering around a theme park.

Other Works by Kristin Durfee:
The Four Corners Trilogy
Four Corners
Two Worlds
One Earth

Other Works from Orange Blossom Publishing

••••••••••◦(◦✐◦)◦••••••••••

Focus Journals
Teachers' Journal for Balance
Mothers' Journal for Inner Peace
Creatives' Journal for Inspiration and Productivity
Quarantine Journal for Sanity

Children's Picture Books
Grumbler
Joyride
Pling's Party

How I Met My Other Series:
True Stories, True Love
Furry Friends, True Tails
True Engagements, Forever Love

If You Enjoyed This Book…

Please consider leaving a review on Amazon or Good Reads. It helps authors sell more books!